"Irresistible!"

Peter glanced at his watch. It was quarter after eleven, time for the morning kindergartners to leave, and the first graders to have lunch. He looked at the phone and drummed his fingers on his desktop. He had a couple of minutes. Should he call Melissa? It would be a casual call, he told himself, just to ask how the dog was. No big deal. Just to find out how the dog was. That's all. Just the dog.

"This is Dr. March."

The instant he heard her voice he knew he'd lied to himself. He was struck silent for a moment, then all of a sudden his voice returned. "This is Peter...Peter Winthrop." He felt like a teenager again, stuttering and shy, as if he was calling a girl for the first time. He had to pull himself together quickly. "I was just calling to find out how the dog is." *Liar,* his conscience taunted him, just like a fourth-grader.

"She's fine." Her voice was pleasant and professional. "She came out of the anesthesia without any problems. She's getting used to the cast, and she's had a small breakfast."

"She must have been hungry after being on her own for a while."

"I'm not sure about that. She threw up as she was coming out of the anesthesia. That's not unusual under the circumstances, nothing to be upset about," she added quickly, her voice losing that professional tone and becoming more like the voice he remembered. The voice that had haunted his dreams.

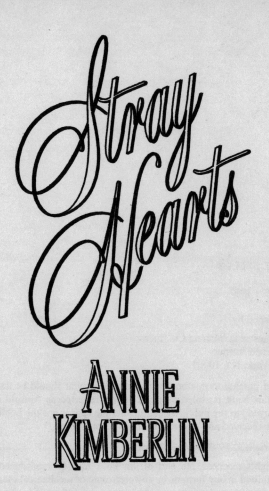

Stray Hearts

ANNIE KIMBERLIN

LOVE SPELL BOOKS   NEW YORK CITY

LOVE SPELL®

October 1997

Published by

Dorchester Publishing Co., Inc.
276 Fifth Avenue
New York, NY 10001

ISBN 0-505-52221-7

To Beth Werking, CLX** and a terrific friend

**Children's Librarian Excellent

All my thanks to Pam Baker for getting lost with me on I-70; to Laurie Grant for her wonderful support, and to Dr. Scott Whiteman, DVM, of Willow Wood Animal Hospital for ten years of giving the best care to my best friends, and for allowing me to "borrow" Woody.

A portion of the author's royalties supports THE COMPANY OF ANIMALS, a nonprofit agency that distributes grants to animal welfare agencies providing emergency and ongoing care to companion animals throughout the United States. Thank you, Michael, for allowing me to help.

Stray Hearts

Chapter One

Melissa March sank into the warm water of her antique bathtub and closed her eyes in absolute bliss. The scent of peaches wafted up lazily along with the steam, accompanied by the strains of the Brahms violin concerto on her CD player. The perfect ending to a grueling day spent in surgery.

The phone blasted, shattering her peace.

It was the clinic phone. She'd forgotten to turn it over to the answering service.

She threw up her arms in resignation, then clambered out of the warm water into the cold air, sloshing suds onto the bath mat. She slung a rose-colored towel around herself as she trailed puddles into her living room to turn down the volume on the CD, then grab the phone.

Hugo, her bulldog, lifted his head inquiringly from his customary spot on the couch. "Sorry, buddy," she told him. "It's not cookie time yet."

Melissa grabbed the phone before it could ring obnoxiously again. Well, she'd wanted her phone to be loud so she'd be sure to hear it. *Be careful what you wish for,* her mother had always told her. She should have paid attention.

"Hartley Vet Clinic."

"Is this Dr. March's office?" The masculine voice was tinny, as if coming from a portable phone.

"This is Dr. March." She swiped the loose end of the towel around her shoulders to catch the drops of water running down her back. Her face was wet with the steam from the bath, so she wiped that as well.

"My name is Peter Winthrop. I got your number from Sally Foster. She said you were the best vet in town." There was a seriousness to his voice, a warm steadiness that she found attractive. It was the kind of voice that could read a person to sleep. "I'm westbound on Route 14, right outside of Hartley." Then she heard him take a deep breath before he continued. "I just hit a dog. A stray dog by the look of it. It was an accident. This dog just ran out in front of me. I stopped and called Sally. Can you help this dog? It's bleeding."

Instantly Melissa shoved all thoughts of returning to her bath to the far recesses of her mind. "Can you tell where the dog is bleeding?" *Please, don't let it be from the mouth*, she thought.

"Leg. Looks broken. She, I think it's a she, was thrown as my car hit her. Look, I feel terrible about this."

"I'm sure you do, but tell me, does she have a collar? Tags?"

"I don't see a collar, but the fur around her neck is full of mats."

Melissa swore softly. "Sorry. Is she conscious?"

"Yes. She's also shivering. I thought a dog in shock would probably be similar to a person, so I covered her with an old blanket until I could get some help. I figured . . ." There was a short pause, then he added, "I figured if I called the dog warden, they'd only put her to sleep."

Melissa grimaced. "You're right about the dog warden. But it really isn't their fault. They just don't have funding to pay vet bills. The blanket was an okay thing to do also. Now, where are you exactly?" She carried the phone across the room to the spot where she'd dropped her clothes a mere fifteen minutes earlier. Scrunching up her shoulder to hold the receiver as she pulled on her jeans, she listened intently to the directions.

"Okay. Try not to let the dog get up, but also, be very careful. Dogs that are hurt don't always know that you're trying to help them and they can sometimes bite. Remember, she has no way of knowing that you're trying to help. Do you

11

know what kind of a dog it is? Poodle? Hound? Some breeds are more sensitive and nervous than others."

"One of those miniature collies, I forget what they're called."

"Shelties." Very sensitive dogs. "Try to keep her quiet, and I'll be there in about fifteen minutes."

"I'll wait."

Melissa hung up the phone and bent down to brush a kiss on Hugo's broad head. "This," she explained to him, pulling a rose-colored turtleneck over her head, "is what it means to have James Herriot as your very own personal hero." *And,* she continued to herself, *why you are no longer married.*

Hugo snorted at her, then tumbled off the couch to follow her into her bedroom, wagging the whole back end of his stubby body so vigorously that he wobbled. He made the grunting snuffling noises that Melissa knew were his way of talking to her.

"I know. It *is* a cold night." She picked a pair of warm socks out of her top drawer. "But I have to go see if I can save a dog." She shoved the drawer closed, then sat on the floor to pull on the socks. Peter Winthrop. She'd heard his name before. He knew Sally. . . . Oh, she grabbed at the thought before it could disappear. He was the principal at the school where Sally taught. Sally had mentioned him several times, saying he was a terrific principal.

Hugo leaned as close to her as he possibly

could, slinging his tongue around, trying to reach her cheek. Ah, dog slobber. Excellent for keeping one's skin young-looking. Better than any high-priced snake oil, no matter what the ads in women's magazines said. She ought to bottle it. Oil of Slobber. She'd make a fortune.

"But Hugo . . ." She held the dog's cheeks in her hands and brought her face close to his so she could look deeply into his doggy-brown eyes. The dog wiggled even more enthusiastically. "Hugo, this dog might be seriously hurt. Keep your fingers crossed and think good thoughts."

Hugo snorted.

Using the corner of her desk to pull herself up, she strode across the tiny apartment. "I might be late," she told the dog as she grabbed her keys from the hook by the door. "Don't wait up."

As she blew him a kiss, Hugo bared his teeth in his doggy grin, his wheat-colored body quivering in his love for her. He truly was an ugly dog, she thought. His ears were set too high and his eyes were too close together for beauty, even in a bulldog, and with their smooshed-in noses and stubby bodies, they were definitely an acquired taste. He was the sweetest thing in the world, truly wise and wonderful, and bright as well, but ugly as an old boot. She absolutely adored him.

Pulling the door to her apartment closed, she trotted down the inside stairs to the clinic. The boarding dogs, evidently hearing her footsteps, struck up an excited chorus.

"Knock it off, you guys!" she called to them through the door. "I'm only here for a minute." She switched on the light in the treatment room and stood for a second, thinking about things that might be wrong with this dog. Then she opened doors to cupboards, choosing specialized supplies and fitting them in her vet bag.

"Hello, Woody," she greeted the clinic cat as he jumped up onto the counter to push against her arm. She ruffled the marmalade fur on his sleek head and bent down to touch her nose to his. "Just be glad you're warm and safe inside."

The cat answered her with his loud and squeaky purr, and followed her to the back door where her winter parka hung on the coat tree.

For once, her battered old mini-van gave no protest at starting up on a cold evening. She patted the dashboard. "Good car," she told it with great enthusiasm as she craned her neck to see out the driveway. *Always pretend that you love your car. You never know when you'll need its goodwill.* Well, this was a night she needed it, she thought, pulling out into the road.

"Just over twelve minutes. Good car!" she praised the van as she caught sight of a man kneeling beside what looked like a lump at the side of the road.

She drew up alongside the car parked on the shoulder of the road. He'd told her what kind it was, but she wouldn't know a Cadillac from a

Mack truck. She could identify a breed of dog at a hundred yards, but cars all looked alike. She maneuvered her van so the headlights would give her the most light as she checked out the dog. She ground to a stop, jerked on the parking brake, then killed the motor. Her battery should last for a while with the headlights on. She hoped.

When he saw the van pull to a stop, like the cavalry coming over the hill, Peter stood up next to the dog. His knees were stiff from crouching in the cold.

"Hello," he called out to her as she strode over to the dog. And to him.

"Hello, I'm Dr. March." After giving him the briefest of nods, she pulled her gloves off and stuffed them in the pocket of her down parka, then knelt down beside the trembling dog. She pulled away the blanket and regarded the creature who watched her with pain-dulled eyes.

Peter breathed a silent sigh of relief, and the overwhelming sick feeling that had enveloped him since he'd hit the dog began to dissipate. Sally had told him that if anyone could do miracles with animals, this was the vet who could. He hoped Sally was right.

"You're right, it is a sheltie," she told him as she set her vet bag down beside her and opened it. "The poor thing looks like she's been on the road for a while. There, baby, it's all right," she crooned softly. "I'm here to help you." Her hands looked gentle as she slipped an elastic

15

muzzle on the dog. "I know it feels funny, but it's just a precaution. You don't know us." The patter became matter-of-fact as she checked the dog over, her hands moving swiftly and surely.

She lifted the dog's lip around the elastic to peer closely at its gums and teeth. "You have all your adult teeth, but they're pretty clean. Not much in the way of tartar, which we'd expect to see in an adult dog. So I'd say you're still a baby, probably not quite a year old. I know you wouldn't really bite, lovely girl like you, but you might forget your manners. I'd understand if you did. You must hurt like the dickens. But we're going to make you right as daffodils in the spring." She obviously knew what she was doing, and as Peter watched her, he started to relax, telling himself that maybe it really would be all right.

While he'd been waiting for the vet something odd had happened. After he'd covered the little dog with the blanket, he'd knelt next to her, his hand on her head, willing her warm. He'd looked into her eyes, knowing that any apology was impossible, wishing with all his might that he'd been able to swerve, to avoid hitting her. He'd told the dog—actually spoken the words— that he'd done the best thing he could do, call for help. The wariness and uncertainty in her eyes along with the pain—pain he was responsible for—had reached deep into his being, and had touched something secret within him. And without realizing it until it was a done deal, he'd formed a bond with this dog. Now the vet was here, and though the sick feeling was still with him, he felt unneeded, superfluous in the face of her competence. *How ridiculous,* he chided himself. *The dog needs a veterinarian, not an elementary school principal.*

He crouched down next to the dog, petting her, careful to keep out of the vet's way as she held a stethoscope to the dog's chest. He watched Dr. March as she waited through the swooshing sound of a passing car, then listened intently, moving the stethoscope periodically, staring straight ahead, at nothing. Her face was framed by a knit cap pulled low on her forehead against the cold, and for a brief moment he wondered what color her hair was. She had a pleasant face, he supposed, but the thing that struck him most was the look of absolute concentration in her large eyes. Every iota of her being was focused on the breathing of this creature, a stray dog, a stranger.

But though he'd never seen this dog before, she was no longer a stranger to him. She was a creature that, in these short few minutes, he'd become responsible for. He looked away from the vet, down at the dog, his hands stroking the dirty matted coat. He wondered what she would look like if she were clean and combed. She was a lovely golden red color, with a white chest and blaze on her forehead. She had a narrow muzzle, and the very tips of her ears were folded over. He wondered what her personality was like. He wondered if she liked children. But somehow, he knew she did. He knew this dog

17

was the answer. Somehow he knew this dog would be perfect for helping him with Angie. And at that moment he knew he was going to keep her.

"She's a lucky girl," the doctor murmured, slinging the stethoscope around her neck in a practiced motion. "No fluid in her lungs, and her heart sounds okay, considering."

The dog seemed to relax as Dr. March continued her examination, evidently understanding that this was help, for the very tip of her tail twitched slightly. Suddenly Peter realized the vet's soft, crooning voice was directed at him. "Excuse me?"

"Can you tell me what happened?" she repeated in a voice that ran over him like honey.

The headlights of her van provided a backlight, giving her a halo. *Fitting*, he thought. *If she has hands like an angel, a voice like an angel, and can work miracles, that's probably what she is.*

He shook his head briefly to clear away the fanciful thoughts. "She just ran out in front of me. There was a car coming the other direction so I couldn't swerve." *How ironic*, he thought, remembering another night two years ago. *History repeats itself.*

The vet sat back on her heels and studied the dog. "She does have a broken leg. I have to take her back to my clinic."

"Will she be all right?"

"I think so. Here, help me put this splint on her leg. It's just a temporary one. That's right.

Hold this very still now while I wrap it. Good. I have to take some X-rays, and then I'll set her leg, but she seems to have been very lucky. Course, we won't know for certain until I can check her out more thoroughly."

He watched her stride back to her van, her bag swinging at her side. He turned his gaze from the vet back to the dog. The dog's eyes were still wary, eyes that did not trust, eyes that pierced his conscience. And there was that odd sensation again, that he and this dog were connected.

He heard a thud, probably her vet bag slung into the van, and glanced over. The vet was fiddling with something that made a metallic sound. He heard her mutter softly.

"Will you need some help back at the clinic? Sally told me this was after your normal office hours." Besides, he couldn't just let this dog disappear, not when he was responsible for her and when he'd finally found the answer to Angie's fear. And this woman, with her air of total confidence, pulled at something deep inside him, something he'd not wanted to acknowledge for two years. He didn't want her to drive out of his life either.

"There," she said with a hint of triumph in her voice. "I got the wretched thing open." She faced him, considering. Then at last she said, "I have to commend you for stopping and helping her. Lots of people wouldn't have bothered. It takes real guts to do that." She smiled, lighting up the darkness, and the sick feeling in his soul began to dissolve. Then she continued. "Yes. In answer to your question I would welcome some help. Let's get her into my van, in this crate here. You can follow me to the clinic."

Once on the way, following the mini-van's taillights, Peter reached for his car phone and punched in the number for his mother-in-law, Gloria, to tell her he'd be later than expected.

"Here we are," Melissa told him as she flipped on the light inside the clinic door. She noticed that he was carrying the dog very carefully. And he'd not been the least bit hesitant about touching a filthy dog, nor had he seemed at all concerned that blood from the dog's wound was on his blanket. When she'd pointed it out, he'd said it was an old blanket, kept in his car for just such emergencies. It would wash. This was an unusual man. Of course, her experience with men was fairly limited, and probably prejudiced.

"Bring her back here, to the X-ray room," she instructed him, her shoes squishing on the institution-green linoleum as she led him through the examination rooms and down the hall to the surgery.

The boarder dogs started their canine chorus again. "Knock it off, you guys!" she called out to them. And this time, they listened to her. Good for them, she thought in surprise. She'd give them an extra cookie when she took them out for one last time later tonight.

Woody, his purr on the way to breaking the

sound barrier, came running toward them to wind around her legs.

"Is that your cat?"

She threw him a grin over her shoulder. "This is Woody. Woody, this is Peter Winthrop who knows your friend Sally." She shoved a door open with her hip, and held it for Peter and the dog. "Woody lives here in the clinic. He's our candy striper. He visits all the animals and keeps them company, keeps their spirits up."

"Unique thing for a cat to do."

"Woody's a unique cat."

"Where did you get him?" he asked as he carried the dog through the door.

"He was dumped. Last winter, during that incredibly cold spell, I found him in a box outside the clinic. He was very sick. Evidently someone wasn't willing to pay the vet bill for him." She let the door go and it thunked closed.

"Do you know who left him?" There was a hint of disbelief in his voice.

"No. He wasn't one of my patients, and I never called the other vets in town to find out. I figured out what was wrong with him and decided that anyone who wasn't willing to take care of him shouldn't have him." She scooped up the cat, rubbed her cheek on his orange fur, and took comfort from the rumbling of his purr. "He needed surgery. Some people aren't willing to spend that kind of money on what they consider a dumb animal. Why spend two hundred dollars to save a cat's life when you can look in the newspaper or go to the Greene County Animal Shelter and get any number of cats for next to nothing?" She realized her voice had become very bitter. "Sorry." She gave him a smile that she hoped conveyed her apology. "This is a very sore point with me."

"So who paid for the operation?"

She cocked her head, considering him for a moment, then turned the cat in her arms so he faced this man, this man who was taking full responsibility for hurting a dog, even if it had been an accident. "Look at this furry face," she said. Woody obligingly closed his eyes in complete satisfaction and turned up his purr. "I decided to keep him. How could I do anything else?"

But Peter was not looking at the cat. He was looking at her, with something very warm in his eyes that made her forget who and what she was. Then she did remember, and the moment was gone, leaving her feeling breathless and flustered.

"I really need to X-ray the dog," she mumbled, trying to cover her emotions as she slid past the man to lead him toward her surgery. This place, her clinic, was where she felt sure of herself. This was what she knew, what she had studied and sweated for, what she had wanted for as long as she could remember. This was her life. Hers alone. She had no business thinking about a man when she had an animal's life in her hands. If she took that responsibility lightly, she would be failing not only the dogs and cats entrusted to her care, but James Herriot as well.

It was eccentric, she knew, but that was just the way it was.

In the X-ray room, she helped Peter set the stray dog on the table, then showed him where he could hang up his coat.

"You know you don't belong in here," she admonished the orange cat gently, picking him up and setting him down outside the door.

"I need to get a picture of her before I go in, to see what I'm working with," she told Peter. "The only obvious thing is her leg, but there might be something else."

She carefully removed the splint so she could arrange the dog's leg in the best position for the X ray. Without saying a word, Peter took the makeshift splint from her, as if assisting a vet were something he did every day. She looked up at him in surprise.

"Thank you," she said, tucking that impression in her memory for future study.

"You're very welcome." Peter said, the warmth of his eyes reaching something deep in her soul. "Where shall I put this?"

"Over on that counter there." She pointed into the surgery room. She noticed the way he raised his eyebrows just a speck when he asked a question. There was something truly endearing about the tiny movement. In fact, he had a very expressive face. The dog, she reminded herself, turning her attention back to the task at hand. The dog.

"That's a good girl, you're not going to fuss." She made her voice matter-of-fact. She'd learned it was better not to coddle her patients too much or they would pick up on her tone of voice and think there really was something to be worried about. "And you're not going to move at all, are you. Good girl. You're going to be just fine. Fine but thoroughly filthy and so we'll have to do something about that as well. I wonder what you'll think of a bath," Melissa added as she took the briefest moment to pet the dog. Poor baby.

She noted briefly that Peter was keeping out of her way. He was interested, obviously concerned, but not intrusive. She liked that. He stepped closer to pet the dog as well, and his nearness hit her like a tank, but it wasn't only his nearness. There was a unique scent about him that made her senses reel out of control. A great feeling of loneliness surged through her. It had been a very long time since she'd been . . . *That'll do, Melissa, you have a dog to save. Get yourself together, girl! What would James think?*

Donning her lead apron and gloves, she motioned Peter out of the tiny room. "Picture time. Nasty X rays you don't want to be exposed to. You can watch through that window, if you want. I need to make sure she stays completely still." When Peter was safely behind the glass window, Melissa pressed the pedal with her foot. The X-ray machine hummed for a moment, then was still. She gently repositioned the dog and took another picture.

"You can come back in now," she called to

him. "The film needs to cook for a moment, then we can see what this girl looks like inside. What we're going to be working with."

We, she thought. How right it sounded, and how smoothly he assisted her, somehow knowing what needed to be done. He seemed to belong in her clinic as if he had always been a part of it. Of her life. She was not sure if this was a comforting thought or not.

Peter liked the way Dr. March moved. She was efficient and certain of her actions. The brief look he'd gotten of her clinic on the way back here confirmed this. It was as sensible and no-nonsense as she was. From where he stood, at the dog's head, his hand continuing to stroke the dirty golden fur, he glanced into the surgery, noting that the walls, though old, looked spotless, the floor squeaky clean. And he could hear the incredibly loud purr of the orange cat, still winding figure-eights around the legs of the surgery table.

Then Dr. March was smiling up at him. Her springy dark curls sort of wisped around her face and he'd never seen such warmth in blue eyes before. She wasn't beautiful, like Claire, but there was a quality about her that attracted him, drew him to her, closer and closer, like the proverbial moth and flame.

She shoved the developed X rays under the clip on the light box and studied them intently. "I think this break in her leg is all we have to worry about." She tapped the X ray with her forefinger, and he noted her nails were short and very clean. No polish. In fact—he took a quick peek just to be sure—she wasn't wearing any make up at all. This was all natural beauty.

"This is definitely a broken leg," she continued, "but there's no splintering, which is lucky. It means it should mend with little or no trouble. Everything else looks pretty good. At least as far as I can see."

She leaned forward, towards him, to get a better look at the X rays. He thought he could detect the faintest scent of peaches. He moved a fraction closer to breathe more deeply. Yes. Peaches indeed. Peaches in the dead of winter. It brought to mind summer, sun, warm days and nights full of promise.

"Are you ready?"

Her voice was like a jolt, shaking him out of his thoughts.

"It's nothing to be embarrassed about," she continued. "If you think you can't deal with an operation."

"I'm an elementary school principal, and I'm a single parent with a six-year-old daughter." He purposely kept the tone of his voice light and he smiled at her, just to see the twinkle come back in her eyes. "I've seen my share of scrapes and cuts and bloody noses." *But*, he added to himself, *I've not seen anything like you in a very long time*. "What do you need me to do first?"

Birdlike, she cocked her head to one side, regarding him for a moment. Then he was rewarded by her smile, wide and infectious and all too short.

"Then let's go. First we put this little girl in one of those cages there while we get ready." She carefully picked up the dog and motioned with her head to one of the cages in the surgery room. "Can you open the latch?"

Holding the door to the cage open, he caught another trace scent of peaches as she put the dog in.

She strode over to a cabinet against the wall. The door screeched when she opened it. "I have to get some goop to put on that door." She shook out two surgical gowns and handed him one. "Here. Ever wear one of these?" She grinned at him, and he was once again struck by the way her eyes sparkled. "Let me assure you that these lovely creations are designed by Madison Avenue's finest. They tie in the back."

"Then I'll need help," he told her, matching his tone to hers. What would happen, he wondered, if her tone were more personal? If his was? He wanted to find out. But now was not the time. He slid his arms into the snowy white cotton and presented his back to her. "I must have been absent the day the teacher taught knot-tying in back."

She chuckled, and he could feel her hands brush his back as she tied the gown. Then she moved away, and he felt a sudden need to have her touch him again. But he wanted her to do more than tie knots. Much more. And he wanted to touch her as well.

27

Down, boy, he admonished himself. *You barely know the lady. What's wrong with you today?* Unfortunately, he knew what was wrong, and it had nothing to do with the fact that Claire had been dead for two years. He gave himself a moment before he turned around and followed her to the scrub sink.

"Mask and gloves," she announced. He put them on, feeling odd and out of place in the regalia of a surgeon, but when he looked up, there was Melissa with the dog in her arms. The filthy, matted sheltie seemed out of place in the immaculate room.

Once on the table, the dog fluttered her eyes open. They were unfocused, and confused, so Peter bent down where the dog could see him. "You'll be just fine," he whispered. "Dr. March said so." He was rewarded by a twitch of the tip of the dog's tail.

It had been a long and tiring evening, Melissa thought several hours later as, book in hand, she sank down next to the heat pad where the sheltie lay sleeping. Melissa leaned back against the wall. Peter had left shortly after the operation, but she had to stay until the dog woke up, to make sure she came out of the anesthesia without any problems. There rarely ever was a problem, but the animals, whose lives had been entrusted to her, came first. Always.

Melissa opened the book. It was Kay Nanling Michaelson's newest, and Melissa had been waiting impatiently for it to come out. Fantasy in the highest degree, with lush writing, more fun than reality. And even if there weren't many dogs or cats in the series, there were nice people. Nice people.

Peter was nice people, she thought. They sure didn't make elementary school principals like they used to. While he was not drop-dead gorgeous, like Charming Michael, he was very nice looking. His eyes were the dark brown of a Newfoundland's, she decided. And his hair was dark and thick with a slight wave to it, like a flat-coated retriever. He was decently tall, looked naturally trim. He moved well, smooth gait, had a very nice rear. *Stop it, Melissa. Sounds like you're evaluating a dog, not a man.* And Peter Winthrop was very much a man. Yet there was about him an air of what she could only call clarity, as if he always had good thoughts, always looked on the bright side of things. As if he were just plain nice.

In that instant, she was struck by how even in the brief hours she'd been with him, he had become familiar to her. And he'd very cleverly let her know that he was single. Whoa! Back to reality time. *C'mon, Dr. March,* she told herself sternly, *his personal life is absolutely none of your business. And it's not going to be, so stop drooling over the man.*

Melissa put down her book to check the dog's breathing again. Sounded good.

When she had finished setting the leg and casting it, she checked the dog more thoroughly and found an identification tattoo on her inner thigh. So evidently someone had once cared about this dog. She'd told Peter what the tattoo meant, that they might be able to trace the dog's owners. Peter had gone down the hall to her office to fetch a piece of paper and a pencil, then had copied down the number.

"Why is the tattoo there?" he'd asked.

"Because people who buy dogs for experimental purposes, usually from people who have stolen them, won't buy a tattooed dog. It's illegal. Dogs used to be tattooed in their ears, but lots of dogs showed up at research facilities with their ears chopped off. You can't chop off a whole leg, so now dogs are usually tattooed here." Peter's face had turned very pale, close to the color of the mask. She'd reached out and touched him on the arm, a comforting touch, nothing more, she told herself, as she continued. "So we call the 1-800 number and tell them we've found a dog with this number, and they get in touch with the people who've registered that number."

"That was interesting," Melissa murmured now, absently tapping on the book's cover in time to the stray dog's breathing.

"Hey, girl," Melissa whispered, knowing the dog couldn't hear her. "You know what happened? His whole face shut down. Yup. Shut up tight. As if he knew he had to do what was right, but he didn't want to." She reached over to stroke the dog's head. The anesthetized dog didn't move. "When we called the registry hot line, and they didn't have your number on record, that was one relieved man. And we didn't find a microchip implant in the back of your neck either. So unless someone has put an ad in the paper, or called the local pound, I think you may have a home with Peter Winthrop." She leaned back against the wall and studied the dog. "I think once we get you cleaned up and brushed out, you'll be a lovely little thing. Just right for a little girl. Peter has a little girl. He told me."

Woody climbed up into her lap with his purr turned to the loudest setting.

"Hi ya, Woody. What do you think of our little stray here?"

The cat arched under her hands. Then he daintily stepped onto her knee and edged closer to the dog, sniffing intently. As if satisfied, he leaped gracefully onto the heating pad, next to the sleeping sheltie, and sat down very close to her, purring loudly. Then the cat reached out one paw and very gently touched the dog's head.

Melissa smiled. This cat was truly an original.

"Watch out, Woody, she'll be waking up soon. I don't know what she'll think of having a cat as a candy striper. Anyway, I want to take the other guys out while she's still asleep."

They all had to go out, one at a time. Hugo, who went back upstairs, and the boarders. There was Baby, a terrier mix, yappy little thing, Melissa thought with affection as she petted the rough head, and Jean-Luc, a very aristocratic-looking but thoroughly silly standard poodle. Her surgery patients had all been able to go home.

By the time they had all been out and settled back in for the night, with the extra cookie she'd promised them, Melissa returned to the stray. "We'll have to think of something to call you," she told the sleeping dog. "We can't keep calling you, 'The Stray.' Naming a dog is a very important thing, not to be taken lightly."

She wondered what Peter would think about naming a dog. She wondered if he was thinking about the dog right now. "From the way he looked at you, he probably is," she told her sleeping charge.

Peter had kissed Gert the Goose good night, and Benjamin the Elephant, Senor Lemon the yellow rabbit, Pink Kitty, and all three bears. Then it had been Angie's turn.

She flew at him exuberantly, planting wet smacks on his cheek, and as he closed his arms around her she chanted, "I want the biggest bear hug of all," and had practically strangled him with her own biggest bear hug. "I love you, Daddy," she sang out.

"I love you too, Angie." It never ceased to amaze him how much.

But now, Angie was finally in bed, under the quilt Claire had made for her. Tucked in tight with every one of her stuffed animals. Her six-year-old eyes tired and droopy at last. She'd been asleep at her grandmother's house when Peter arrived to pick her up, but she woke while he was trying to slip her arms into her coat. And when Angie woke up, she was, as usual, cheerfully wide awake. No "I-just-woke-up" blues for this child.

Angie had chatted merrily all the way home. She didn't seem to notice it was the middle of the night. But then, she didn't have to get up the next morning and be a principal. She could sleep late because she went to afternoon kindergarten.

Once they were home, it had taken Peter four times through *The Runaway Bunny* before the little blue eyes started to relax.

"Daddy," Her soft voice came to where he was still standing in the doorway, watching over the miracle that was his daughter.

"Yes, my tulip."

She giggled sleepily. "Not a tulip."

"Then what kind of a flower are you tonight?"

"I'm a snapdragon."

"Yes, my snapdragon."

"Where were you?"

"When?" But he knew when.

"Tonight. Where were you tonight?"

With a sigh of resignation, he came to sit down on the edge of her bed. He had to do this carefully, he knew. Given a choice, he would have waited until tomorrow. Or the next day. But Angie had a kind of unerring sixth sense when she thought he was trying to hide something. And then she did a terrific imitation of the Spanish Inquisition.

He might as well get it over with. At least he had time. In all probability, the dog wouldn't be able to leave the clinic for a couple of days.

Melissa—he'd stopped thinking of her as Dr. March—had run several tests to make sure the dog didn't have any infectious diseases. The sheltie had checked out clean. Still, it might take a couple of days to truly assess her condition. He refused to think they might find the people who owned her.

"Angie, tonight I helped take care of a hurt creature."

"A hurt creature?" Her eyes opened in wonderment. Angie was an exceptionally nurturing child, loved taking care of things. "What kind of a creature?"

This was the tricky part. He took a slow breath. *Don't blow it, Peter.* Hoping to seem casual and matter of fact, he took hold of her little foot through the blankets, wiggling it back and forth as he told her the next part. The important part. The difficult part.

"It is a very hurt dog." There. It was out. Now for the rest of it. "She ran out in front of my car and I hit her. It was an accident, but I am responsible. So I called Miss Foster's vet and told her what happened. Then I helped the vet take care of this dog."

He continued to move his daughter's foot back and forth like the pendulum of a clock. Rhythmic, steady, comforting. At least he hoped it was. "She's a young dog, still mostly a puppy, probably not quite a year old. The vet says you can tell from her teeth. She's pretty too. But she needs a bath. She doesn't have a home, doesn't have anyone in the world to love her. So I thought that when the dog is better, perhaps tomorrow, or the next day, you and I could go visit her. We could take her a dog biscuit or something."

He watched her eyes as they turned expressionless and flat. The interest in a hurt creature disappeared. He'd hoped she'd want to do something to help the stray dog, to take care of it. He should have known better. They'd been through this before.

"I don't like dogs," she announced stonily. "A dog killed my mommy."

Chapter Two

"I hate mornings, even Fridays," Melissa muttered to Hugo as he enthusiastically stuck his nose into her face, his way of asking her if she was awake yet.

"Go away, Hugo," she told him as she rolled over, knowing that it was a lost cause. She was right. The bulldog just trotted over to the other side of the bed and put his front paws on that side and, once again, stuck his nose into her face.

"Oh, all right," she told him as she flopped onto her back and blearily stared up at the ceiling. There was a crack in the plaster. She'd have to get it fixed. She'd never ever live in another house that had plaster walls. "I know, I know," she told her wiggling dog. "It's not perfect, but it's above the clinic." Which made it practical, affordable, and saved on gasoline.

"But someday," she told Hugo as she shoved back the blankets, "we'll live in a real house, and we'll have a huge fenced-in backyard where you can wander around for hours on end if you like."

Her dog just wiggled harder.

Melissa pulled her jeans on over her long-johns. "Okay," she said through a giant yawn. "Let's go out."

Hugo's response was immediate and totally predictable. Hugo loved mornings. Of course, Hugo loved everything. "Should have named you Pollyanna," she grumbled as she stumped downstairs. "You're so blasted cheerful all the time. And look," she added when she opened the door to let her best friend out into the tiny fenced-in area to do his morning routine, "it even snowed. Just for you," she muttered. She really hated mornings, she thought, as she stood shivering while she waited for Hugo.

Hugo loved the snow, prancing through it with utter glee, turning the smooth white stuff into a mash of paw prints and Hugo-type angels. And of course he didn't want to come back inside, so she had to remind him it was time for breakfast. That worked like a charm. Hugo loved breakfast.

Once back inside, Melissa scooped kibble into Hugo's bowl. It was, as usual, empty within two seconds of hitting the floor. She smeared cream cheese on a bagel for herself, making a note that this was the last one. Grocery shopping tomorrow. A fate worse than fleas. The only thing she hated more than mornings was grocery shopping.

When she turned around she noticed the flashing light on her answering machine. She must have been so tired last night she hadn't even seen it. She pushed the button and slumped down on the couch, still chewing her bagel, as she waited for the machine to stop rewinding.

Hugo parked himself at her feet, stared at the piece of bagel left in her hand, and drooled.

Hi, Melissa, this is Sally, the voice said, sounding as cheerful as Hugo, Melissa thought sourly. *It's a little after nine o'clock p.m. Hope you don't mind that I gave my principal your number. He's really a nice man, and he sounded like he needed help. I'll call you sometime tomorrow, or you can call me. Hope things went well, even if it was a dog. Bye.* Sally was a dyed-in-the-wool cat person.

"Well, James," Melissa said to the poster of her hero which hung on the wall. "You'd be proud of me. Things did go well, and the dog should be fine." *And the man, well, the man had been fine too. Very fine, in fact.* But that wasn't the sort of thing she could say to James Herriot. Even in her imagination. Besides, men could *appear* to be nice all they wanted to, but that didn't change the fact that they were still men. While she knew all about the temperament and anatomy of various kinds of animals, men had not been taught in vet school. All she knew about men she'd learned from Charming Michael. Now she stayed away from them.

Melissa took a final bite of bagel and tossed the last bit for Hugo. He caught it in midair.

Peter loved mornings. He loved sitting here, in his bathrobe, beside these windows, drinking coffee and watching the birds at the feeders in his backyard. There were sparrows, juncoes, and in the spring there were hummingbirds and doves. It was usually a time of peace, a time to breathe in calm and rightness and the sensual fragrance of coffee, before his day began.

But this morning, pondering last night, he was unsettled. He'd been over it and over it with Angie for the last two years. It had been an accident, pure and simple, if an accident could ever be considered pure. Claire had swerved to avoid hitting the dog and had lost control of her car and slid into the other lane. Claire loved dogs, had wanted one more than anything when she was little. In fact, they'd been planning on getting a puppy that spring. But when Claire died, a puppy had been the last thing on his mind. How ironic that something his wife had wanted for so very long had been, however indirectly, the cause of her death. Now another accident, another dog, and another change for his life.

He was about to take in a stray dog. He'd never expected anything like this to happen to him, and now as he watched the birds search for seeds under the fine coating of new white snow, he wondered about the twists and turns of life.

It was by the merest chance that he'd taken Route 14 last evening, instead of his usual way home from the school board meeting. *The road less traveled*, he thought pensively, *making all the difference*. Because of that one bit of chance, or fate, or whatever one chose to call it, he had met the dog that was going to help Angie get over her fear. He was sure of it. And he'd also met a woman.

Oh, he'd met women, lots of them, in the past two years. After all, he was a principal of an elementary school. Teachers, secretaries, administrative aides, members of the PTA, room mothers. Some of them were not very subtle about their interest in the recently-and-tragically-widowed-principal-with-a-young-daughter.

Thing was, he wasn't interested in any of them. Not that they weren't attractive, some of them. It was that he wasn't Peter Winthrop to them, he was the recently-and-tragically-widowed-principal-with-a-young-daughter. He was fair game. He was the prize. He was a "good catch," or so he'd overheard one morning when he'd arrived at school earlier than usual. It had made him feel slightly sick to his stomach.

But this woman, Melissa March, DVM—he'd noticed the certificate from the university that was framed and hung proudly on the wall of her office—this woman was different. She'd treated him as an equal, instead of as a potential bread-winner. It was refreshing, unusual, and he found that intriguing.

He wondered if there was a man in her life, and his thoughts snagged. There had been something else on the wall of her office. A framed photograph of a man wearing a tweed jacket, a dog at his side, standing among a flock of sheep. He wondered who that man was. He looked too old to be a boyfriend. Her father, or an uncle perhaps? He didn't think so. In the brief moment he'd been in her office, he'd gotten the distinct impression that the photograph had been taken in England. Well, whoever it was, Peter guessed, the man was important to her.

A cardinal flew down to find some sunflower seeds. Cardinals were so striking, with their brilliant red against the white of winter. Claire had called them brazen, but it had always been said with affection. Like blood on snow, she'd always said.

The thought screamed into his brain. Blood on snow. What would have happened if he'd not stopped last night? The dog might have died, its blood mixing with the newly fallen snow. Just like Claire.

Suddenly he didn't want any more coffee.

He set his cup in the spotless sink and left the kitchen to finish getting dressed.

He had lots to do today, he thought as he pulled his suit from the closet. He'd promised Melissa he'd do all the things that one does when one finds a lost dog. Look in newspapers, call the animal shelter, call the other vets in town. After all, it was the honorable thing to do. But he didn't have to hope he'd find the people who'd owned the dog.

They cared enough to get her tattooed with an identification number. The thought wound itself around and around in his mind, much as Woody had wound himself around the table legs the night before. *But they didn't register the number,* he reminded himself sternly. How much could they have cared if they hadn't even registered the number?

Besides, Angie needed this dog, she just didn't know it yet. Angie was tenacious, yes, but she'd inherited that trait from him. He could be just as stubborn as she could be, and he was sure that this was the dog to help her. He also wanted another reason to see Melissa March.

Ten minutes later, Peter sat on the living room couch tying his shoes—knots he could see, he thought to himself, remembering the slight touch of her hands as she had tied the strings of the surgical gown. He felt a smile form on his face, and he let his eyes drift closed so he could better hold onto that memory. Just for a second, he thought he caught the faintest whisper of the scent of peaches.

The front door opened, bringing in his mother-in-law and a blast of frigid air.

"Good morning, Gloria," he said, trying to control his irritation that even after Claire's death she continued to walk into his house without knocking.

"Good morning, Peter," she returned, beaming at him as she set a shopping bag by her feet and slipped out of her coat and hung it up. As soon as she closed the closet door she marched over to the rocking chair under the window and whisked yesterday's suit jacket off the back of it. "I'll hang this up for you, dear. You must have been so tired last night that you just left it here, not thinking."

That was the problem, he thought. She was so nice. If she were nasty, or mean, or imperious, he could deal with it. But she was a nice pleasant woman. It was like trying to fight a feather pillow. One with a core of iron. "I'm sorry, Gloria," he apologized, squashing down the little sniggle of irritation.

She held out a shopping bag from Hartley's finest department store. "You also must have forgotten the dress I bought for Angelina."

Yes, he had forgotten it. Deliberately. *But*, he reminded himself, *you catch more flies with honey than with vinegar*. "Thank you for bringing it this morning. Ang . . . Angelina's still asleep, so I'll put it in the closet until later." He moved past her to the closet to put the bag inside, and took out his coat.

"Well, then, after I hang up your clothes, I'll make her breakfast and have it ready for her when she wakes up." Gloria floated upstairs, a study of grandmotherly concern.

Suddenly, he felt suffocated by her care. Gloria felt it her duty to come over every morning and stay with Angie until it was time for her to go to school. Then she picked Angie up after school and kept her until he arrived home in the late afternoon. Gloria didn't want her granddaughter, Claire's daughter, she said, being raised by a series of baby-sitters. So here she was, in his house, fixing breakfast for his daughter, as she did every morning. She loved Angie, and Angie loved her. It was small of him to not appreciate her more, he always told himself. He was really very lucky that she was willing to do so much for them.

Gloria did have one quirk, though—dresses. Gloria, claiming Peter couldn't possibly know about such things, was the one who bought all of Angie's clothes. Gloria believed in dresses. All little girls belonged in dresses, all the time, no exceptions, no matter what. At least he'd finally been able to convince Gloria not to buy any more frills and lace. He'd gently pointed out that fancy things were just not suitable for kindergarten. Angie needed to be able to run and play and jump and spill paint on herself like the other kids. So the frills had stopped, but not the dresses.

Last night Melissa had been wearing jeans. They had fit very well, he'd noticed. *Better not follow that train of thought,* he cautioned himself. Then he silently counted to ten before he started his usual discussion with his mother-in-law, who had come back downstairs to start Angie's breakfast.

"Gloria," he called to her quietly, not wanting to wake his daughter. "It looks cold today. Did you have any trouble starting your car?"

She reappeared in the kitchen doorway, paring knife and an apple in her hand. Evidently Angie would have sliced fruit with her oatmeal this morning.

"Oh, yes," Gloria told him. "It was very cold indeed. I hope I don't need a new battery for my car before the winter is over. Thank goodness that will be very soon now," she fussed.

"I think," he said, trying to make it appear if he'd just had the thought, "Ang—" He stopped, and went on carefully. "Angelina will be warmer wearing her flannel lined pants to school." He purposely did not call them jeans. "If there is outdoor recess I don't want her to be cold."

Her forehead wrinkled, and for a moment he thought she might give in without an argument.

But then her face cleared. "I'll just make sure she has her knit tights on. They'll keep her plenty warm. I remember Claire always wore knit tights when it was cold. Even as a child Claire was always a lady." She beamed at him as if she had just solved the problems of the world. "Have a good day, Peter, and remember to wear your scarf." She returned to the kitchen to prepare a thoroughly nutritious breakfast for his daughter.

He dropped his coat on the sofa and followed her. "Gloria?" *Be firm, but kind, Peter*, he reminded himself.

"Yes, dear?" she said, not turning around

from where she now stood at the kitchen sink, peeling the apple. He noticed that the coffee cup he'd set there earlier this morning was nowhere in sight.

"I would like Angelina to wear her pants today."

This time she did turn to face him, and there was a look of hurt in her eyes. "Oh, Peter, it's just not ladylike for girls to wear pants. She'll grow up to be a tomboy, or worse." Her chin trembled slightly as she looked at him imploringly.

Why did he always feel like a heel when they went through this? *Remember, firm but gentle, as if you're dealing with recalcitrant fourth-graders*. But this was not a recalcitrant fourth-grader, he reminded himself, this was his mother-in-law, who loved Angie. "I know you care about her very much, and want what's best for her." Peter reached out to touch the woman's arm, to try to soften his words. "But believe me, at school Angelina is much happier wearing pants like the other girls. She doesn't have to worry about keeping those lovely dresses you buy for her clean."

"It isn't ladylike," she protested.

"But it *is* childlike," he insisted gently. "Please, let her be a child."

"But Claire always—"

Suddenly he was impatient with her. "But this is *not* Claire. This is Angie!" As soon as the words were out he regretted them.

He watched as two tears made their way

down her soft cheeks, feeling guilty because he knew he'd put them there. But he wanted her to stop trying to make Angie into another Claire.

"I know she's not Claire," she whispered, and her fingers clenched on the fabric of her apron. "But Peter, I miss my daughter so very much. Angelina is all I have left of her."

"I know you miss her, Gloria. I do too." He put his arm around her sagging shoulders, patting the soft back for a moment. "But I owe it to Claire to help Angie grow up to be happy."

"I wish you wouldn't call her by that name," she said at last, sniffing.

He gave her a very slight grin, knowing that she would be all right now. "Angie prefers it."

"It's not ladylike."

"But she's not a lady yet, she's still a child. Perhaps when she's grown up she'll want to be called Angelina. But for now, pants today, all right?"

She nodded, eyes downcast, and with a sigh that he thought just a tad bit theatrical, presented her back to him, her attention once more on the breakfast she was making. He was obviously dismissed, he thought with amusement.

Peter made an about-face and headed for the door, shrugging on his coat. On his way past, he pulled his scarf, the one Gloria had knitted him for Christmas, from the closet. Time for work, and the many things he had to do that day. He would call Melissa, after she'd had time to get started on her day, just to find out how the dog was. *Be honest,* he told himself with a grin. *You also want to hear her voice again.*

"Good morning, little stray one," Melissa crooned. "Looks like you're standing up just fine, even on that cast. Why are you back in the corner? I won't hurt you." She opened the latch to the pen and entered, deliberately acting casual. The sheltie tried to back up further, her expression noncommittal. "You can't back up any further, I'm sorry, the wall is in the way." She stooped down, offering her hand. "Look. Remember me? I'm the good guy. Go ahead, sniff. You'll smell Hugo, and he's a good guy too. So whaddya say? Can we be friends?"

The stray dog watched her for a moment longer, then reached out her nose to sniff delicately at Melissa's hand.

"That's right. Good girl." Shelties could be shy around strange people. It sometimes took them a while to warm up, but when they did, they stuck fast as fleas.

Moving carefully and slowly so as not to startle her, Melissa slipped a leash loop over the dog's head and patiently drew her out of the pen. "Let's go outside for a minute. You remember outside from last night. I know you do," Melissa said, keeping up the encouragement as she led the stray to the exercise pen outside. "Good girl," she said, putting quiet praise in her voice.

A few minutes later, she led the stray back into the treatment room and lifted her up on an exam table. "Let's take a look at you this morning." The dog made no protest as Melissa prodded and felt around her abdomen. "You're being a very patient girl," Melissa said, looking into the dog's eyes.

The dog seemed to be reserving judgment, holding herself aloof enough for any royal family. Well, that was typical of the breed, Melissa thought as she continued her exam.

"Hello," a woman's voice called from the front of the clinic.

The stray looked startled, fear returning to her eyes. She let out a warning yip.

"It's okay, it's just Jessie, my vet tech," Melissa told her. "I'm back here, Jess."

By the time Melissa had convinced herself that the dog would be fine, the heady scent of freshly brewed coffee filled the clinic and she closed her eyes for a moment in anticipation. "You're doing so well, there, girl," she told the dog. "I think we can take you out of intensive care, and put you in one of the cages in this room. There you go, up and in. Look, here's a nice comfy blanket to nap on and here's some breakfast. I'll be back in a bit. I need my morning coffee fix so I act like a reasonable human being."

The dog wouldn't look at her. It would take time for the dog to develop trust. Time and patience and lots of it, Melissa thought as she made her way to her office, and a blessed cup of coffee.

* * *

"Oh, Jessie, you make the best coffee in the world!" Melissa inhaled the fragrant steam that wafted up from her mug. "Your coffee makes mornings bearable."

From the front desk, she could hear Jessie snort. "What's the matter? You stay up too late reading that new Michaelson book? You only think it's the best coffee in the world because you didn't make it."

"My coffee always tastes like old tires."

"It wouldn't if you learned to make it properly."

Melissa, now fortified with the best coffee in the world, looked up as her good friend came in to drop the appointment book on her desk. "The books on small-business management always say to praise your workers for what they do well. It makes them feel needed and valued."

Jessie snorted again. "They should also say not to lie."

Melissa set her mug down. "Yeah. I know." She sighed morosely. Then she brightened. "But you still make the best coffee in the world. I can't cook. I admit it."

Jessie chuckled. "Coffee isn't cooking. It's putting grounds in the coffeemaker, adding water, and turning the thing on."

"Like I said, I can't cook." But fun and games were over for the morning. It was time to get some work done before patients started arriving. Melissa pulled her pen out of the pocket of her lab coat and studied her appointment book.

"Oh, and uh, M'liss," Jessie stammered, "Mrs.

Shoemaker called a couple of minutes ago."

Melissa jerked her attention from the appointment book over to Jessie, still standing in the doorway.

"She says Sandy still isn't eating." Jessie's normally cheerful face was drawn with concern. "I told her to bring him in early this morning, we'd make time to see him, no matter what."

Melissa nodded. "Absolutely," she agreed firmly. "No matter what."

Jess turned to go, then whirled around again to face Melissa. "Oh, and who is that filthy little sheltie with a cast on her leg that I just saw in the treatment room? I don't remember her from yesterday."

"She was an emergency, brought in last night." Melissa noticed Jessie's eyes narrowing, body becoming alert, like a hunting dog on point.

"Brought in by who?"

"Whom."

"What?" There was confusion on Jessie's face.

"You use 'whom' in that sentence. It's the object, not the subject. 'Brought in by whom.' Not 'brought in by who.' "

Jessie took the stack of clinical textbooks off the chair and deposited them firmly on the desk, then decisively sat down. Woody promptly jumped up on her lap and started his motor.

"So, Dr. March, cut the grammar lesson and spill it." The emphasis was on the "Dr." And though Jessie's voice was teasing, Melissa noticed her hands were very gentle as she rubbed the cat under his chin. Woody blissed out. Still, the speculative gleam in Jessie's eyes was something to avoid.

"There's nothing to spill. Oh, remind me to call Bollard Pharmaceuticals, will you? We need more heartworm pills. Spring is coming—that means mosquitoes and heartworm checks. April is National Heartworm Prevention Month, you know."

"I'm well aware of National Heartworm Month. Stop shoving that paper around," Jessie ordered with the familiarity of an old and dear friend. "Who is the sheltie and where did she come from? And why is she here?"

Melissa sighed, then grinned at her friend. "Let's go look at her. She's something special. I want to introduce you to her. Why are you always such a bully?" she added as they made their way down the hall to the treatment room followed by the clinic cat. "You're supposed to be my friend."

"I am your friend," Jessie pointed out reasonably. "That's why you have to tell me things. If you tell me nicely I don't bully you."

Melissa stopped at the treatment room door. "I suppose you want the truth?"

"The whole truth and nothing but. Just make sure it's juicy," Jess added cheerily.

Melissa chuckled as she opened the door and held it for Jessie. "Nothing juicy about this one, my friend, sorry." Nothing but a man who smelled incredibly good, and who had kind hands when he picked up a hurt dog. But she had no business thinking about that, she reminded herself. "Sally Foster's principal accidentally hit a stray dog in the road last night. He called Sally, she gave him the clinic number. I went out to take care of her and brought her here, that's all."

As she moved over to the cage Melissa heard Jessie's derisive snort, but she decided to ignore it. Her attention was on the dog. "See, Little Stray, I told you I'd come back. And I brought a friend."

"No, no, Woody," she heard Jessie say. "We don't know if this dog likes cats yet. Even a cat as terrific as you are. Let's you stay out here in the hall till we find out." The door clicked, then Jessie continued. "Okay, Melissa, so he's Sally's principal. So tell me about him. How does he fit into things?" Jessie was not going to let this go.

"Jessie, this is Little Stray. Little Stray, this is Jessie. She's really a nice person, but she doesn't know when to quit sometimes. She was probably a terrier in a former life. Probably a kerry blue terrier. They're one of the most stubborn kinds." Melissa lifted the dog out of the crate and set her on the floor.

"Don't change the subject," Jessie groused, squatting down to let the dog sniff her hand. "Hey Little Stray, what's your real name? It's okay, you can tell me. You're sure a timid little thing. I know. Let's call you Spike, or Rambo. Oh, you're a girl. I know, why don't we just call you Rambette? Sniff away, that's it. You smell Woody. He likes dogs." Jess continued her patter as the little dog sniffed her hand. "Who is this man who you decided to run into, eh? Or should I say 'whom'? Melissa is being very secretive about it. She keeps trying to change the subject. But at the same time, she's turning pink. So I guess I have to ask you."

The little dog backed away from Jessie a few steps, then stopped and let out a few sharp barks. Typical sheltie temperament, Melissa noted.

"Why are you so obsessed with the man who brought her here?"

Jess trained her gaze on Melissa. "Because now you're turning from pink to red, that's why."

Melissa could hear the amusement in her friend's voice and she felt her face grow even hotter. "Let's start her on shots. No way of knowing what, if anything, she's had." She carefully picked up the dog and set her on the table. "Up we go, Little Stray. You're an incredible romantic, you know that."

"You're an incredible cynic, you know that?"

They grinned at each other with perfect understanding. They'd known each other for a long time.

"M'liss." Jessie's voice was tentative as she opened a drawer and took out a syringe and a tiny bottle. "Some men are okay people."

"You really think so? I hadn't noticed." Melissa placed the stethoscope on the dog's chest.

"Still sounding good," she told the dog, giving her a pat on the head. "Let's see if we can get you looking good as well. Jessie, what do you think? You think this dog needs a bath, or what?"

When Jessie didn't answer right away, Melissa looked up to see Jessie standing still, all levity gone from her freckled face. In fact, she looked downright serious as she handed Melissa the filled syringe.

"I think," her friend said, "you'll never notice that all men aren't jerks until you're willing to let one close enough to find out."

"I did that once," Melissa replied shortly. She pulled up the skin at the back of the dog's neck and injected the needle. The little dog didn't flinch. "I found out. He was a jerk."

"All men aren't Charming Michael." Jessie's voice was very quiet.

Pain ripped through Melissa as if she'd been punched in the stomach. "That's just it, Jess," she said, feeling tears suddenly threaten. "I didn't know Michael was either. I thought he was perfect." She looked down at the dog's head. Such lovely golden fur.

Michael had golden hair also, long and luxurious. Lying in bed with him, streaming her fingers through the silky stuff, she used to tell him he looked like a lion. She'd thought he was majestic and regal. She'd thought he was the sun and the moon and the stars. "But I was wrong. I was so very wrong." She disposed of the needle, keeping her face from Jessie. She was careful to keep all emotion out of her voice as she continued. "You see, Jess, if I was so wrong about him—and I was, I really was—how can I ever trust my own judgment again?"

"So," her friend answered quietly, "it's easier to think all men are jerks than to risk being wrong again." She nodded her head sagely. "Yup. Makes sense to me. But M'liss, it makes for a very lonely life."

"Mr. Winthrop." His secretary stuck her head through the door to his office. "The librarian said they have two books on shelties and that she'll save them for you. Are you getting a dog for Angie?" she asked enthusiastically.

He should have remembered that Mrs. Calloway loved dogs. She and Sally Foster thought the greatest indoor sport was to discuss the merits of dogs versus the merits of cats, each insisting their own favored species was the greatest on earth. At times it became positively obnoxious. Now Mrs. Calloway was beaming as if he'd given her the moon.

"I'm thinking of it," he admitted. "But please, whatever you do, don't tell anyone. Especially my mother-in-law." Peter shuddered at the thought. He knew what Gloria thought of dogs. "Or Angie. It might not work out and I don't want her to be upset."

"Don't worry, Mr. Winthrop, I'll not tell a soul. You know I wouldn't do anything to hurt your little angel." With her fingers to her lips and a gleam in her eye, she withdrew back into the outer office.

He hoped she *could* keep this secret.

He glanced at his watch. It was quarter after eleven, time for the morning kindergartners to leave, and the first-graders to have lunch. It was a noisy time in the school. But more importantly, today at eleven-thirty, he had to leave for a meeting with the president of the school board. He looked at the phone and drummed his fingers on his desktop. He had a couple of minutes. Should he call her? He'd studied the slip of paper that had her phone number on it so many times that the number was imprinted in his memory. It would be a casual call, he told himself, just to ask how the dog was. No big deal. Just to find out how the dog was. That's all. Just the dog.

"This is Dr. March."

The instant he heard her voice he knew he'd lied to himself. He was struck silent for a moment. Then all of a sudden his voice returned. "This is Peter . . . Peter Winthrop." He felt like a teenager again, stuttering and shy, as if he were calling a girl for the first time. He had to pull himself together quickly. "I was just calling to find out how the dog is." *Liar*, his conscience taunted him just like a fourth-grader.

"She's fine." Her voice was pleasant and professional. "She came out of the anesthesia without any problems. She's getting used to the cast, and she's had a small breakfast."

"She must have been hungry after being on her own for a while."

"I'm not sure about that. She threw up as she was coming out of the anesthesia. That's not unusual under the circumstances, nothing to be upset about," she added quickly, her voice losing that professional tone and becoming more like the voice he remembered. The voice that had haunted his dreams. "She threw up tiny bones, so I think she had probably been eating mice, or other roadkill. Not the most balanced diet for a growing dog, but I don't think it'll hurt her in the long run. As long as she gets quality food from now on."

He swallowed convulsively, feeling a little sick. He didn't know what to say.

"I know," she continued in a more personal tone, evidently knowing what he was feeling. "It is awful to think about, isn't it. It makes me cringe as well. My first dog, when I was seven, was a stray. The same thing had happened to her. I mean, she wasn't hit by a car, but she had survived on her own for a while and had been eating roadkill. She'd been poisoned and was almost dead when I found her. That's why I became a vet. To save the lives of other dogs, like Doc Fields had saved Shirley."

He cleared his throat, strangely moved by her words. "I called the pound, and I looked through the newspaper. No one has reported a lost sheltie for several weeks."

He heard her sigh. "Then we can assume she has no home. Poor thing. She is such a lovely dog." Her voice grew in animation as she continued. "We gave her a good combing and a bath. We had to cut out some of the mats so she has some spots that are pretty bald, but Peter, she is lovely And she's beginning to know us. Jessie and Suzette—they work for me—and I have been spending time with her in between patients. I think she's just looking for someone to love. Dogs are like that, you know?"

He knew from her voice that that special sparkle was in her eyes, and he hungered to see that sparkle, to be near her again. "Do you think it would be all right if I stopped over to see her this afternoon after school is out? I'd like to bring my daughter."

"That would be fine. My last patient is at five, so it would be best if you could come soon after that." There was a slight pause. Then she continued. "Tell me about your daughter. Does she have any experience with dogs?"

He had to be honest with her. There was no way he couldn't. He owed it to her, and besides, she needed to know what she was getting into. "My daughter is six. She's in Sally's class, in fact. She loves cats. Angie does, I mean." *You're stalling, Peter,* he told himself.

"But?" she prompted.

"She's afraid of dogs." He said the words without emphasis.

"Why?"

"She thinks a dog killed her mother."

Her gasp came over the phone lines clearly. "Is that true?"

"No. Not really. Claire died two winters ago. It was very late at night. She swerved to avoid hitting a dog and slid on a patch of ice into an oncoming car. It really was an accident, but for some reason Angie is convinced that a dog killed her mother. Now, two years later, another accident involving a dog. Ironic, isn't it? Even if this time there's a different ending."

"Oh, Peter." The concern in her voice was almost a palpable thing, almost as if she were touching him, and he closed his eyes as if he could make that touch a reality. "If she's afraid of dogs, do you think bringing her here is the best thing?"

"Melissa . . ." He realized he'd never said her name out loud before, but he liked the way her name felt. "Melissa, I've talked to her about dogs, we've read stories about dogs, gone to see movies about dogs. She's still nervous around them. But she also has great compassion for hurt things, like that cat Sally found, the one that had to have its leg amputated."

"Ah, yes, Troy. He's a nice cat. So you think by bringing her to visit this hurt dog, she may get over her fear of them in general? Peter, this is a stray dog. We don't know anything about her background. Shelties as a breed are usually fine with children, but there is no way of knowing if this particular dog is."

"This dog will be fine. I'm sure she will."

"You're not thinking clearly." Her voice was emphatic. "Let me repeat this. There is no way of knowing anything about the background of

61

this dog. The way people treat a puppy can affect that dog for the rest of its life."

"But you said this dog is still a puppy," he insisted, knowing that he was being stubborn.

"She is, but we have no idea how she has been treated up until now." Her voice was as emphatic as his had been. "There are breed clubs all over the country who have committees of people who rescue their breed and find them homes. They are very good people, and care deeply about their dogs. I'm sure there are lots of sheltie people who will be only too happy to foster her until they can place her. They'll probably even pay her vet bill. Don't feel you have to take on that responsibility."

"But I *am* responsible!" he burst out.

He raked his fingers through his hair, and frowned in concentration. How could he make her understand what he'd felt for that dog when he didn't understand it himself? "Melissa, this sounds bizarre, I know, but I honestly think that this dog is the one to help Angie. Last night, while I was waiting for you . . . Look, I know it sounds totally off the wall, but I looked into her eyes and I felt as if I recognized her, and she recognized me." Yeah, it really did sound off the wall. Melissa probably thought he was a total kook. He took a deep breath before he continued. "I just have this gut feeling that she'll be okay. The dog has no home, you said so yourself. Well, I *am* responsible for her, and I want to give her a home. I want to keep her."

"Whoa! Let me get this straight. You want to

keep her," she repeated. "I don't mean to sound rude, but . . . No, on second thought, I don't care if I do sound rude. Too many people take on puppies and kittens without knowing what is involved. That's why they end up hit on the road. And in shelters, and . . ." She broke off again. "Sorry. This is a big thing with me. I tend to get carried away." She sighed. "I'll try to be more tactful. Have you ever had a dog? Do you have a pet now? Why do you think yours would be a good home for this dog?"

"Angie and I don't have any pets now, but I had a dog while I was growing up. I want to give Angie a best friend, like my dog was my best friend. And this is the dog I want. If she needs medicine, I'll get it. If she needs another operation, I'll pay for it. Whatever it takes. Melissa, I *know* that she is Angie's dog." He was suddenly aware of just how strongly he felt.

There was silence on the other end. He was determined not to be the one to break it.

"You're real stubborn, aren't you?" Did he detect slight amusement in her voice?

"Yeah. I am. Especially when it concerns my daughter. But I'll need help with this. I know I don't know everything about dogs, but you do. So, will you help me help this dog? And help Angie get over her fear?" Even as he said the words, he knew they were only half the truth. Just as he somehow knew that this dog was meant for Angie, he knew that this woman was meant to be part of his life.

"Such a deal. How can I resist?" She chuckled, and once again he was struck by the intimacy of her voice. "I'll see you here about five-thirty. And Peter, I think it would be best if I first introduced your daughter to a dog that positively likes children, so I can get a better feel for how she'll react. I don't want the sheltie to be upset, any more than I want your daughter to be frightened."

"Do you have a dog in mind?" It was going to work! He knew it!

"Hugo. My dog. He loves everyone. And while we're making deals, if she gets nervous around Hugo, the sheltie is off limits this time. Agreed?"

"Agreed." She'd said "this time," as if there would be other times.

"And Peter . . ." There was a pause before she continued in a slower, more serious voice. "What you said a minute ago about recognizing this dog. It doesn't sound bizarre. Not to me. Not at all."

Melissa hung the phone up with a sigh. After Jessie's insinuations, *which were nothing but insinuations,* she told herself firmly, she had decided that if he did call—to check on the dog, of course—she'd be coolly professional. At first she had been. But when she heard his voice she couldn't seem to help herself. "Dumb, dumb, dumb, Melissa," she muttered. She swiveled back and forth in her chair while she continued to lecture herself. *Sure, he's a nice guy, they all are until you get to know them better, and they start to take you for granted. And then they take advantage of you, and they start using you. They make you over into what they want you to be, because what you are is not good enough for them. And then you find yourself forgetting all about your dreams, your goals, to help The Man with his. Forget it, girl. Men are simply not in your picture. Stick with dogs; they're much more dependable and loyal, and they don't leave the toilet seat up.*

But this man had a daughter. A little girl who thought a dog had killed her mother, and was now afraid of dogs. This man had done everything he could to help his daughter get over her fear of them. Now he'd found a dog he thought would do it, but he needed her help. And she'd ended up grilling him about what kind of home he'd give that dog. All of Karen's canine militancy was evidently rubbing off. Karen would be so proud when she found out. "Interestinger and interestinger," she murmured as she tapped her pen on a notepad. "Decisions, decisions." *Okay*, she told herself firmly. *This is the deal. You can help him with his daughter, and with the dog, but you are absolutely not going to get involved with him on a personal level.*

She craned her neck around so she could see the photograph on the wall. "Well, then, James, I have something to do. Sally has been trying to talk me into this since September."

After a good look at the rest of the day's patient schedule, she looked up a number in her rolodex and dialed the phone. "Suzette," she called to her receptionist while she was waiting for the phone to ring. "I'm going out for an hour at lunch."

"Good morning, Montrose Elementary School," the voice said over the line. Melissa recognized that voice.

"Hello, Mrs. Calloway. This is Melissa March. I'd like to get an important message to Sally Foster, please."

Chapter Three

They're after him again, he thought sourly as he pulled into his parking space. When would the school board realize that he was not interested in being the next superintendent of schools? He liked being a principal, and he was good at it. They thought he was good at it too, which was why they wanted to put his name forth for discussion. They wanted him to turn the whole school system around, as he had Montrose Elementary.

After stomping the light snow off his shoes, Peter entered the building. Ah. He breathed in the smell of his school and let it banish all thoughts of the school board. The fragrance of finger paints and cleansers and worn sneakers. There was nothing like it in the world. He stood for a moment, his hand on the door to his office, and gazed down the hall where the lower-grade rooms were. He could hear the faint chanting from Miss Manchester's class, and Ms. Leslie was pounding out a tune on the piano while the second-graders sang along. The halls were lined with collages from art classes, and there were poems, posters and maps drawn with colored pencils and crayons on brightly colored construction paper. His school really should buy stock in a company that made construction paper.

"Oh, Mr. Winthrop." There was delighted surprise in Mrs. Calloway's voice as she came bustling out of the office and spotted him. "I didn't know you were back. Have you stopped in Miss Foster's room? She has a visitor. It's so exciting. You know, she's tried to get Dr. March to come to her class since school started."

Peter stared at her. "Dr. March?" he repeated, immediately feeling foolish.

"Yes. She's the veterinarian I take my Clarence to. I wouldn't take him anywhere else." Mrs. Calloway beamed at him.

"You're saying Dr. March is here? In Sally's class?"

"Yes. And Dr. March brought her cat and her dog. Isn't it wonderful? Mrs. Field's class is there also. Mr. Winthrop, where are you going?" Her voice trailed after him. "I have those figures you needed for the school board meeting next week."

"That's great, Mrs. Calloway," he called over

his shoulder to her, softly so he wouldn't disturb the classrooms, even though there was an assortment of voices coming from them. "I'll be back in a moment. I just want to look in on Sally's class."

It would only be a moment, he promised himself. After all, it was his duty as principal to greet any guests who came to his school. Nothing personal about it.

But when he reached the door to Sally's classroom, he knew he was fooling himself. Looking in the window, he could see giggling children from both kindergarten classes sitting on the large rug at the back of the room. Melissa sat in the Guest Chair, laughing with them. The ugliest dog he had ever seen was sitting at her feet, though the word "sitting" was stretching it. The dog, who was gazing at her with something very akin to adoration, was wiggling so much it was a miracle it didn't fall over.

Then Melissa said something to it, and the dog instantly dropped to the ground and rolled over. The kids roared with laughter. The dog stood up, snuffled and snorted at the kids, as if agreeing with them, then shook its ugly body and sat down again to continue its worship of Dr. March.

Peter searched the seething throng of kindergartners for Angie and finally saw her, by the row of easels, standing next to Sally. He watched her carefully for a moment, looking for signs of stress, or nervousness. She didn't laugh with the others at the antics of the ugly dog, and he noticed her hand was clutching Sally's. Then he saw Woody, doing precise figure-eights around the two of them. Winding around and around, rubbing against their legs.

An excited roar from the kids jerked his attention back to the ugly dog. It was sitting up on its rump. He stared as Melissa tossed something up in the air and the dog caught it.

He opened the door and slipped inside.

"This is Hugo's favorite trick of all," she was saying. But then she happened to glance his way and their gazes locked. For one breathless moment they stood as if in a tableau, as if the rest of existence had simply ceased to be and there was only the two of them drowning in each other's eyes.

The dog barked. The moment was lost. Suddenly Melissa looked nervous as she wiped her hands on the legs of her jeans. He watched in fascination as a tinge of red flooded her cheeks and she looked away from him, back to the children.

"What's his favorite trick?" little Jeremy asked her. Jeremy and Mrs. Calloway traded dog stories, Peter remembered.

Melissa looked startled for a second, he thought. But then she evidently pulled herself together, for she stood up, said, "Stay," to the dog, and waded through the kids to Woody, still figure-eighting around Sally and Angie.

"Woody here," she said to the kids after picking up the orange cat, "is very unique. I don't know where he came from, or if he ever lived with dogs before, but now Woody and Hugo are best friends." She made her way back through the mass of five-and-six-year-olds.

"He's purring!" Joshua Martini called out. "He's as loud as a tank!"

"Wow, it's so loud!" and "Cool," the kids said in amazement. Even from the door, Peter could hear the cat's squeaky purr.

"But boys and girls," Melissa said. "This is what Hugo loves best. Hugo." She paused and waited for the dog to look up. "Hugo, stand."

The ugly dog lumbered to his feet and stood. "Stay!" she told him. "Hold still, don't wiggle, you silly thing. There, that's right." The dog was making an obvious effort to hold very still and at the same time wag his corkscrew of a tail.

"Woody, up." The cat lightly jumped on the dog's massive back and sat down as calmly as if he were sitting in a patch of sunlight.

The children stared, the silence broken only by the purring of the cat.

"Now, remember," Melissa cautioned them with a smile, "don't try this at home with your dogs and cats. They might not like it. Okay, who remembers what to do if a strange dog comes up to you?"

Peter immediately glanced at Angie while a little voice sang out, "Be a tree!"

Even though Angie wasn't moving, he could tell by the set of her shoulders and the tilt of her head that she was listening intently.

"Right!" Melissa announced. "Who remembers what *not* to do if a strange dog comes up to you?"

"Don't run!" It was Katy, who loved to run, waving her arm frantically in the air. "And don't look him in the eye."

"What else?" she asked them.

"Don't scream!" several children called out at once.

"Wow!" Melissa looked at them with wide eyes. "You guys really listened well. I'm very impressed! Okay, now, let's get Woody off Hugo's back. There you go, Woody." She picked up the cat and handed him across the kids to Sally, then sat back down. The ugly dog was still standing, only his tail moving. "Hugo," she told him. "Okay!" The word released the dog from his position, and he immediately started wiggling and snuffling so enthusiastically that he wiggled right into the front row of the children. They, of course, loved it.

"Hugo, come over here. Good boy. Now, sit." Even though the dog was sitting, he was still wiggling in enthusiasm, and as he watched Melissa his eyes were so full of such reverence that even from the doorway, Peter couldn't miss it. *Yeah, pal,* he said silently to the dog, *she is something special.*

"I would like to thank you all for asking Hugo and Woody and me to come visit you at school today."

"Kindergartners," Sally called to them, Woody still in her arms. "What do we say to Dr.

March for bringing Woody and Hugo to school?"

The children chorused a loud *Thank you, Dr. March* right on cue. Sally had taught them well.

"Kindergartners," Sally called over the din, "Miss Foster's class needs to stay sitting so Mrs. Field's class can go stand in line next to Mr. Winthrop." Sally was speaking of herself in the third person as kindergarten teachers always seemed to do.

The kids jostled and thronged around Hugo to pet him. What an incredibly patient dog he must be to withstand the enthusiastic and affectionate mauling of thirty-nine five-and-six-year-olds. Some of the children were at Sally's side petting Woody, who did not seem the least perturbed by it all. Peter noticed that Angie was still next to Sally, petting Woody with the other children.

Melissa was just as patient, listening carefully to those who asked her questions. He could see her answering them, could see her mouth move, but couldn't make out the words.

"Miss Foster's class," Sally's voice called, soaring across the room, "when you have petted Hugo and Woody, I want you to stand in a line next to Mrs. Field's class so we can all go to the rest room. Jenny, I like the way you're standing in line. Jeremy is also standing quietly."

Ah, yes, standing quietly in line, Peter thought. *One of the most essential skills taught in kindergarten.*

He felt a tug on his hand, and there was Angie. "Hi, Daddy." She pulled on his arm.

"Hi, Angie. What do you think of Hugo there?"

"He sure is ugly."

Peter chuckled as he drew her away from the door where the others were lining up. "Yes, he is, but he's also very patient. See how he likes being petted?" Peter pointed to the dog. "I bet he thinks this is really fun, doing tricks for your class."

"I like Woody better," Angie announced decisively.

There was a hint of pugnaciousness in her eyes that he recognized as something he himself had on occasion. "Well, you know, some people like cats, and some people like dogs. And some people like them both."

"I like cats."

He stooped down to her level. "I know you do. Angie, do you know that your mom liked dogs?"

The look she gave him was one of pure disbelief.

"It's true. She always wanted a dog when she was your age. Did I ever tell you that we were going to get a dog?"

"I don't believe you."

"Well, we were. Look at Hugo. He is shaking hands with Joshua Martini."

Angie looked, then looked pointedly away.

Peter sighed. This might be more difficult than he thought it would be. With a pat, he sent his daughter out the door after the other kindergartners.

*   *   *

Finally, Melissa thought, blessed silence. All the children, herded along by the other kindergarten teacher, were on their way to the rest room. How did Sally manage the noise? It would drive her crazy.

"Thank you so very much, Melissa," Sally enthused as she brought purring Woody to the front of the room. "They all learned so much, and I know they had a good time."

Melissa took Woody, holding him close, conscious that Peter was still standing at the door, silently watching her. She hoped she wasn't blushing, and she rubbed her cheek on Woody's vibrating orange fur.

Sally bent down to scratch Hugo's head. Hugo, of course, adored Sally and gave her his ugly grin.

"Hugo," Sally said with affection, "you really are an ugly dog."

"He's bright and beautiful," Melissa warned teasingly. "Remember, I'm your vet."

"And you're the best vet in the world." Sally had the widest, most infectious grin Melissa had ever seen. "I can't thank you enough for finally coming to my class. But, I have to be off now to rescue my little darlings before they drown each other in the water fountains. Talk to you later. Bye, Hugo, bye, Woody. Hi, Peter, bye, Peter," she sang as she breezed out the door.

They were alone again, she thought. She and Peter. They stood gazing at each other from across the room, in silence. Silence except for Woody's continuous motor, Hugo's panting, and the distant clamor of daily life in an elementary school.

"Hello, Dr. March." Peter came up next to her, his voice as warm as she had tried to forget it was, the scent of him once more teasing her sensibilities.

"Hello, Peter." Color once again flooded her face as her sensibilities ran amok. *Melissa, you're being very very dumb here. Grow up. It's probably only his laundry detergent that smells so good.* "This is Hugo. You didn't meet him last night. Hugo, this is Peter Winthrop. He's the principal here, so you better behave." Still clutching Woody, she sat back down in the Guest Chair.

Peter hunkered down on his heels in front of the dog. "Hello, Hugo."

Hugo fell in love with Peter Winthrop on sight. Of course, it was to be expected. Hugo would fall in love with a turnip. The dog slung his tongue around, trying to reach Peter's hand.

"Why Hugo?"

"What?"

"His name."

She chuckled. "He was even uglier when he was a puppy. But I didn't want to call him Quasimodo."

"Ah," Peter said, as if it were all clear. "And somehow you didn't like the name Victor."

Why did he have to be so charming, Melissa thought in dismay. Charming men had always

76

been her Waterloo. Look how hard she had fallen for Michael. Well, it wouldn't work this time. She had learned her lesson. She would be friendly, but she would not, under any conditions, fall under his spell. She absolutely refused.

"Good for you," she told him keeping her smile friendly yet noncommittal. "Not many people are that quick."

Woody arrived, and turned his purr up loud enough for any teenager's boom box.

"Hello, Woody, did you enjoy visiting school?"

Woody's answer was to squeeze his eyes shut in bliss.

Peter's eyes crinkled in a grin. Yes, she thought, his eyes really were the color of a Newfoundland's. But it was his laugh lines that really got to her. Only someone who had spent a lifetime smiling had laugh lines like that. In fact, he was smiling now. At her. He was casting his spell, and he'd caught her in it. But those lips, finely chiseled and full, lips that looked just right for spending the night with, they were moving. He was speaking.

"What?" She felt a blush rage up her neck and face again. This was getting ridiculous. She really had to snap out of it.

"I said, what brought you to this school on this particular day?"

"Oh. Well, since the summer, Sally has been asking me to visit her class. She wanted me to talk to her kids about dogs and cats, and to bring Hugo and Woody." She felt her heart pounding, and her voice was breathless. "Normally, I would have talked about how cats and dogs are not the same as stuffed animals, you know, pet responsibility. But I thought that if you were going to bring Angie to the clinic, I could start the ball rolling by introducing her to Hugo in a group of fellow children, and I could talk a little bit about what to do around strange dogs. I thought it might give her some confidence. She could see that the other kids were not nervous around him. And then it might make it easier for her to meet Little Stray."

Those lips, the ones that fascinated her, quirked in amusement.

"Little Stray?"

"Yes." She grinned ruefully. "Jessie, my vet tech, wanted to name her Rambette, because she is so timid." Melissa shook her head. But Peter chuckled, an intimate sound. She had to keep talking or she'd turn into a puddle on the floor. "When I said no, Jess suggested calling her Spike, but I told her we'd call her Little Stray. End of discussion."

"I take it your Jessie has a warped sense of humor?"

"Very warped. But anyway, I watched your daughter very carefully. I'd talked to Sally about her before I came, and when I got here, she pointed Angie out."

"So what do you think?" Though his voice

sounded casual, Melissa knew it wasn't a casual question at all.

"I think," she answered, "that if you bring her by the clinic tonight, she'll be okay. Not terrific, not yet, but I really think she'll be okay. I didn't see the kind of fear that is debilitating. And after all, Little Stray is a sheltie, not a boxer, or something equally large and powerful. And she's not rowdy and rambunctious. Not a monster dog at all."

The relief in his face was visible, and as she saw it, Melissa's heart filled. It struck her how incredibly concerned he was for his daughter. And she knew that if anyone could help his daughter conquer a fear, this man could.

"Come on, you guys, let's get home, I have patients this afternoon." She stood and gathered up Woody to put him in a carrier. "Hugo, come get your leash on."

"Do you need help carrying anything?"

Woody and his carrier were not very heavy, and Hugo walked, but the thought of leaving the school by herself made her feel oddly alone. "Thank you," she said, handing Peter the cat carrier. "That would be nice."

Melissa, she cautioned, *you're in big trouble*.

Chapter Four

"Melissa, you were terrific!"

Sitting at her desk, her head in her hands after a tiring afternoon, Melissa jerked her eyes open to see Sally Foster leaning against the door holding Woody and a little white paper bag. "Suzette said you were in your office and I could come on back."

Sally dropped the little white bag on Melissa's desk and cuddled Woody, rubbing him under his chin. Woody's purr was predictably loud. "Jelly beans, to thank you for coming to my class. The kids loved you. Woody and Hugo too. I don't see why it took you so long to do this. I've been asking you since September to come talk to my kids." She finally ran out of breath.

"I'm glad the kids enjoyed it."

"Enjoyed it?" Sally gushed. "Woody and Hugo. Woody and Hugo. That's all they talked about all afternoon. They talked about you too. Melissa, you're a natural with kids. You should've been a teacher."

"No, Sally, I'd never be a good teacher. I don't know anything about kids. I just know dogs and cats." Melissa carefully picked out a red jelly bean and popped it into her mouth.

Sally rolled her eyes dramatically. "Listen to you. You don't know anything about kids, my foot. Let me tell you, there are lots of teachers who know less about kids than you do."

"They shouldn't be teaching."

"You're right. But you, my friend, should."

"Naw, I'm too good a vet. You told me that yourself."

"What did she tell you?" Jessie stuck her head in the door. "Hi, Sally, I thought I heard your voice."

"Hi, Jess. Melissa brought Hugo and Woody to my class today and the kids loved it. She says she doesn't know beans about kids, but she took to it like a duck to water."

Jessie nodded in agreement. "Sure. She does a real good job with the kids who bring in their puppies and kittens. Say, speaking of beans, are those beans of a jelly kind?"

Melissa pushed the bag towards her.

"Thanks." Jessie shook out a couple and crammed them in her mouth. "I love jelly beans," she mumbled.

"Don't talk with your mouth full," Melissa cautioned.

"Say, M'liss." Sally moved from Woody's chin to his head. "Where'd you get the idea you're no good with kids?"

"Another legacy from *Charming* Michael," Jessie answered for her, fastidiously licking a sticky finger.

Melissa watched as Sally caught Jessie's eye, then the two of them nodded in blatant and dramatic understanding.

"*Charming* Michael again," Sally said. "What a bottom-feeder."

"Yeah," Jessie added, reaching for the jelly beans again. "And to think he beat out ten thousand other sperm. Scary thought, isn't it?"

"Probably *charmed* them out of even trying to go for it," Sally agreed.

Melissa, watching her two friends, burst out laughing. "Okay, you guys, I realize he's not your favorite person."

"Pond scum," Sally corrected. "Not our favorite pond scum."

"No, lower than pond scum," Jess asserted. "*Charming* Michael is the stuff the bottom-feeders feed on."

"No." Sally started giggling so hard she almost dropped Woody, and he squeaked in protest. "*Charming* Michael is the stuff that even bottom-feeders won't eat."

"Stop it!" Melissa tried to sound gruff.

"But bashing your ex-husband is such fun," Jessie pointed out reasonably.

"He's not pond scum," Melissa insisted. "He's just a man. He can't help it if he's a jerk, it's part of the breed standard."

"Ah, no, Melissa," Jessie corrected her. "This is where we and you part ways. You think all men are jerks, we just think Charming Michael is pond scum. Slight difference here. Sally and I don't hold his behavior against all men. We just hold it against *him*."

Melissa stood up pointedly. "Well, I'm afraid I don't have a sense of humor where Michael is concerned. Sally, come on back. I want you to meet the dog your principal saved last night."

"Okay," Sally said cheerfully, setting Woody down on Melissa's desk and shrugging out of her coat.

"Yo, Sally," Jessie stage-whispered. "Tell me about this principal of yours. Is he single? Is he cute? Melissa won't tell me. She just gets all embarrassed."

"Yeah, he's cute," Sally stage-whispered back. "And he's wonderfully nice, and single, and oh, so sexy."

Melissa whirled on them both. "Will you two please stop it."

Instantly they were both the picture of innocence. "Stop what?" Jessie asked, wide-eyed.

From down the hall, they heard the front door open. "Saved by the proverbial bell," Jessie crowed. "Duty calls, O Great Doctor." She salaamed theatrically, then whirled around to trot down the hall to the reception desk where they could hear doggy toenails clicking on the linoleum.

"It's only because we care about you," Sally said gently. "We both want you to be happy."

"I am happy."

"But you're alone."

"Maybe I like alone. Besides, I'm not *really* alone. I have Hugo and Woody."

Sally glared at her witheringly for a moment, then said, "You've been divorced for several years now. When are you going to quit letting Michael ruin your life?"

"He isn't ruining my life anymore. That's why I left him. So he couldn't."

"He is too," Sally was insistent. "M'liss, you may be a brilliant vet, but you're not very smart when it comes to people sometimes. Every time you hide away upstairs in your apartment with Hugo, you're letting Michael win. Every time you refuse to go out with a man because you're afraid that he'll be a jerk, you're letting Michael win. Right now the score is *Charming* Michael fifty-eight, Melissa zip." Her eyes were full of sympathy as she leaned close enough to Melissa to lay her hand on her arm. "You're too special a person for that. You have too much to give. Don't let him win anymore. He's not worth it. Never was."

Melissa leaned her head back against the wall staring at the ceiling. "I don't exactly see any men beating a path to my door." She hoped her voice didn't sound as clogged as it felt. "Besides, I really don't think all men are jerks. It's just that

you're right. I'm not very smart about people.
When I get the least bit involved with them I
don't know how to see them clearly. That's why
it took me so long to see what Michael was doing to my life."

"That's because"—Sally's voice was warm
and it sounded as if she were smiling—"because
you're also the most intensely loyal person I've
ever known. Look, Peter Winthrop is a terrific
guy and I think the world of him. He's been
alone for a while too. He could use a little female companionship," she added with a sug-
gestive wiggle of her eyebrows. "Just give him a
chance, okay?"

"Enough." Melissa held up her hand. She
wiped an eye surreptitiously as if she had a
speck in it. She didn't think Sally was fooled.
"Let's go see this dog your principal saved. And
Sally, you've known Angie for a while now. How
do you think she did today?"

Sally tapped her finger against her cheek, a
sure sign she was thinking.

"She loved Woody, of course. She likes cats a
lot. She wasn't exactly afraid of Hugo, just not
very trusting."

"Hmm. I thought so too. Well, come see this
girl. She's gorgeous."

"For a dog," Sally pointed out.

"Someday you'll learn that dogs are special
too."

"And someday" her friend answered loftily,
"you'll learn that cats are the ultimate race on
the earth."

*   *   *

It was a silent trip to Dr. March's clinic. Stopped by the umpteenth red light, Peter glanced over at his daughter. Her shoulders looked set even under the layers of her winter coat. She was staring out the window. She was ignoring him. They'd stopped by the library—the books about shelties they'd checked out were on the seat between them. Angie was ignoring those as well. Suddenly he wondered if this was a good idea after all. Maybe she needed more time, maybe she needed some professional counseling. But the light turned green.

"Angie, this dog is really special. I hope you'll like her."

"I told you, Daddy, I don't like dogs."

"Your mother was killed in a car accident. You know that, don't you?"

His daughter nodded.

"It was at night, she swerved to avoid hitting a dog and slid into an oncoming car."

"I know." Her voice sounded small and miserable.

Even though she was looking away from him, he knew her forehead was wrinkled. This is the part that always got her stuck, the part he'd never been able to get past before.

"Honey, this happened two years ago when you were only four years old. Please, believe me. It wasn't the dog's fault. It was no one's fault, really. Not your mother's, or the person who was driving the other car. If there hadn't been an icy patch right there, it all would have been okay. It was just an accident. Can you understand that?"

She sighed, a heavy sigh that seemed to include him as well.

"Will you at least think about trying to like this dog?"

"No."

It was his turn to sigh. She really was as obstinate as a mule. *Patience, Peter,* he cautioned himself, *she gets her obstinacy from you.* "Well, I'm going to make friends with her. She needs friends right now. Look, the clinic is just past this park. See how most of the snow has melted off the sidewalk over there? And here we are."

He pulled in, stopped the car, and turned off the engine. He sat for a moment, studying the outside of the small clinic. It had been too dark to see much the night before. The clinic was set back from the road, winter-bare trees lined the driveway, and a split-rail fence, covered by vines, edged the parking lot. The building itself was white with blue and white striped awnings over the door and the big window, giving it a cheerful look. The upstairs windows had curtains that repeated the blue and white stripes. While the building was obviously old, it was clean and well kept. "Looks like there are roses here in the summer. See how they've been taken care of?" He was sure this would get a response since Angie loved plants. But he was wrong. His daughter remained silent and forlorn.

He tried again. "Do you think those are lilacs

over there on the side of the clinic? I wonder what color they are."

This time, Angie at least looked where he was pointing. Nothing more.

"Let's go," he said at last to his daughter.

"Can I wait in the car?"

There was no fear in her voice, thank goodness. Obstinacy, but no fear. He smiled at her affectionately. "No, you can't. And you know it."

Finally Jessie, the last of her staff to leave, had gone home. Melissa hadn't told her Peter was coming by, or she'd never have left. Jessie had convinced herself that there was something "juicy" going on. And being positively obnoxious, she wouldn't want to miss a second of it. Melissa took Hugo out, then sent him back upstairs with the promise of a walk later on.

Coming back downstairs, she heard a car drive up and stop. They were here.

"James," she said to her hero, "wish me luck."

Her insides were quivering, and she realized she was nervous. "Stop it, Melissa," she told herself firmly. "Don't be silly. He's here to see the dog, that's all." But in her heart of hearts, she knew that she wanted him to be here to see her as well.

"Miss Foster says she likes you," Angie said solemnly.

Melissa hung the little girl's coat—plaid wool—on a hook in the waiting room, then stooped down so she was on eye level with her.

89

Woody came running, his motor full volume, to wind around their feet. "I like Miss Foster also. She and I have been good friends for many years."

"She says you have a girls' club."

Before Peter could stop his daughter, Melissa held her hand out to him. She glanced a smile at him, trying to let him know that Angie could ask all the questions she needed to. She hoped he'd understand. Evidently he did. He stooped down to scratch under Woody's chin.

"It's not a formal club with dues or officers. It's just a group of friends, all of us women, who go out to dinner together, and to movies. Things like that."

"She says you take care of her cats."

"I do."

"She says she trusts you."

So that was it, Melissa realized. Angie wanted to know whom to trust. Melissa slanted another glance at Peter, to see if he understood the importance of this question. As their eyes met he gave her the slightest of nods.

This had to be done carefully, and in words a six-year-old could understand. "Angie, after I went to college I went to a special school, a veterinary college, for several years. At that special school I learned how to take care of animals when they are sick or hurt."

Woody made his way over to Angie. The little girl wasn't the least hesitant about petting him, about rubbing his ears, Melissa noted. This was a good sign. It meant that she was not afraid to touch an animal. There were actually some people in the world who didn't like animals at all, didn't want to touch them, and when forced to, touched them as little as possible. Angie was not one of them.

"When I completed my studies, I took some tests to prove that I knew what to do, and I earned the title of Doctor. When you're sick you go to a doctor that takes care of people. I'm a different kind of doctor. I take care of people's pets when they're sick and hurt. Mostly cats and dogs, but some other pets also. People like Sally—Miss Foster—and Mrs. Calloway trust me to help their pets stay healthy."

The little forehead wrinkled in concentration. She'd stopped scratching Woody, and now he butted his head against her hand. "Do you know lots about dogs?" She went back to petting Woody again.

Melissa smiled to herself. "Yes, I do. Especially dogs that are hurt."

"Daddy says he's responsible so we hafta visit that dog."

Melissa snuck a quick peek at Peter, catching his eye briefly before returning her attention to Angie. "Your father has done everything he possibly could to help this dog. It's a very responsible thing to do."

"Well . . ." Angie sounded like she was waffling. "I don't like dogs."

"That's okay," Melissa assured her. "Some people, Miss Foster for instance, like cats. Some people like Mrs. Calloway prefer dogs.

Some people like them both. I like both. And I'm glad you came to visit anyway. It looks like Woody is also glad you came." Glad was putting it mildly. Woody was rolling on his back, blissed out.

"I like cats," Angie announced firmly.

"I know," Melissa agreed. "Miss Foster told me."

Melissa had been right, he thought, watching her lead the stray dog out of the cage and into the exam room. The little sheltie *was* lovely, even with clumps of her coat trimmed away. The cast on her front leg made a quiet tapping sound on the floor.

"Hey there, Little Stray." He held out his hand. "Remember me?" The dog sniffed politely, then backed away, not too far, just enough to make a point. Then she barked. A high-pitched yip.

"She doesn't like you, Daddy."

Before he could figure out what to say, Melissa settled down cross-legged in the middle of the room. She beckoned Angie over to her.

His daughter moved hesitantly towards the vet.

"She doesn't not like your father, Angie, she's just shy. You see"—Melissa's voice became very serious—"once she had a home, where people loved her. Then—I don't know how—she got lost. She's been on her own for a couple of months, probably since January from the look of her. She had no home, no nice warm bed, no one to hug her and play with her, feed her, take care of her. No one for her to love either. She had to catch mice to eat."

Angie's eyes were becoming round and wide. She seemed to be intently listening to the vet. Peter backed up, very quietly, not wanting to break the spell the vet was weaving around his daughter.

"She was just a puppy, a baby, and was all alone in the world. And it was winter. She was very cold, and wet. When it snowed, if she couldn't find shelter, she would have been pretty miserable. She might have seen a house somewhere on her travels, and thought there might be people there like her own family. Maybe they fed her, maybe not. Maybe they thought she might be sick and they threw sticks at her to make her go away. Sometimes people are afraid of stray dogs. So you see, Angie, she is shy around people right now."

Peter's heart went out to the little dog all over again. More than ever, he was determined to give her a home, so at least this little dog would never know hunger or cold again. Never be lonely again. If only his daughter could—

Melissa drew Angie down next to her on the floor, and as Peter watched, a miracle happened.

Angie's shoulders lost their tension, and she started to relax, to lean into Melissa, and the woman's arm wrapped naturally around the little shoulders. His daughter seemed to become hypnotized by Melissa's voice. She seemed to begin to look at the little stray not as a dog, something she feared, but as an individual creature that was hurt. Melissa was able to do what he, with all his training in early childhood development, couldn't, help Angie see through her fear, to empathize.

"But there is something amazing about dogs. See how she's standing? See how she's sort of leaning towards us instead of pulling away from us? She's not holding her head up high like a challenge, there's no sign of aggression there. See how she's sort of dipping her head and sniffing the air? That means she's curious about us."

Peter felt himself join his daughter in the web of that calm voice. He let the rhythm and sound of her words wrap around his senses, soothing his soul. He wondered if hypnotism was something one learned in vet school, and he could imagine that voice calmly explaining a difficult procedure to a client. He could see why people thought she was the best vet in the world.

"Now look at the expression on her face," she said, continuing her magic with his daughter. "It isn't hard and suspicious, nothing to be nervous about there. Look closely and you'll see the longing in her eyes, see? She wants to be part of a family again. Look, she took that tiny step forward. She wants very much to come to you, but she's not sure yet what your reaction will be. Dogs are pack animals, you know. They need to live in families. They need companionship as much as they need food. And she's been starved for that also. But even though she wants to be your friend, she is a little shy. You see, she doesn't know if you'll throw a stick at her."

"She's afraid of me?"

Peter could hear the tremble of his daughter's voice, and he longed to take her in his arms and comfort her, but he stayed where he was, leaned up against the wall, with Woody winding around his legs, and he watched something he thought he'd never see.

"Not you specifically, but people in general," was the answer.

"Is she afraid of you?"

"No. Not anymore. But she was this morning. Since then she's learned that I bring her snacks, and I pet her, and I talk to her, and I want to be her friend. But most importantly of all, she has learned that I won't hurt her."

"I wouldn't hurt her," Angie said stoutly.

"I know you wouldn't. Miss Foster said you like animals very much."

"I do. Mostly. But not dogs."

"Well, you know, Miss Foster doesn't like dogs in general."

"She likes cats."

"Yes, she does. But Miss Foster would never hurt a dog. In fact, she helped your father when he wanted to help this dog."

"She did?"

Peter could hear the amazement in his daughter's voice.

"Yes. She gave your father my phone number so he could call me."

"Well, I'd never hurt a dog either, but I just don't like them."

"You know, sometimes people don't like dogs in general, but like one dog in particular. Even Miss Foster likes Hugo, at least a little bit. There are a couple of other specific dogs that she likes also."

Peter watched the dog inch closer and closer, a step at a time, until now it was within arm's distance from Melissa, and also Angie.

"Look, Angie. Little Stray has come closer to me. She knows that I have cookies for her in my pocket."

"How does she know that?"

"Dogs have a very good sense of smell, much better than people, and she can smell them. Besides, I've given her several cookies today, and they always come from my pocket." Melissa pulled something out of her pocket and held it out to the dog. He couldn't see what it was, it was too small.

"That doesn't look like a cookie to me." Obviously his daughter could see it better than he could.

Melissa chuckled again. "It's really a piece of dried cat food. But she thinks it's a cookie."

"Gross!"

She sounded like a typical kindergartner, he thought in amazement.

The dog came closer still, then gently took the piece of cat food from Melissa's fingers and crunched delicately.

Woody left off his winding and was over to her like a shot.

"Here, Woody, you can have a piece too."

"Can I give it to Woody?"

"Of course." Melissa reached into her pocket again.

"Here you are, Woody," Angie crooned in a high voice. She giggled as the cat took the food. "It tickles," she said in obvious delight.

"Another piece for our Little Stray here." Melissa held out another piece, and the dog obligingly took it.

"See, Angie, dried cat food is tiny enough that even fifteen pieces are fine for a dog. But if I gave her fifteen dog cookies, she'd be very fat in no time."

The dog came even closer, watching Melissa intently.

"She wants another one," Angie said.

"That's right. You're pretty good at interpreting the expressions on her face. Here you go, Little Stray."

The dog was close enough for Angie to touch, and for a brief second, Peter thought she might. There was a hint of indecision in the way she held her shoulders and arms, but then it faded. She held out another piece to Woody. And she had a question.

"Why doesn't she stink?"

But before Peter could react, Melissa was answering.

"Because she's clean. You know, dogs are like people They come in all different shapes and sizes and colors. Just like people, if they're not clean and healthy they begin to smell bad. But dogs can't go to the store to buy soap and towels. They need their people to help them keep clean and healthy. Then they don't smell bad. Unless they find a skunk." Her voice took on amusement as she continued to dole out pieces of dried cat food to the dog. "Have you ever smelled a skunk before?" she asked conspiratorially.

Angie nodded. "Pee-yoo!"

"I agree," Melissa said laughingly. "Not much you can do about a dog that gets hit by a skunk. Except special shampoos. Say, Angie," Melissa said, "I promised Hugo I'd take him for a walk, and Little Stray here needs to go for a walk too. Even though her leg's in a cast, she has to get a little bit of exercise to keep her muscles working. If your father says it's all right, would the two of you like to come with us? We're just going to go over to the park next door. It can only be a very short walk until she's more used to her cast."

Angie's forehead wrinkled. "I don't know," she said at last. "I don't like dogs, you know."

"Yes, you've told me. But I like you, and Hugo likes you, and Little Stray doesn't seem as afraid of you as she was when you first got here."

"Well, I guess it would be okay, if my dad says so."

Melissa's eyes met his. "Well, Peter, what do you think?"

He thought she was the answer to his prayers.

She had been able to do in thirty minutes what he'd not been able to do in two years. He thought she was certainly a magician, or at the very least, a witch, able to cast spells, or perhaps an angel, or any other of the myriad of miracle-makers that inhabited the folklore of humanity. But then he knew she wasn't supernatural at all. Sitting on the floor, her arm around his daughter, dried cat food in her hand, wearing jeans, a sweatshirt, and a question in her eyes, she was very much a woman.

"When the student is ready, a teacher appears," he murmured.

"What?" she asked in amazement.

He started. "Sorry. I was just thinking out loud."

"Well? Would you like to walk with us in the park? As I said, it can only be a short walk. It's still pretty chilly, and I don't want to tire Little Stray here, she's been through a lot."

He'd follow her anywhere, he thought. "Yes. We'll come with you."

The radiance of her smile washed over him like the sun in summer. "Hugo will be thrilled. He likes you so much, Peter."

But before he could reply, the phone rang in Melissa's office and she whisked away to answer the call.

They were going out the door, like a family, he thought a few minutes later. Two adults, two dogs, a child. Melissa led them through a break in the fence, on stepping-stones, to the paved path, cleared of snow, that led through the park.

Melissa had a thin leather leash in each hand, Hugo was prancing at the end of his, but Little Stray walked by her side somewhat gingerly on her cast, the metal tip tapping lightly. Angie trotted ahead, but not too far. A casual observer would think all was right with the world. However, he didn't think that was quite the case. When Melissa'd returned from the phone call there had been a change. She was quieter for one thing. Her smile was not as frequent as it had been. But the most damning evidence was she wouldn't quite meet his eyes, as if she knew something she was not telling him. Now, after he had felt so close to her, as if the two of them were beginning to weave a bond, she seemed to be shutting him out. He did not like it. Maybe the phone call was from one of her patients, he thought. Maybe another dog got hit in the road. He fervently hoped not, yet at the same time he hoped there was another reason for her changed behavior.

"Why do I have the feeling you're hiding something from me?" he finally asked.

She stopped, as did Little Stray, but Hugo reached the end of his leash and bounced back at the sudden halt. "Sorry, Hugo," she said absently, while intently studying a spot on the ground.

Then she looked up, her eyes meeting his for the first time. "I think I've found her owner."

Chapter Five

He was staring at her blankly, as if he didn't know what to say. She understood completely. So she continued, knowing what this would probably mean to him. "This afternoon I realized that Little Stray's tattoo might be a Social Security number, so I called my cousin Madeleine. She lives out West and has some connections with some cops. I told her about Little Stray. She's a dog person too. I asked her if she'd run the number through the police computers to see if she could find a match. Anyway, that was Madeleine on the phone. She said she'd found the number."

By this time Peter had shifted his gaze away from her. She followed his gaze to the figure of his daughter, her plaid coat a splash of dark red against the white expanse of the park. Angie was doing some kind of six-year-old dance, lifting her booted feet high and stomping down in the snow that lined the walk. Her voice wisped back to them, the words indistinct, but there was a definite rhythm to her song as she stomped and pranced in time.

Melissa took a deep breath, knowing that she had to finish telling him. "Madeleine wouldn't tell me who the number belonged to, of course, that's pretty confidential information. She said she'd try to track them down on Monday, but it might take a few days."

For a few heartbeats longer, Peter's whole being was still, unmoving. Empathy for him surged through her. Knowing how he felt about his daughter, knowing how responsible he felt about this dog, she felt her heart go out to him completely and without hesitation. She transferred Little Stray's leash to her other hand, then reached out to touch his arm. It was the touch of a kindred spirit, of understanding, of comfort.

His hand came to cover hers, an answer, an acceptance of what she was offering.

Little Stray was sitting quietly by her left side, as if she'd been taught some basic obedience. Hugo was also still and quiet, though he normally pranced and danced his ungainly way along the sidewalk. She glanced down at her dog. He was watching her intently, concern in his big brown eyes. He was truly a sensitive soul, she thought, wise and wonderful. She smiled at him, to let him know that everything was okay.

Like a miniature whirlwind, Angie was suddenly in front of them. "Daddy, I'm hungry," she announced stoutly.

Melissa felt Peter jerk his attention to his daughter. "You are?"

"Yes." Angie was certainly a definite child, Melissa thought. Nothing wishy-washy about this one.

"Well, then," Peter answered, "we'll have to fix that, won't we."

Though his tone was cheerful, Melissa knew what it cost him. Her respect for him grew, as she watched him put aside his own feelings to take care of his daughter.

"Maybe Dr. March would like to join us for pizza, do you think so?"

Angie's face wrinkled up in concentration as she studied Melissa for a moment. Then she made her pronouncement. "I think Dr. March would like pizza."

Melissa chuckled.

"Well, Dr. March?" Peter still had not released her hand, and now he gave it just a little squeeze. "What do you think? Do you like pizza?"

"I love pizza."

"So you'll join us?"

Melissa felt a jerk on Hugo's leash and looked down to see that Hugo was wiggling, obviously understanding that his people were happy now and wanting to be part of whatever it was. Little Stray moved her eyes from one to the other of them, uncertain about what was going to happen. Hugo pranced over and nudged Little Stray with his nose. She jumped back in surprise. Hugo sat down and grinned his doggy grin at her. Then he quickly leaned close and licked her muzzle.

Angie's bright laughter filled the air.

"Look, Daddy, Hugo wants to be friends with Little Stray. Are they friends, Dr. March?"

She smiled at the little girl. "They are getting to know each other. Watch what she does now."

Little Stray leaned her head tentatively toward Hugo. He snorted at her. She dropped her head and twisted it so she was looking at him almost upside down.

"Look, Angie," Melissa said softly. "Little Stray knows that Hugo is older than she is, so she's telling him she's not going to try to be the boss. She's telling him she wants to play with him."

Hugo nudged Little Stray again, this time with more force, almost knocking her off her feet. Little Stray bounded up in spite of her cast, tail wagging, and leaned against Hugo.

"How does she know Hugo is older?"

"I'm not quite sure. It has to do with survival in the pack, though." Melissa had never tried to explain pack behavior to a six-year-old before. She was not quite sure how to go about it. But this six-year-old solved it for her.

"Are you coming to pizza with us?"

"Please." It was Peter, his voice rich and full, adding his plea to his daughter's.

"How can I resist?" she answered lightly.

"Oh, goodie!" Angie jumped up and down.

But at Hugo's first wild bark, she stopped still, her eyes full of fear. "Is he going to bite me?"

"Oh, dear, no. Hugo, quiet!" Melissa quickly knelt down next to the little girl. "He will *not* bite you. You can tell, because he's wagging his tail. Look how he's wiggling all over. He is excited. He knows that you're happy, and he's telling you that he's happy too."

"Why did he bark?"

The fear in her voice was unmistakable. "It's his way of talking to you. Hugo, come. Sit. Good dog. See, Angie, Hugo is happy. When you were happy just now, you jumped up and down and said, 'Oh, goodie.' This was Hugo's way of jumping up and down and saying, 'Oh, goodie.' "

Peter knelt on the other side of his daughter, and now he reached out to pet Hugo. "See Angie," he said. "Hugo likes you."

Hugo swiped Peter's hand with his tongue.

Then Peter reached out to pet Little Stray. This time the little dog did not pull away. Though she did not completely relax her stance, she did wag her tail. It was a small wag, but a wag nonetheless. "I think Little Stray likes us too."

But Melissa saw the reserve in his face. She knew that he was steeling himself against disappointment, and the words he'd spoken to her earlier that day came back to her now. He'd said he'd recognized this dog, and he thought the dog had recognized him also.

Melissa knew that feeling, knew the bonding that accompanied it. She'd felt it the first time she'd seen Hugo. It was at the Greene County Animal Shelter. She was there to consult about a cat, and she'd been reading the medical report as she walked by the bank of dog cages. For some reason she looked up from the report. Right in front of her, hunched up in a tiny cage, she saw the ugliest bulldog puppy she'd ever seen, behind bars, miserable, his very soul in his eyes.

From the instant her eyes met his, there was no doubt in her mind that she and this dog belonged together. It didn't make any difference that she had just moved to Hartley the week before, right out of vet school—she hadn't even unpacked her boxes yet. No matter that she'd never imagined in her wildest dreams that she'd have a bulldog, that she'd always been partial to the herding breeds. She knew that vets usually inherited dogs and cats, it came with the vocation, and she knew eventually she'd end up with lots. That was just fine with her. She loved dogs and cats.

Still, nothing in vet school could have prepared her for that instant in the animal shelter when her gaze connected with the gaze of that young and incredibly ugly bulldog. She slid the card out of the holder on his cage and turned it over to read the other side. His owners had turned him in because he'd chewed one shoe too many. Well, what did they expect, she thought in exasperation. He was a puppy.

When she finished the consultation about the cat—it was a very nice cat, she remembered—she left the building with the bulldog in her arms.

Yes, she knew how it felt, bonding with a dog. And she could imagine what Peter must feel, knowing that this dog he'd bonded to might belong to someone else. Someone who might want her back.

Still kneeling, she drew Hugo to her, to hug him, to press her cheek against his broad head, to whisper in his ear that she loved him. Hugo grunted. All was right with the world. She smiled over at Peter.

"Let's go get pizza," she said.

"You mean she only had pizza for dinner?" Even over the phone Gloria's voice had that concerned disapproval. "Peter, pizza is not a nutritious dinner for a growing child. She needs vegetables as well, and fruits. Peter, you know that Claire would never have approved."

There was much he could say to that, but he let it pass, and at the same time held his temper. Gloria was really getting out of hand. He'd have to do something about it, but not over the phone, so he changed the subject.

"We saw the Ballentines at the pizza place. They came over to say hello."

"The Ballentines?" Her voice was suddenly more cheerful. "Did Harold Ballentine say anything more to you about the superintendent position?"

Peter let out a silent sigh. "I had lunch with him today. We talked about it then. Listen, Gloria, I'm glad you called, but you know we just now got in the door and I need to get Angie into the tub and then into bed."

"Well, Peter, I was just concerned when I called earlier and you weren't home. I was worried, you know. Ever since the accident, I worry about my little angel. You're all the family I have now."

"I know," he said soothingly. "But we're just fine. We visited a friend and went out to dinner." *Damn!* He said to himself. He shouldn't have let that slip.

"Friend? What friend?"

He could almost hear her ears perk up. This was where Angie got her Spanish Inquisition act.

"A veterinarian." He wanted to leave it as vague as he could.

"Veterinarian? I hope you're not thinking of bringing any animals to school, Peter. You know they carry disease, and parasites, and who knows what else. What if one of them bit one of the children? It would not look good to the school board."

Tolerance, he reminded himself. "I appreciate your concern, Gloria. You know I do care very much about the safety and well-being of my students. I really have to go now. Angie is waiting for her bath. I'll see you Monday morning."

"But what about—?"

"I'll be in touch with you, Gloria, good night." He was firm with her.

"Good night, Peter," she said at last.

He set the phone down with a sigh of relief. Gloria needed something other than Angie to occupy her life, poor soul. She used to play bridge, used to take senior-citizen tours, but that was before Claire died. Gloria had to get back into her own life again. Not only for her sake, but for Angie's as well. It was not good for her to have her grandmother hovering over her so closely. It was not good for him either. Especially if he was going to pursue a relationship with Dr. March.

His thoughts shifted to the woman who had worked such a miracle. She had a natural knack with children, and he was an authority on knacks with children, or the lack of them. She would have made a terrific teacher. The ability to interact with children was something society expected women to have instinctively. But Peter knew firsthand that not all women knew what to do with kids. He saw it every day. Women who loved their children, no doubt about that, but just didn't know how to interact with them, how to talk with them, how to help them grow up to be terrific adults.

But Melissa, now she knew exactly how to talk to Angie, and the other kids in Sally's class.

Sally had told him Melissa was divorced with no kids. He wondered if she'd wanted children. She'd be a terrific mother, he thought. He imagined Melissa settled in a rocking chair with a tiny scrap of a baby nestled against her breast. His tiny scrap of a baby.

"Daddy! I'm ready."

Peter came out of his reverie with a start.

"Okay, my tulip," he called up to her. "I'll be right there."

He stood for a moment with his hand on the light switch. As he looked around the living room it felt, for the first time, lonely. His whole house was sparkling clean and orderly, the furniture still exactly as Claire had always arranged it—Gloria saw to that. Yet it was empty. No purring cat wound figure-eights around his legs. There was no dog to curl up beside him as he watched the evening news, to be taken out one last time. There was no wife waiting upstairs for him, to stretch out against in bed, warm skin pressed to warm skin. A wife to hold into the night, and most wonderful of all, wake next to in the morning.

After Claire had died, Peter had thought he'd die too, from loneliness. But he hadn't. He'd had Angie to take care of, and while he would always mourn Claire's loss, it was part of his life, part of who he had become. Now, suddenly, once more, he felt totally alone. And he knew it was because of a woman with warm blue eyes, and dark hair that wisped around her pixie face. A woman who had held his daughter close as she discussed dog behavior, and made Angie feel safe. A woman who took in an abandoned cat needing surgery. A woman who smelled like peaches.

"Daddy!" Angie's voice was impatient.

He cleared his throat. "Coming," he called to her as he switched out the light.

Melissa turned out the light in the clinic. "Good night, guys," she told the boarder dogs. "Sleep well. Your moms will be here for you soon."

But she paused at the stairs to her apartment. She just couldn't go to bed without one last check on Little Stray. Okay. Back to the treatment room, Woody following. Woody loved Little Stray. And it appeared that Little Stray liked him as well.

She opened the door and switched on the light. "How are you, Little Stray?"

The sheltie clambered to her feet, still clumsy because of the cast, and greeted her with a slight wagging of tail.

"I think you're glad to see me, aren't you?" She opened the cage door, and helped the little dog out.

They looked at each other for a moment. The little dog was still aloof, which was not unusual for this breed. What is this little dog thinking? Melissa wondered as she pulled a "cookie" out of her pocket and held it out to the dog.

Little Stray regarded her seriously for a moment. Then, suddenly, subtly, there was a change in the little dog's manner. Her posture, her shoulders, relaxed, her expression softened, and her tail wag was without hesitation and in full force. Melissa understood what had happened. The little dog had just accepted her as leader. Until the end of time they were of one pack.

"So I'm no longer a stranger to you, eh?" she asked, opening her arms to the little dog. "Just now you decided to join my pack, didn't you?"

Little Stray threw her head back and yipped. It was a yip of recognition, of joy.

"You're right, Little Stray," Melissa agreed, feeling bursting with happiness. "It is magic— members of two totally different species becoming family, totally devoted to one another. Thank you," she whispered. Then, "Look at this tail wagging. Well, what a good girl. I guess that means I'm sort of your mom, eh?" The dog's head felt solid and natural under her hand.

The dog leaned against her leg and looked up at her with a brightness in the brown eyes that were almost human. Melissa loved looking into a dog's eyes; they told her so much about that dog. And this one was telling her through her eyes that she trusted. Implicitly. Completely. And forever.

Melissa stood for a moment in indecision. She really shouldn't do this. After all, the dog had a home. Madeleine had found the person that had that Social Security number. Still, it might take several days to track the person down. And what would it mean to Little Stray to be so alone for all that time? If Little Stray had decided to trust her, how could she deny that trust? She couldn't. James would have been proud of her.

"Little Stray, would you like to come upstairs with me?"

Little Stray wagged her tail and bestowed on her a look of utter devotion.

"Okay, then. It's settled. C'mon, Woody, you want to come too? It'll be like a slumber party. Hugo will be thrilled. But you guys have to promise not to stay up all night telling ghost stories. I want to read my new book. Here, Little Stray, I don't think you can do stairs with your cast, let me carry you."

It was noon on Saturday. Clinic hours were over. The last client had left, and so had the little terrier mix. But Jean-Luc was still with them.

"Howdy, Jean-Luc, old guy." Melissa truly enjoyed the standard poodle. "Your mom should be home sometime late tonight. Unless she misses her plane again. I really like your mom a whole lot. But," she added in a whisper, "she's very distractible." Melissa made another futile attempt to smooth the curls on the dog's head. "Who in their right mind would name a poodle after a bald guy?" she asked him rhetorically. She knew. Sylvie would. Wagging his tail, Jean-Luc leaned against her leg and sighed noisily.

"Okay, buddy, let's take you outside for your noonly constitutional."

While she stood waiting for the dog, Melissa leaned against the chain-link fence, pooper-scooper in hand, her gaze far beyond the park next door. Peter Winthrop was in her thoughts once again. Of course, he'd been with her, at the edges of her mind, all morning. Now she invited him into the forefront. She liked what she saw. He was probably the kind of guy who picked up spiders to take them outside instead of squishing them. What a wonderful thing to do. She was really tired of men who had alpha male confused with bully. Honest to jiminy, if more people would study the pack behavior of wolves, they'd understand their own lives better.

Jean-Luc, having done his duty, bounced over to her, ready to play. "You're not an alpha male, are you, Jean-Luc?" She leaned down to the dog. He took advantage of the moment to swipe her cheek. His tongue was almost as fast as Hugo's. "Yes, you're truly a wuss of a guy," she said, making use of the scoop.

"Who're you calling a wuss?"

Melissa turned to see Jessie standing in the doorway. "Lovely day, isn't it, Jess?"

"Yeah. Lovely day. Who's the wuss?"

"Jean-Luc here." The curly fur bounced back against her fingers.

"Jean-Luc," said Jessie, and the poodle pranced over to Jessie for a greeting. "Jean-Luc, you are such a great guy dog. Very studly. Not a wuss at all." Jessie bent her head down so Jean-Luc could give her kisses. Jean-Luc obliged. "But speaking of wusses, *Charming* Michael called a little bit ago."

Melissa jerked her head up. "He's not a wuss." At the sound of her voice, Jean-Luc trotted back to Melissa for another scratch.

"I know. He's the opposite of a wuss. He's a caveman. You know"—she mugged—"the old *'me big-strong-handsome-male-stud, you lowly female'* type."

"When did he call?"

"While you were with that black and white cat, lancing that abscess. Suzette took the call and asked me if she should interrupt you, but I decided you should only have to do one gross thing at a time. So I told him you were with a client, and that I'd leave you a message that he'd called. He was not pleased."

"No, he never did want to come second to what he considered a 'dumb animal.' "

Jessie snorted loudly.

"I wonder what he wanted. Did he say?"

"Only that it was important. So I've told you. Now," she added airily, "I can forget that he walks on the face of the earth," She smiled beatifically at the prospect. "So, Jean-Luc, this is the night your mom might be home. If she remembers which airline to take, eh?"

Jean-Luc immediately abandoned Melissa for Jessie.

"Just like a man. Can't be faithful for one second," Melissa muttered, only partly in jest. No one, not even Jessie, knew what she'd suspected. She'd never told anyone that more than once Michael had come home smelling faintly of perfume. Even now, after all this time, those memories still had the power to hurt. Not that she wanted Michael back, she wouldn't take him back on a bet. No, what hurt was the knowledge that evidently she hadn't been woman enough for him.

"Infidelity is just part of the breed standard, m' dear." Jessie ruffled the poodle's curls. "You know, when Sylvie gets home—assuming she actually does get home and doesn't end up in Timbuktu—and when Karen gets back from that dog show, I'll tell you what. Let's call Sally and have a Girls' Night Out. We need to go see that new Mel Gibson film. That'll give us all fodder for our fantasies. Oh, Mel," Jessie swooned melodramatically à la Scarlett O'Hara, accent and all. "It doesn't matter if you are short. You have the bluest eyes." She fluttered her own eyes outrageously.

Melissa laughed fondly. "You're a nut."

Jessie abandoned her faux swoon. "Speaking of which—blue eyes, not nuts—any new developments with your principal?"

"Nope. Besides, his eyes aren't blue. They're the exact color of Brian Boru's."

"I sure hope he's not as hairy as Brian. Karen's Newfoundlands have gorgeous coats, but it wouldn't look good on a man. Hair like Jean-Luc's here, now that would be quite the handsome man about town." Jessie tried to gather Jean-Luc's curls into a topknot. "Hey, M'liss. Whaddya think. Karen names her dogs after Celtic music, Sylvie named Jean-Luc after a starship captain. Sally names her cats after characters in Thomas Hardy novels. You named Hugo after Hugo. Didja ever wonder if people think we're eccentric? Oh, no." Her eyes got round. She let go of Jean-Luc's curls. "What if your principal thinks we're eccentric? Maybe we should just all be invisible until you've hooked him. But, oh, dear, he already knows Sally. I guess there's no hope then." Another dramatic sigh, hand to forehead. "Your principal is doomed to think us all dotty as hatters."

"That's mad as hatters, you idiot," Melissa said with a chuckle. "Besides, he's not *my* principal. He just dropped a dog off." *Liar*, she taunted herself.

Jessie reached to the heavens, the exasperation in her posture too melodramatic to be real. "She is still evading me. What shall I do?" she beseeched. "Please, O Great Spirit of the Dogs and the Cats and All the Other Various Creatures on the Earth, give me a sign."

Jean-Luc leaped straight up in the air and barked.

Jessie left the Great Spirit, and looked down at Jean-Luc, who was trying desperately to engage her attention. "This is a sign? He wants to play b-a-l-l is a sign?"

"He can't spell, Jess," Melissa said drily.

"Yes, he can. Poodles are very intelligent.

Sylvie has taken this dog to school. He graduated at the top of his class. She once told me she needed a brilliant dog so it could take care of her. Besides, look how excited he's getting."

"Well, that's because you're getting him all riled up. But there's not enough room here to play b-a-l-l. He'll just have to wait until Sylvie gets home. And you get no sign."

"Well, that's okay," Jess announced pertly. "I took things into my own hands last night. I called Sally, and she told me that Mr. Peter Winthrop is the best principal she's ever had, and that if she didn't work for him she'd have gone after him herself. Evidently it's not a good thing to be romantically involved with your principal. She said it was her rotten luck. She also told me that she thought the two of you would be perfect together. So there." Jessie looked quite pleased with herself.

Melissa was so filled with dismay that she couldn't speak for a minute. Evidently Jessie figured that out, because she spoke up again.

"It's okay. Not to worry. Sally won't do anything to embarrass you. I won't either. You know that."

Melissa found her voice. "Sure. Like the time you called The Guy with the Irish Wolfhound." She didn't have to say more. Jessie's mishap with The Guy with the Irish Wolfhound was practically a folk legend among their friends. Melissa didn't even remember the man's name, and if Jessie did, she wouldn't admit it. As far as any of them knew, his name was The Guy with the Irish Wolfhound.

Jessie sighed. And squirmed a little bit. "No," she admitted. "Not like that at all. Besides The Guy with the Irish Wolfhound was just so incredibly cute. And I *told* you I was sorry. I must've told you at least a million times already. Look. I'll butt out. I promise. I really will." Her brown eyes were bright, and sincere, just like the eyes of a beagle. "I only want you to be happy. I've been trying for days to cheer you up."

"I am happy."

"No. You're not." There was no teasing in Jessie's voice now, no impish clowning, no playing around. "I've known you for a long time. I've seen you happy, and I've seen you not happy. And you're not happy now. Don't try to argue with me, M'liss. You're hiding it, and hiding it well. Probably someone who didn't know you as well as I do wouldn't even catch it. But this is *me* you're talking with."

Melissa felt a trembling in her heart. She had to change the subject very quickly, for Jessie did know her too well. "I see. So, if I'm so unhappy, let's get Jean-Luc put away, and then I can take off my vetting clothes and go grocery shopping. That'll make me truly happy."

"You hate grocery shopping," Jessie scoffed.

Melissa ushered Jean-Luc through the door. "But I'm out of raisins. A big box of raisins will make Hugo happy, and that will make me happy."

119

* * *

So Michael had called again, Melissa thought sourly as she lugged the bag of groceries upstairs. What did he want this time? He probably thought she was just waiting to run right back into his faithless arms. Hah! His most recent girlfriend had probably just found out what a faithless jerk he was and had left him. So the poor baby was lonely. Let's just call up Good Old Melissa. Double hah! She should sic Hugo on him! Of all the things in the world Michael hated most, doggy slobber headed the list. And Hugo was a master at spreading around doggy slobber.

Speaking of Hugo, she could hear him on the other side of the door. He always recognized her feet on the stairs. "Hi, honey, I'm home!" she called out as she shoved the door opened with her hip.

Hugo's greeting was enthusiastic and unmistakable.

Melissa set down the groceries, then turned to shrug out of her jacket. "Not too cold today, Hugie, in fact it's almost warm. That means that later on we can w-a-l-k in the p-a-r-k. We have to help Little Stray get her exercise."

She chatted to him as she put her new CD in the player. Vaughn Williams' Sea Symphony. Loud. Music was one of the few luxuries she allowed herself to spend money on. Music and books. Everything else she earned went to paying back her school loans, and the mortgage on the clinic. At this rate, she mused morosely, she should have it all paid off by the time she was seventy-two.

Hugo was very much under her feet as she danced around the minuscule kitchen putting the groceries away, singing along with the chorus on the CD. "Yes, I got some goodies for you." She punched her thumb in the perforations on the raisin box, then ripped the top back. "Here, Hugo, want a raisin?"

It was a totally rhetorical question.

Tossing him a second raisin, then a third, Melissa noticed the light on her answering machine. She read the display. Three messages. "Last one, Hugo." She lowered the volume on the CD player, then pressed the rewind button on the answering machine.

Hello, Melissa. It's Michael. I called your little clinic, but your assistant refused to get you. You have to sign some papers for me, but I'll be out of town for the next couple of days. I'll call you when I get back. Ciao, darling.

The nerve of him! Papers she had to sign. What papers? The jerk didn't tell her, of course. True to form, he'd leave her wondering. Well, she simply refused to wonder. She snorted in disgust as the next message started. It was Madeleine. *Hi, M'liss, I got the phone number for the person who owns that dog. I called in a few favors.* Typical of Madeleine. She was crazy about dogs too. Must be a dominant gene in the March family. *I tried the number, but it's been disconnected, so I have to do some more tracking down. I knew you'd want to find that dog's*

*home as soon as you could. I hope she's doing
well. Give her a kiss from her Auntie Madeleine.
Kisses for Hugo and Woody too. I'll get back to
you. Love you a lot. Bye.*

"So, Little Stray," Melissa murmured to thin
air. "We may find your home after all." Somehow that thought did not bring any joy. But before she could go any further, the third message
started. *Hello, Melissa. It's Peter.* Even on the
machine tape his voice sent mushy feelings
through her body. Stop it, she told herself. Behave. *I got your home number from the phone
book. Angie is visiting a friend for the afternoon.
I thought if you were going to take the dogs for a
walk you might like some company. My number
is . . .* She pulled the grocery store receipt out of
her pocket while she scrambled for a pencil.
She muttered the number to herself rapidly
again and again until she found a pencil that
had enough of a point on it so she could write.
There. She had it.

She sank back on the couch in thought while
the tape rewound.

"So, James," she said to the poster of her
hero. "He wants to go for a walk with us. What
do I do?"

James, in his great wisdom, did not answer.

Hugo frolicked over to her with his ball in his
mouth.

Absently, she took it. "Here you go, Hugie."
She tossed it down the hallway, Hugo in hot
pursuit. Well, hot pursuit for a bulldog—which
really wasn't saying much. Hugo brought the

ball back to drop it on her lap. She tossed it again, in time to the music.

What did she know about this Peter Winthrop anyway? How did she know he wasn't just a jerk in waiting? She didn't.

Oh, yes, you do, she reminded herself gently.

Once more she looked up at the poster of her hero. As she had many times throughout her youth, she imagined James Herriot speaking to her. But this time, he was speaking about trust. He was comparing her to Little Stray. The need to be part of a pack countered by the fear of being hurt. It all came down to trust. Trusting yourself that you're making an intelligent decision. Trusting that the other person will honor your trust, and won't hurt you. But finally, and probably most importantly of all, knowing that you're strong enough to deal with any hurt that might occur. After all, packs are not just for dogs. Homo sapiens is basically a pack animal, meant to live not alone, but in a group.

But was she willing to trust her own judgment again? Growing up deep in the country without brothers or sisters, the farm animals as best friends, did not exactly help one grow up to be a prom queen, or Miss Popularity. "I was a litter of one, and I suppose I just wasn't properly socialized when I was little," she told Hugo, tossing the ball again.

Hugo came back with the ball in his mouth, thrilled to pieces. She took the ball, by now gooey with slobber, and heaved it down the hallway for him again. She wondered what Peter Winthrop would think of doggy slobber. Yesterday he hadn't wiped his hands after he met Hugo. At least, not while she was there. Who knows. As soon as she'd left he might have run to the washroom to scrub his hands with some of that institutional soap. The thought depressed her.

"Well, Hugo," she said to him when he dropped the ball in her lap again. "There's only one way to find out." Melissa tossed the ball down the hallway for the last time. Then, wiping her hands on her pants once more, she reached for the grocery receipt where she'd written Peter's phone number.

She stared at the number. The pencil marks were soft and fuzzy. *I really need to get a pencil sharpener*, she thought. *One of the electric kinds. I could put it over there, on my desk . . .*

Coward. You're trying not to make a decision.

Exactly right.

You big wuss, she taunted herself. *I thought you'd given up being passive when you left Michael.*

It was merely an aberration.

Guano.

"Hugo, I once read somewhere that the sign of someone who is truly insane is that they answer themselves. So whaddya think? Am I insane?"

Hugo shoved his wide smooshed-in muzzle into her face. "You love me, even if I am insane, don't you? And even if I'm a coward."

Yes, Hugo most certainly did.

She studied the ugly face for a moment, running her hand over the wrinkles in his broad head. She most certainly loved him too. The wide-spaced brown eyes, the protruding lower jaw, the wrinkles. She'd let him make the decision. "Do you want to invite Peter for a walk?"

It was a lovely day for a walk, he thought. A warm front had come through during the night, melting what little snow remained, and the sun was bright. It was one of those days that promised spring would not be long in coming. So here he was on a lovely walk in the park with a delightful woman and two dogs. What more could he want? He stopped himself before he started thinking of just what more he did want.

"No, Little Stray," Melissa cautioned. "Not in the mud. You'll get all dirty and we'll have to bathe you again. You won't like it." She glanced up at Peter. "She didn't like having a bath yesterday morning. Jessie and I had to argue with her about it."

"Evidently, you won."

He watched Melissa step back for a moment and study the dog. "Well, we really didn't have a choice. We had to get her clean."

"She was rather filthy, wasn't she."

"Yes, and Jessie and I ended up getting a bath too! She shook water all over both of us."

As he caught Melissa's grin, Peter had a sudden vision of her in his tub, rising from a mountain of bubbles, her skin all slick and glistening from the soap. *What is wrong with you, Peter?* But he knew. To deny it would only be foolish. He wanted her. In every way that a man wants a woman. No matter that they'd just met. He knew more about her than she probably realized. He'd spent his adult life studying people, teaching people, managing people. He had a terrific gut instinct. He trusted it implicitly. Now his gut instinct was telling him that Melissa March DVM was going to be more to him than a casual friend, certainly more than a fling. At least he'd like her to be.

Then he realized she'd said something.

"Excuse me?" he asked in surprise. "I'm sorry. What did you say?"

"You're smiling. What are you smiling about?"

He bent down to play with Little Stray's silky ears, hoping he hadn't turned red. No way could he tell her what image had made him smile. He'd have to change the subject. "You asked me why I thought I could give Little Stray a good home. I'd like the chance to show you the home I'd give her. I would like very much for you to come home with me for dinner."

She stilled, as if she were suddenly wary. On guard. He wondered why, and decided to proceed slowly, but as if he hadn't noticed her wariness. "We can pick up Angie on the way. And of course the dogs could come also. I have a large backyard that's fenced in, so they can run around if they like." She didn't look convinced. Instead, she was looking out over the park, almost ignoring the dogs at her feet. It was not like her, and he wondered if he was perhaps moving too fast. But the offer had been tendered, and he wouldn't back out now. Besides, he wanted her to accept. And this was the first time since Claire's death that he'd wanted anything like this.

"Well, what do you say? Will you and the dogs have dinner with Angie and me this evening?"

She nudged a stone with the toe of her shoe. "Do you really think it's such a good idea? I mean, yesterday was the first time Angie met the dogs. Do you think it's a good thing if suddenly they're at her home?"

"I think Angie will be fine," he said, trying to put all possible sincerity into his voice, willing her to know it.

This was how it started, Melissa reflected before she gave him her answer. A charming man, a conversation or two. A walk, then dinner, then another dinner, or perhaps a lunch. More and more time spent together until the man was part of her life, more of her life than her friends. And then, when she'd fallen madly in love with the man, he'd begin to subtly alter. To expect more and more of her time, rather than ask for it and thank her for it. And then, she would end up compromising the things she held most dear, just to please

127

him. Instead of paying off her clinic, she'd buy silk underwear. Instead of having a Girls' Night Out with the gang, she would spend every available evening with him. He would become the focal point of her life. There would be nothing left of her. The irony was, he wouldn't even see it. He would only see that she had become what he wanted her to be. That was how relationships always evolved.

Was she ready to give up her life? No. She refused to be anything other than what she was, what she had become. She was proud of herself, and her accomplishments. So let's see if he was willing to accept her. As she was. No frills. Complete with dog hair on all her clothes.

Chapter Six

"I have a boarder dog that might be picked up this evening. He belongs to one of my best friends. And in case there's an emergency I'd have to give your phone number to my answering service." Why did she feel like she was drawing a line in the sand and throwing down her gauntlet? Why did she feel she was challenging him? Because she was. *Because Michael would never have allowed your practice to interfere with his life,* she told herself.

"That's fine," Peter assured her. "Then you would also want to take your own car, so you could leave quickly if you got a call." There was a hint of a twinkle in his eyes as he continued. "In case you got a frantic call from the principal of Candlewick Elementary School."

He was quick, she thought. Using the same future perfect case she'd used. He seemed to understand that she was hedging, unsure, not quite willing to commit herself. "I don't think he's one of my clients." She was stalling, she admitted to herself.

"Neither was I," he said, the twinkle becoming something else, something that caused her pulse to speed, her breathing to become slightly irregular.

Suddenly she was very aware of how close together they were standing. She could feel the heat from his body. *That is absolute nonsense*, she told herself wildly, struggling for composure, trying to mentally step back away from the line she'd drawn in the sand. She'd seemed to be trying to see how close she could come to that line without actually stepping over it. *Unless he had a high fever you wouldn't be able to feel his body heat. You're imagining things.* Yes, she was imagining things, and oh, what things they were. Things having to do with those finely shaped lips, and those long hands that she just knew could hold her with as much care as he'd held a hurt dog. How long had it been since she'd been held? It was too depressing to think of. After the first year of her marriage, Michael had done very little holding. At least of her.

The leash in her hand jerked. Her attention was ripped away from her maudlin thoughts and onto the dogs.

Hugo and Little Stray had decided to play a game of Knock-Me-Down. Little Stray was losing. And obviously enjoying it thoroughly.

From beside her, Peter's chuckle was warm. "They're having a good time."

"Yes, they've become special buddies."

"Here, let me help you with that," he said as he reached for one of the leashes. He had no idea which leash it was, since the dogs were still dancing around each other, paying no attention to the twists and wraps they were making in the thin leather—paying no attention to Melissa and now Peter trying to untangle the leashes. As soon as he thought they had them untangled, the dogs would twist around again and all would be for naught. No, for knot, he thought with a chuckle as once more the dogs wrapped around and around each other.

"You sillies," Melissa grouched good-naturedly at them. "You're both gold medal leash tanglers."

"How nice it would be if they could play like this and run without leashes." He tipped his head in her direction. "If you would come for dinner they would be able to play in my back-yard."

"I've always promised Hugo that when I can afford a real house he'll have a big fenced-in backyard of his very own," Melissa told him as she unwound her leash. "My friend Karen has the most wonderful fenced-in yard in the world for her dogs. Hugo is incredibly jealous of that fence." Then she noticed the wistful sound of her voice, and continued in a decidedly brisk

131

tone. "Someday he'll have a yard just as wonderful."

"That's a good promise. He'll like that."

"Yes, he will."

"I have to warn you, though, as an owner of such a backyard, there's a lot of mowing involved. Unless you can teach this wonderful fence of yours to mow the lawn."

Her heart caught at his grin. She hadn't noticed it before now, but Peter grinned with his entire being. It was infectious, it was encompassing, it was inviting, it was the most wonderful grin in the world. It was the kind of grin that bound two people together. A grin that reached out to her across lines drawn in the sand.

"I grew up on a farm," she answered. "I learned how to mow the lawn when I was ten."

"Then you must be an expert on lawns."

"I know a good lawn when I see one," she quipped.

"I have an idea," he said, snapping his fingers as if the idea had suddenly come to him. "Why don't I take you to see my backyard so you can give me your expert opinion."

His eyes were imploring, and playful, and excited all at once, just like Hugo's when he was trying to promote a game of b-a-l-l. She'd never been able to resist Hugo, and she found she couldn't resist this man either.

"Your yard instead of your etchings? Now there's a new one." She couldn't believe that she was actually flirting with a man.

"Oh," he said softly, "I will show you my etchings after you have been impressed by my yard."

There was silence between them, unless he could hear the beating of her heart.

She stepped over the line. "Okay."

"Okay?" His eyes became bright as the sun. "You'll come for dinner?"

"Yes. I will. But," she warned him before he got too carried away, "rule number one. I will have to take my own car. Number two, if there's an emergency, I'll have to take care of it, which means the answering service gets your phone number. And three, if my boarder dog's mom comes home this evening, I'll have to meet her at the clinic."

"Of course." He sounded surprised, as if there could be any other possibility. "Dr. March's rules for an evening out with an elementary school principal. Tell me, Doctor. Is there a rule number four? Or five? A rule about turning into a pumpkin, for instance? Or into a duckling? You're already a swan, you know."

An hour later, she was driving her battered van through the streets of Hartley. Peter had given her directions to his house, then left to pick up Angie.

Melissa had tended to the clinic chores, called her answering service, then gone upstairs to change her clothes—she didn't want to arrive at Peter's house smelling like animal chores, she'd thought as she tossed her dirty clothes in the hamper. She'd washed her face, then run a comb through her unruly curls. "Totally point-less thing to do," she'd told her reflection in the mirror. "Dr. March, your hair needs obedience lessons. It is totally out of control." She'd put a handful of dried cat food in her pocket, and then she'd been ready.

Little Stray had gone in the crate that was bolted down in the back of her van, but Hugo had been allowed, just this once, because the crate was now occupied, to ride in his favorite place. The front passenger's seat. He'd thought this was a great treat, almost as good as raisins, but much more rare. "Just don't get used to it, buddy," she'd admonished him. "If we're going to do much driving around with Little Stray, then we'll have to get another car crate for you."

Hugo had been suitably impressed.

"Look, Hugo, there's the grocery store. Peter said there was nothing I could bring, but I think I'll stop anyway. See if something looks partic-ularly good." She pulled in the parking lot and nosed the van into a space close to the front. "No," she told Hugo, who started bouncing around. "You need to wait here while I do battle with the Horrible Grocery Store. I'll be right back. I promise. Guard the car."

"Sorry, folks," she muttered under her breath as she hurried through the automatic doors and was hit with a whoosh of warm air. "I hate gro-cery shopping and there's nothing you can do to convince me otherwise." The grocery store was bustling with shoppers. The lights were bright, and the aisles sported a circusy look, as if this were the most exciting place in the world to be. But Melissa would rather be anywhere else. Grocery stores always reminded her that she was a failure as a homemaker, as a cook, as a woman. If she could get her bagels and raisins at the feed store along with her dog food, she'd never enter a grocery store again as long as she lived. But right now she had to make the effort. For Peter and Angie.

Five minutes later, she emerged triumphantly from the grocery store, a plastic bag in her hand.

"Okay, sweeties," she told the dogs cheerfully as she clambered up onto the driver's seat, "a cookie for each of you." She brought forth two cookies. "Real dog cookies this time. I vanquished the grocery store and it looks like you did a good job of guarding the car." Little Stray gently took the cookie from Melissa. Hugo didn't even bother to chew.

"Next stop, a big fenced-in backyard."

But her cheerfulness was short-lived. Consulting the piece of paper where she'd scribbled down directions to Peter's house, she turned down a tree-lined street, then another. Soon she was following his directions deeper and deeper into the kind of life she'd never had, yet had longed for with all her heart. Neighborhoods where children played together in tree-filled yards until dusk, when the sounds of their names wafted through the streets as their parents called them in for perfectly prepared dinners. Where children could have a dozen best friends within shouting distance, and probably did. Where there were tree houses, and swing sets, and where all the little girls grew up to be the kind of girl she hadn't been. And had wanted desperately to be.

She had written the directions on a pad of paper from a veterinary pharmaceutical company—a promotion for their newest product. The irony of that small piece of paper was not lost on her. On one hand, printed in ink, there was her life as a vet, a life where she felt secure and confident. Then there was the life that she both wanted and feared, a house with a family— represented by the handwritten directions to Peter's house. In pencil. Easily erasable.

Suddenly feelings of complete inadequacy careened wildly through her mind. "Oh, Hugo," she whispered. "What have I done?"

Hugo's answer was to snuffle and lean towards her, almost falling out of the seat. She reached over to steady him, and he took the opportunity to slurp the part of her that was closest, her hand. And Little Stray, not wanting to be left out, gave a bright little yip.

The kids who had teased her all through school had come from these kinds of neighborhoods. They wore the newest fashions, knew the latest styles. They were popular. She mostly wore jeans, and had no idea what style was. Yet she'd so much wanted to know, to be popular. Once, in junior high, she'd read a magazine article about makeup. She'd gone to the dime store and used up her allowance on eye shadow and blush and lipstick. She'd spent all weekend long trying to follow the instructions exactly, so she could go to school Monday morning with the poise and confidence the article promised would be hers if only she had the makeup know-how. But that high school student—one of the In Crowd—who'd worked at the tractor shop had come out to the farm to drop off some part. He'd seen her. And he'd laughed.

In sheer mortification she'd scrubbed her face until it hurt. She'd shoved the makeup to the bottom of the trash bag vowing never to try it again. After that, at school she'd kept her nose in her books, and out of the way of Those in the Know.

Most of her clients were from these kinds of neighborhoods, but as long as she was in her clinic, where she felt sure and confident, she was fine. But now clinic hours were over. She didn't have her surgical tools and her lab coat to shore up her confidence. Now she was in their world.

"I'm really out of my element, you guys. You'll have to help me through this."

Hugo snorted.

Little Stray yipped again.

"Thanks. I knew I could count on you."

Peter's house had obviously come right off a greeting card. It was a two-story, with a large bay window in the front, flower beds that promised to be full of color come spring, and a large maple tree whose branches sheltered the house. There was even a bird feeder, full of seeds, hanging from the lower branch.

"I don't know why it didn't occur to me," she said to the dogs as she set the brake and sat for a moment looking at the house. "I never even thought about where he might live."

Hugo started prancing on the seat, and Little Stray, knowing something was up, started pawing at the crate. "Stop it," she said to both of them. "Wait."

For one brief moment her lack of confidence got the best of her. What if she just turned tail and ran? She could say an emergency came up. But then she caught sight of the dogs, their expressions full of anticipation, knowing they were somewhere special and wanting to know where it was. Waiting anxiously to be let out of the car. She'd promised them an adventure in a large backyard, and she couldn't let them down.

"You win," she told them, resigned. "Besides, there isn't room in my freezer for the ice cream."

She was here. From his lookout at the bay window, he watched her for a moment. She was just sitting in her van, not moving. For an instant, he thought she was going to leave, and he wanted to protest. But then her door opened and she hopped out.

"Angie," he called. "She's here."

His daughter clattered down the stairs, her face a study in contradictions, excitement and apprehension, joy and fear. "Did she bring the dogs?"

"I don't know," he said. "Would you like to come to the door with me and we can see?"

There was a tiny hesitation. "I don't like dogs," she reminded him.

"Yes, you've made that perfectly clear."

"Even if I like Hugo and Little Stray just a little teensy-weensy bit, I still don't like dogs."

"I understand completely."

"I like Woody a lot."

"Yes, you do like cats."

He opened the door, and there was Melissa, one hand upraised as if to knock, the other swinging a plastic bag to and fro. But this he took in only peripherally. His gaze met hers and held. There seemed to be as much contradiction, as much uncertainty on her face as on Angie's. He wondered why.

"Did you bring the dogs?" Angie asked.

He lost her gaze as she stooped down to greet Angie on a six-year-old level. It was very perceptive of her to understand what would make Angie most comfortable. Yet he felt a loss, as if a door had been shut. He wanted to open that door again.

"Yes, I did," Melissa said, her voice serious. "Your father said it was okay."

"Then where are they?"

"They're in the car."

"Are you going to bring them in our house?" It wasn't confrontational, more hesitant.

"Angie, that's enough of the Spanish Inquisi-

139

tion bit," he said gently, reaching out for Melissa's elbow as she stood up. "Angie has been reminding me that she doesn't like dogs in general," he said.

"I told him," Angie broke in, "that I only like Hugo and Little Stray a little teensy-weensy bit." She grinned with the utter charm of a six-year-old. It was a grin that she'd obviously inherited from her father. "But I like Woody a lot. Did you bring Woody too?"

Melissa chuckled. "Well, you know, Angie, I like Woody a lot also, but cats are different than dogs. Cats don't like to go visiting very much."

"Oh. Well, then, what's in the bag?"

"Angie, your manners," he reprimanded her quietly but firmly.

"Sorry, Dr. March. I didn't mean to be rude."

Melissa smiled at her. "That's okay. And Angie, if it's all right with your father, why don't you call me Melissa?" Once more her gaze flew towards his, this time in question, and he nodded.

"Good. Then you shall call me Melissa. And I brought some ice cream. Would you like to put it in a place where it can stay very cold?"

"Oh, goodie, I love ice cream, I love ice cream," Angie chanted as she took the proffered bag and disappeared with it into the kitchen.

Peter felt foolish and excited all at once, as if he were poised on the edge of something big, something important, with only a hairsbreadth between something glorious and something full of despair. And Melissa, she looked just as nervous. *Why, she's just as rusty at this as I am,* he realized in amazement.

"Now, why are your dogs in the car?"

"You invited them to play in your backyard. I wasn't sure if you wanted them in your house or . . ."

He wanted to dispel her uncertainty, make her feel comfortable and at ease. "Of course they're welcome in my house. Why wouldn't they be?"

"Some people don't like dogs in their houses."

"Some people should stick to pet rocks."

She burst out laughing. "You're right."

"And besides . . ." He stepped out onto the porch. "Come on, let's go get your dogs. Besides, I told you I wanted to adopt Little Stray. Did you think I was going to give her a yard but never let her in the house?"

"Adopting a dog is a big commitment," she commented.

"You're right. It includes all the things I try to give my daughter."

"Remember, though, we might find her owner."

He felt she was trying to warn him not to get too attached to Little Stray, not to set himself up for disappointment. "Then again, you might not find the owner. Or the owner might not want her. If that's the case, I would like very much to adopt her. Would you help me make that possible?"

She tossed him a grin. "If we can't locate her owner, I'll spay her, and then she'll be yours."

When she opened the door to the passenger side, he reached around her to pet Hugo, who was practically falling out of the car in his excitement.

"Wait, Hugo," she told the wiggling creature. "No, wait. Let me help you down. It's too high for you to jump, you big doofus, hold still."

She hefted the dog and set him down with a soft oomph. Hugo shook himself soundly. The ritual to starting something new.

"How much does he weigh?"

"About fifty pounds." She clipped a leash on his collar. "Here, will you please hold him while I get Little Stray?"

He heard yipping and pawing from the back of the van. Melissa slid back the door and he could see the sheltie.

"Hi, Little Stray," he said softly. "Welcome to my house."

The dog closed her mouth, sat down on her rump, cocked her head, and gazed at him in speculation.

"How does Angie feel about having the dogs in her house?" Melissa asked, unfastening the latch and slipping a collar and leash on Little Stray.

"I think she's okay with it, as long as we remember that she does not like dogs in general."

Again she chuckled, and the rich sound entered his heart where it lodged firmly, filling a spot he'd not known was empty.

* * *

She and the dogs followed Peter around the side of the house, through a gate, and into the backyard. No, not just a backyard. It was a gloriously huge yard, Melissa thought reverently. She breathed deeply as she took in the masses of flower beds, trees, and the expanse of flat lawn. It would be barefoot-green in the summer, she just knew it would. Without a single mole hole.

She caught sight of the fence, a fence that was just as nice as Karen Matheson's—and Karen had the nicest fence any vet could ever lust after.

She peeked at Peter. He was watching her. She nodded. "Very impressive."

"Wait till you see my etchings," he answered softly.

She felt her face grow hot. But there was the grating sound of a screen door sliding shut. Angie was with them.

Melissa bent down to unsnap Hugo's leash. "Go explore, buddy. But remember, this is a huge yard, so don't get lost or we'll have to call in Auntie Madeleine and her rescue dogs."

Hugo took one incredulous look around and then waddled off ungainly. His head was up and he was ready for adventure.

Angie stood close to her father, noncommittal. Well, Melissa thought, that's very good coming from a child who up until yesterday was afraid of dogs. How to get the child to empathize with Little Stray. That was her mission right now.

"Angie," she began. "You see Hugo pretending to be a great explorer? Dogs are very curious creatures. They like to know what's what. Hugo can sniff all the bushes and trees and know who's been here. He probably won't smell any dogs unless there have been other guests in your yard. But if there is a neighbor's cat who comes through, or squirrels or rabbits, he'll find that out." She took a quick look at Angie, to see how she was doing. The little girl was shifting her gaze between Melissa and Hugo, and Little Stray.

"Several neighbor cats come traipsing through," Peter offered. "Rabbits, yes. What about squirrels? Angie, do you see many squirrels in the backyard?"

She nodded silently.

So, Melissa thought. This is very different. The dogs are in her space now. This is different from meeting them on neutral ground. She is unsure, she is timid, just like Little Stray. Angie also needed to learn how to trust. "Well, Angie, you see how Little Stray isn't exploring?"

"Because of her cast?"

"That's a good possibility, it was very clever of you to think of that. That shows lots of perception, and it may be part of why Little Stray is not exploring. But there's another reason as well." She bent down, somehow knowing that she could best communicate with Angie if they were on the same level, knowing that this was important. "Little Stray is feeling unsure of herself. She's been through a lot recently, and all of this is very new to her. She doesn't quite want to trust her own instincts yet, doesn't know for sure what will happen to her here." *Gee, Melissa,* she thought. *Are you talking about the dog, or are you talking about yourself? Well,* she answered herself, *if the shoe fits . . .*

"Does she think we'll throw sticks at her?"

Good, Melissa silently praised the little girl. *That's right, put yourself in her place. Empathize.* "I think she knows that I won't let anyone throw sticks at her. This little dog doesn't have much self-confidence."

She pulled a piece of dried cat food from her pocket. Little Stray sat immediately, eyes trained on the treat. Melissa gave it to her. "Shelties can be timid sometimes, and remember she's still mostly a puppy, and she hasn't had a home for a long time. So she needs to learn to trust people again. We have to be patient, and give her time to come to trust us. I think she will. But it might take a while." Melissa gave Little Stray another piece of dried cat food.

"Angie, why don't you show Melissa around the garden while I put the chicken on." He smiled at Melissa. "I hope you like chicken on the grill. I know most people think of grills as summer food, but I use mine all year round."

"It's almost spring," she said lightly. "And I love chicken."

"Good. I'm glad."

Once again their eyes met, and held, in that way that was almost becoming familiar to her. That way that left her feeling trembly in her soul, mushy inside, and full of longings that were finished with their winter weathering and were ready to blossom forth.

"C'mon, Melissa." Angie was tugging at her hand. "I'll show you the garden."

"I'll hold onto Little Stray's leash, if you like," Peter offered.

Melissa understood it was his way of making his daughter more comfortable, and she nodded, trying to tell him silently that she understood. "You stay with Peter now, Little Stray. Guard him well. I'll be right here in the yard with Angie. Peter, hold out your hand."

Eyebrows raised in question, he nevertheless did as she asked.

"Here. Dried cat food."

The coals were just about perfect, he thought as he shut the top of the grill. He'd give them about fifteen more minutes. The afternoon was just about perfect as well. His daughter was becoming more and more comfortable around the sheltie, and he was becoming more and more comfortable around Melissa.

He settled down on the porch step, leaning against the post. Little Stray watched him uncertainly. "Come here, little puppy," he murmured. "I won't hurt you. I need you to help my daughter. And to keep this woman in my life." He held out a cookie. Would he ever get used to thinking of dried cat food as dog cookies? He had no choice.

Little Stray considered her options, looking across the yard at Melissa, then back to the cookie in Peter's hand. Finally, she crept closer to him, uncertainty clearly visible in her expression.

"That's it," he said softly. "That's right. Come closer."

She did. Close enough so that she could take the cookie. Her furry muzzle brushed lightly against his fingers as she took her treat. He wondered if she was always this ladylike. "Can I pet you?" he asked. "There, doesn't that feel good? It's been a long time since you've had anyone to pet you, hasn't it? Well, it's been a long time for me too. I guess we're alike, you and I." Odd how comforting it felt talking to a dog.

The little dog met his gaze, watching him carefully, a puzzled look in her eyes as if she was trying to understand what he was saying.

"I would like to be your friend. I would like it if you could come live here with my daughter and me. We would take care of you. We would feed you, and brush you, and take you for walks."

The little dog came even closer, then carefully sat herself down at his feet. She wasn't touching him, but she was close enough so that he could continue petting her while he talked.

"I know I should feel terrible about the accident, and should probably tell you that I'd give anything if it hadn't happened. But you know, girl, I can't do that. It sounds awful, I know, but I'm glad. Oh, I'm very sorry you were hurt, but if it hadn't happened I'd never have met Melissa. Or you."

The little dog gave a soft sigh and settled herself more comfortably. This time she ended up leaning against Peter's knee.

He understood. "Thank you," he whispered. She had accepted him. It meant he wasn't alone anymore. It meant that he had a dog. He bent his head down so he could look her in the eye. "But what about the lovely vet?"

He'd been alone for the two long years since Claire's death. Was he ready to begin a new relationship? Was he ready to let the past be the past? He was certainly attracted to Melissa, physically as well as emotionally. No doubt about that. Just being around her made him feel alive, made him feel aware of his body in a way he hadn't felt for two years. Yet it was more than just hormones. He liked the way she was able to interact with kids, with Angie in particular. The change she'd brought about was nothing short of a miracle. But was he confusing gratitude with attraction?

At the other end of the large yard, Angie was pointing out the row where they planted giant sunflowers every year. His daughter was standing on tiptoe, her arm upraised as high as it could go, obviously demonstrating the height of the sunflowers. Melissa, even from here, looked suitably impressed. Yes, she was wonderful with Angie.

If he pursued a relationship with her she'd bring changes to his life. Animals for one thing. Lots of them. While that didn't bother him—he'd always liked animals, had grown up with pets—it would bother Gloria. She was vehemently opposed to pets, always had been. Claire had never been allowed so much as a goldfish, which was why she had wanted to get a dog for Angie.

Look at his house, he thought. It was exactly as Claire had left it. The furniture in the same place, the curtains the same. Did he think by making a change he'd be betraying her memory? Was this really the way he wanted to live? No, it wasn't. But he knew if he wanted to make any changes, especially something as radical as getting a dog, he'd have to deal with Gloria's disapproval.

But this was *his* house, *his* daughter, and *his* life. Not Gloria's, he thought emphatically. He was finally ready to make some long-needed changes in his life. If Gloria didn't like it, she'd have to deal with it. He couldn't spend his life looking over his shoulder at Claire's mother. Claire had spent her life trying to make her mother happy and proud, and had ended up with a very low self-esteem. He would not raise Angie in the shadow of Gloria's disapproval.

So what was he to do about this budding friendship with Melissa? If he pursued it, he would offend Gloria, and she could be a formidable opponent. Yet if he didn't pursue it, he would never know what might be possible. It might not work out. Melissa might decide she wanted more than a prosaic and unexciting elementary school principal could give her. After all, there were many men who would find her very attractive, and some of those men would certainly be more qualified than he to give her the happiness she deserved.

Little Stray butted her head under his hand. She wanted him to pet her again. "Sorry, Little Stray," he apologized. "I was thinking."

From inside the house, he heard his phone ring. "Sorry, again, girl, I'll be right back."

"Angie," she heard Peter call.

"Let's go see what your father wants," she suggested. She took a look around for Hugo, and saw him busily investigating some bushes. She decided to let him have his adventure.

As she and the little girl made their way up the center of the lawn, towards Peter and Little Stray, Melissa felt a strange sense of possibilities hovering about her. How close to this man did she want to get? How close was possible? Like a life in slow motion, she saw Peter reach down to pet Little Stray. She glanced at the child beside her. There would be no possibility of a relationship with a man whose daughter was afraid of dogs. Dogs and cats were too strong a part of her life. Correct that. They *were* her life, as much as breathing. She was a veterinarian, devoted to helping hurt animals.

They were a given. Just as Angie was a given for Peter. Melissa knew this on an intellectual level, but suddenly it struck her on an emotional level. If Angie didn't get over her fear of dogs there would be—could be—no relationship with Peter.

A sense of overwhelming loss tore at her insides, ripping down the half-formed dreams that had been tacked up on the walls of her heart.

Thank goodness Peter had his attention on his daughter, giving her time to compose her face. She was a lousy poker player.

"Kaitlyn's mom just called, asking if you could come over for a little bit," Peter said to Angie. "They're going to go see the kittens and Kaitlyn wanted you to come to help her pick one out."

Angie hopped up and down. "Oh, yes, yes, yes. Please, can I go, Daddy?"

"I told Mrs. Elliott you'd be ready in five minutes. Give you time to wash your hands and face." He turned to Melissa as Angie scampered up the porch steps and into the house. "Kaitlyn and Angie are best friends, and Kaitlyn is getting a kitten for her birthday next week."

"I take it Angie is as excited as Kaitlyn."

"That's putting it mildly," Peter said with a grin.

"It's good for children to have pets," Melissa noted. "It gives them someone to love when all the world seems arrayed against them. It gives them a connection with another species, and it

151

gives them something outside of themselves to look out for."

He nodded. "You probably see lots of kids and pets every day."

They were quiet for a moment, but it was a companionable silence, not clumsy or awkward. Then Peter spoke. "That's one of the reasons I want to adopt Little Stray. To give those things to Angie. I know I could get her a cat, but it's like falling off your bike. You have to get right back on and ride it again. She's afraid of dogs, and she needs to have a dog to deal with or she'll always be afraid of them." He shrugged, his shoulders expressive, even through his jacket. "Maybe I've waited too long as it is. But somehow it never seemed right until now. Until this little dog came running into my car."

He bent down to pet Little Stray.

His words echoed in Melissa's mind, but she was applying them to her own life and his arrival in it. She too was afraid to deal with men, after her disastrous stab at marriage. Or after her stab at a disastrous marriage. Perhaps she too should have gotten right up and back on that bike. That's what all her friends kept telling her. Jessie had even tried to fix her up with The Guy with the Irish Wolfhound. Her friends, Jessie, Karen, Sally, and Sylvie, were terrific friends. She couldn't ask for better. But doing the single thing, dating, hadn't seemed right for her either, not until now. Now it seemed right. Maybe. At least there was a possibility for it being right.

*   *   *

Kaitlyn, and her mother arrived moments later and took Angie off with them. The kittens were just over on the next block, on the other side from Mrs. Calloway, so they were walking. Mrs. Elliott promised to have Angie home within an hour.

Then he was alone with Melissa.

Suddenly, feeling shy, he didn't know what to do, what to say.

"Hugo is in love with your backyard," she said.

He grinned. "I like it myself."

"That's obvious. You've done wonderful things with your garden. I'm impressed by how much Angie knows about plants and flowers."

"She's a good helper."

They wandered back into the yard. Melissa bent down and unsnapped Little Stray's leash. "Now, little girl, go play. Explore and see things. There's a whole exciting world out there and you just need some courage to find it." Why, she wondered, did everything she said to this dog seem to apply to herself?

Little Stray looked up at her questioningly.

"It's okay. It's safe. Go ahead." Was she referring to Little Stray, or to herself? She shoved her hands into the pockets of her jacket.

The little dog tentatively set out, glancing back every few moments to make sure she was still there.

Peter pulled two chairs out from the garage and set them on the porch near the grill. "Come have a seat while I start the chicken. It'll just take a minute." He ducked into the house, and was back again bringing a platter of chicken in one hand and a drink in the other, which he offered to her.

"I think Little Stray is feeling more comfortable here," she said, taking the glass and settling down in the redwood chair. "It's so nice of you to invite us to share your backyard."

"It's so nice of you to bring us company on this lovely day," he returned, sliding the chicken onto the grill. Instantly fragrant steam rose up spreading scent.

"Smells good." She smiled appreciatively. "I can't cook worth beans. I burn everything."

"Cooking is something that one learns to do." He raised his eyebrow at her. "If you had to, you'd learn to cook easily. You're intelligent, you can read a cookbook and follow directions. You can learn to cook."

She blushed under his scrutiny. "Yes, but there's following the directions in a cookbook and then there's cooking."

"Once you follow directions enough times, then you start to understand the concepts, and you start taking off on your own. Soon, you're cooking." He settled down in the chair next to her. The chair legs grated against the concrete. "My mother was a terrific cook. She made sure all of us learned our way around a kitchen."

"All of you? Do you have brothers and sisters?"

He nodded. "Two of each. I'm in the middle. What about you?"

She studied her fingernails. "I am an only child. I grew up on a farm outside of Hartley. No brothers or sisters, but cows and horses and dogs and cats and things. And I have two cousins. My folks still live there. But they don't have as many animals now."

Angie would love the farm, she knew, and would love the cows and horses. She felt the urge to invite Peter to bring Angie out, when the weather was warmer. But it still seemed too soon. She didn't want to make plans for next month, not when she didn't know what next week, or even tomorrow, would bring.

He asked her a question about growing up on a farm, and she found herself opening up to him, telling him of her childhood, while he told her of his. She told him about the tree house she and her father had built, and he told her of a fort he and his brothers had built in their backyard.

That's what we're doing now, she thought. *We're building something*. Talking with each other—no, it was more than mere talking, it was sharing their lives with each other—they were building the foundations for a relationship, just as she and her father had built the foundation for her tree house on two strong branches.

"Look," he said suddenly, and it was perfectly natural for him to lean forward and touch her arm as he pointed with his other hand.

Little Stray was in the back of the yard, clumsy because of her cast, chasing Hugo. Though the dogs were her life, she only gave them half of her attention. The other half was on his hand, his hand still on her arm, touching her. She wanted to close her eyes, to better capture this perfect moment in her memory, but she kept her eyes open, and concentrated on the sensation of his touch. This was the first time a man had touched her, deliberately, in years. And it felt good. It felt wonderful, right. It felt natural as breathing. It felt as if she wanted to touch him back, to let him know that his touching her was welcome.

Melissa leaned her forehead against the cool glass of the sliding doors staring out into the night. The dogs were making yet another exploration of the backyard, in and out of the floodlights. Hugo seemingly everywhere at once, Little Stray, finally over her hesitation, hobbling on her cast and struggling valiantly to keep up. Hugo thought this yard was absolutely terrific. Well, she had to agree. There were trees and shrubs and flower beds, and a great big lawn just right for two dogs to tear around in. Even at this time of year. Someday she'd have a yard with just such a fence. "Maybe some fruit trees as well," she whispered to no one. "And spring bulbs."

Peter was upstairs putting Angie to bed. She could hear snatches of his deep voice accompanied by Angie's childlike tones. The little girl was singing some sort of song evidently. Melissa listened intently, but couldn't quite make out the words. Behind her, in the fireplace, a fire popped cheerily, and from the hallway the tick-tocking of the grandfather clock reminded her that time moved ever on. The answering service had reported, when she'd checked in, that the only call was from Sylvie. She'd missed her flight, and the new one would get her home very late, so she'd pick Jean-Luc up tomorrow. Melissa was free. Free to enjoy the evening.

"She's finally tucked in tight." Peter's voice came from behind her. "But," he added as she turned to face him, "she wants you to come upstairs to tell her good night one last time. Do you mind?"

Did she mind? For one instant, Melissa got a faint sense of what it might mean to have a child, to have a family of her own, and her heart clutched in a sudden pang of longing. Longing made all the more bittersweet because she had given up all hope of it ever happening. "No, I don't mind at all."

He grinned. "Last door on the left. There's a night-light in the hallway. And, don't let her keep you too long."

By the time Melissa had returned downstairs, Peter had put on a CD, and the dogs were curled up in front of the fireplace as if they belonged there. When they'd first come into the family room, after dinner, Hugo had tried to promote himself a place on the couch, but Melissa had told him absolutely no way, and though he'd looked up piteously now and again, he'd not argued. Little Stray had immediately claimed an obviously well-loved old teddy bear to curl up with. Angie had said it was okay, as long as Little Stray didn't chew on Mr. Blue. Melissa had assured her that Mr. Blue would be safe.

"I hope you like Brahms." Peter rose from the couch and came to her.

"I love Brahms," she answered sincerely, and was rewarded by the light in his eyes.

"Come, sit here with me and let's listen to Johannes and stare into the fire thinking deep thoughts."

"What an invitation," she answered lightly, not wanting to reveal the sudden rushing of her pulse, the flutters in her heart, the reeling senses.

The dogs merely opened their eyes, only to close them again in great contentment.

Peter chuckled. "The brave explorers look worn out from all their expeditions of the Great Backyard."

She nodded. "You must remember that Hugo doesn't have a backyard, and Little Stray hasn't had a home for quite a long time. This is new to them."

"Is it new to you as well?" His eyes were dark and his voice, oh, his voice had somehow become velvet, caressing her senses as much as the symphony.

"Is what new?" she whispered, unable to tear her gaze away from his. "I know what backyards are. I grew up with one. Some of my best friends are backyards." She found herself babbling.

"Being alone with a man, away from your clinic."

Oh, if he only knew. She felt a flush sweep over her face, burning hot. But as if he sensed her discomfort, he changed the subject. "Thank you for reading that book to Angie. She loves *The Runaway Bunny*. I've read it to her so many times I could recite it with my eyes closed."

Melissa cocked her head in thought. "It's probably a very important story to her. It's about the constancy of a parent's love. I imagine that would be very important to a little girl whose mother had died."

His eyes widened, and then he smiled at her with great approval. "You're right," he said softly. "Claire gave that book to Angie for her birthday. It's her comfort book. You know, the one she wants read before bed, or when she doesn't feel well. Other than me, you're the only person she's ever asked to read it to her."

He reached out to capture her hand, holding it lightly in his. "She thinks you're pretty special."

Angie thought she was special. It was one of the greatest gifts she'd ever been given. A great lump formed in Melissa's throat as Brahms led up to a crescendo. She'd never again be able to listen to this music without remembering this moment. Tears welled up in her eyes. She fought them back, blinking rapidly. "I think she's pretty special also," she managed. There. She had control of her voice now. "You've done a super job with her. It must be difficult raising a daughter on your own."

"Oh." His thumb traced an unseen pattern on the back of her hand, keeping time with the strains of the violin. "I've been lucky. Claire was a terrific mother, so Angie had a very secure toddlerhood."

"Did she make the lovely quilt on Angie's bed?"

He nodded. "The pictures in the quilt represent all the good things Claire wished for Angie. Flowers, blue skies, nature, peace, stability, and all the love that could possibly exist." He was silent for a moment, his thumb still keeping time with Brahms. Maybe, she wondered, when thoughts were difficult, music gave him a quiet space in which to breathe, before he thought again. Music did that for her.

"It must have been horrible for you when she died."

He nodded again. "It was." He was silent for a moment, and she wondered if she'd overstepped some boundary.

"I won't lie to you," he said at last. "I loved Claire very much. We had a good marriage. Not perfect, no marriage is, but it was good." He grinned at her, but the light in his eyes was not as bright as it usually was. Instead she found a depth that she'd rarely seen in people's eyes. She'd learned that unlike dogs, most people shuttered their eyes, keeping their deepest selves protected from casual view.

He moved his gaze to the fire, but he still kept her hand in his. "And Claire's mother helps me with Angie."

She detected a slight hardness to his voice. Not sure whether or not to ask him about it, she merely waited. Her whole being was attuned to him, wanting to learn all she could about him. If he'd been a dog or cat, she'd know what to do to find out if he was hurt. But he was a person, a male person, Homo Unfamiliaris. And people were much more complex than cats or dogs. So she waited.

Finally he sighed, and as if making up his mind about something, he returned his gaze to hers, and once more she felt a sense of connection, as if their lives were becoming woven together. And the warp was strong.

"Gloria, Claire's mother," he started, "has become something of a problem. Or rather, she's always been a problem. I've just not realized it until now."

"Sometimes . . ." She was hesitant, not wanting to appear as if she were an expert on human interactions. "Sometimes we don't see things until we're ready to deal with them. It's a way of protecting ourselves, I think."

He smiled at her, but it was a smile tinged with sorrow. "If you're right, then I'm evidently ready to make some big changes here."

"In what way?"

"She comes over to take care of Angie in the

mornings when I leave for school. She puts Angie on the bus for kindergarten, and then takes her after school until I get home."

"But?"

"Yeah." He grinned ruefully. "There's a very big but. She wants to recreate Claire."

"How do you feel about this?"

He shrugged expressively. "Angie is not Claire, and never will be. But nothing I say seems to make any difference to Gloria." He sighed. "She behaves as if Claire is just off visiting, or shopping, or something. As if Claire will be home tomorrow."

"That must be very difficult for you. For getting on with your life, I mean."

"I have gotten on with my life. But I do have to do something about Gloria."

"What will you do?"

"That's the thing. I don't know. At school I deal with personnel issues every day. Teachers, administrators, parents, students, support staff, you name it. Every one of them has a problem. And those I can solve. No sweat. That's what principals do. But my ex-mother-in-law, I can't deal with."

"Maybe that's just it."

"What's it?"

"She isn't your ex-mother-in-law. You didn't divorce Claire, so technically, she still *is* your mother-in-law."

His gaze once more held her captive, and she felt as if she never wanted to be set free. The fire crackled and popped, sending a shower of sparks up the chimney. From the corner of her eye, Melissa could see Little Stray start, then settle back down. Hugo's only response was to snort in his sleep. Neither of them had so much as opened an eye.

"You're pretty wonderful," Peter whispered, his free hand reaching out to gently stroke her cheek. "You know, since Claire's death, I've not gone out with anyone. Not out of any sense of loyalty to her, but because I never found a woman I wanted to be with. Not until I met you."

His hand on her cheek slowly, mesmerizingly, moved to the back of her neck, his fingers tracing their way up through her hair.

As a deer on the road at night is frozen in the headlights of a car, so was she stilled in the brightness of the light in his eyes. Like the deer, she had only a fraction of a second before her fate was sealed. Like the frightened deer, she had the power to flee, to break the spell, to run to the shelter of the trees.

But she was a human, meant to live in a pack, a family, not alone in the woods.

Knowing that she risked her heart, she reached out to touch his cheek, barely inches from her own. His skin was slightly raspy, yet soft at the same time.

At her gesture, the light in his eyes softened, then deepened as his lips came closer and closer to hers until at last, they lightly touched. It was the lightest kiss imaginable, a butterfly's kiss, a whisper of a kiss that seemed to hold an infinite number of possibilities. And Melissa, no longer the least bit unsure, found herself smiling against his lips.

Then, with a swiftness that left her breathless, the butterfly became a falcon, the whisper a crescendo, building higher and higher. Melissa felt her whole being surge towards him, her mouth answering his. Yes, her heart cried out at the rightness of it all.

"Peter!" A woman's strident voice shattered the moment.

Chapter Seven

Peter wrenched his mouth from Melissa's as the dogs started a canine commando act. Little Stray yipped for all she was worth, and Hugo added his basso-profundo woof. As if getting into the spirit of things, Brahms chose that moment to wind up to his final climax. Peter recognized fright in Melissa's eyes, as if the hunter had found its prey and she was it. "It's Gloria, my mother-in-law," he said to her, as he rose to his feet. "Stay here."

"Hugo, Little Stray, come here! Be quiet!" she commanded the dogs. Hugo obeyed, but Little Stray kept up her vocal protests at the intruder.

This was the last straw with Gloria, Peter told himself grimly as he cut Brahms off and then took his position in the center of the room to wait for his mother-in-law. Changes were going to have to be made, big changes. And soon.

"Peter!" Gloria called out, fear in her voice. "Are you there?"

"Yes, Gloria, I'm here. Please, come in." He heard the sarcasm dripping from his voice before he could stop it.

"Peter, I hear barking."

"Yes, Gloria, I have company. Please, come in and meet them."

"Maybe I should go," Melissa's voice came to him over Little Stray's barks.

"No. You're staying right here." It was a command, and more forceful than he would have liked. "Don't you dare run away." And as he said the words, he realized they were true. He realized she would run away, as a wounded animal, in fear and in pain, to hide. He could see it now in her eyes. "Please," he said to her in a gentler tone. "Please, don't leave me. I want you to stay."

In answer, she grabbed Little Stray's collar and wrapped her hand firmly around the dog's muzzle. "Quiet! That means stop barking." Little Stray struggled against her hand, but he could tell it was a halfhearted attempt.

"Gloria," he said, leading her by the hand into the room. "Please, come in and meet my guests. Melissa, this is Gloria."

As Gloria nodded her head stiffly, he could almost tell what she was thinking, and it wasn't very nice. Too bad. "Gloria, this is my very good friend Dr. Melissa March. And her two dogs,

Hugo and Little Stray—she's the noisy one."
Though he knew Little Stray was not really Melissa's, he felt that was beside the point at the
moment.

"Hello, Gloria." Melissa's voice was firm and
steady. He felt very proud of her. He watched
her gather her courage, no longer the frightened
creature, but someone who had a place in his
house. She was indeed his very good friend. Her
short curls were tousled, and her lips were swollen with the interrupted passion they'd just
shared, but she held her head high. Yes, he was
very proud of her indeed.

Gloria was another matter. "Hello, Dr.
March," she said stiffly, all but pulling away
from the dogs. "I am Peter's mother-in-law."

Trust Gloria to get that in, right away, he
thought sourly, as if it gave her life meaning and
focus, connected her to him, gave her rights of
possession.

Hugo, deciding that the excitement was over,
hunkered back down in front of the fire with
great sighing and snorting, but Little Stray was
the epitome of alertness, her watchful eyes
trained constantly on Gloria.

"Was there something you needed?" Peter
asked her.

"Oh, Peter." She smiled at him sweetly. "I just
stopped by to see how you were."

"As you can see, I am fine."

"Where is Angie?" She had lowered her voice
slightly, as if trying to keep her words from Melissa. "Are you sure it's wise to have these ani-

mals here when you know how frightened she is of them?"

"Angie is in bed. And she likes these two dogs. At least a little teensy-weensy bit."

"But Peter, dear," Gloria continued, her voice soft and gentle, as always. "What if one of them would—"

"I invited them here," he said firmly, cutting her off. "They are my guests. And"—he was annoyed with her enough to say it—"I am thinking of adopting Little Stray."

Gloria put a hand over her mouth in shock, her eyes becoming wide and astonished. He was just beginning to realize what an excellent actress she was. "You can't be serious. Why—"

"I most certainly am." He cut her off, knowing he was being rude but beyond caring. "Now, Gloria, I know it's late, I'm sure you want to get home."

"Grandma!" Angie came rattling down the stairs and over to her grandmother, arms outstretched.

Hugo staggered to his feet to waddle over towards Angie, his stub of a tail going mightily, snorting and snuffling all the way, his lips turned up in his peculiar expression of glee.

"It's going to attack!" Gloria cried, sweeping Angie up off the floor.

The look of delight in Angie's eyes turned to pure terror as she flung her arms around her grandmother and buried her face in the fake fur collar of her grandmother's coat.

"Hugo, come here," Melissa ordered quickly.

Hugo stopped halfway to Angie, turned around, and looked inquiringly at his boss.

"Come," she repeated, this time more quietly but just as firmly.

As the dog maneuvered his body around and staggered back towards Melissa, Peter intervened.

"Hugo was not going to attack." He barely managed to control his anger as he reached out and took Angie, now shivering in nervousness, from Gloria's arms. But he had to deal with Angie's fear, not his own anger. He sat down, Angie on his lap, deliberately ignoring Gloria. "Look, sweetie, Hugo was happy to see you. Did you see his tail wagging? And did you see the expression on his face. He wanted to tell you how glad he was to see you."

As Angie, trembling on his lap, shrank back into his arms, Peter's heart sank.

"It was snarling at her. It looked so fierce." Gloria certainly had her act down pat, he noted. She said everything with that sweet-little-old-lady inflection in her voice, so people assumed she was harmless. As he had for so long. How could he have been so blind?

"He wasn't snarling," Melissa answered evenly, an arm protectively around each dog. "Hugo is a smiler. Some dogs are able to smile when they're happy to see people they like. They lift their lips in a true smile, just as people do. Hugo was very happy to see Angie so he was smiling at her."

"But forgive me, Dr. March, it looked so frightening."

"That's a matter of opinion," she answered in clipped tones. "I think he's bright and beautiful."

"But isn't it a pit bull?"

"No. Hugo is a bulldog. They are very gentle and sweet. Hugo would *never* hurt Angie. He loves her."

"Hugo loves me, Daddy?" His daughter's soft voice came to him.

"Yes, my tulip," he answered with all the assurance he could. "Hugo loves you."

"And he would not hurt me."

It was Melissa who answered. "Angie, I promise you this. Hugo would never *ever* hurt you." Though her voice was gentle, Peter could hear her intensity, as if she was willing Angie to believe her.

"What about the other one?" Gloria was not going to give up.

"Little Stray has a big mouth," Melissa told her evenly. "But shelties are not attack dogs."

"Why does it have a cast on its leg?"

"She was hit by a car." Peter's admiration for Melissa took one giant leap forward as she continued. "Her leg was broken. Peter called me. He probably saved her life."

"Peter." Gloria pinned him with those eyes he'd once thought gentle. "You can see how upset Angie is to have these animals in her house."

From across the room he could feel Melissa bristle, but Angie was still on his lap, still unsure, once again a frightened child. "Gloria, Melissa and the dogs are my guests. Angie and I invited them here. We have had a wonderful time together today. Angie has not been the least bit upset until you arrived. I think it would be best if you left now." He wanted to see her to the door, to speak his mind to her once and for all. But that would mean putting Angie down. Angie was still trembling.

As if reading his mind, Melissa solved his dilemma. "Hey, you guys, why don't you go explore the backyard again." The dogs followed her willingly to the sliding door, though Little Stray's gaze darted from Melissa to Gloria, as if unsure whether or not to leave her boss unprotected. But the boss was certain. "Go on, Little Stray, it's okay. We'll be all right."

As the sliding door whooshed closed, Peter set his attention on his daughter. "I need to show Grandma to the door. I want you to stay here with Melissa for a moment. I'll be right back. Okay?"

"Okay, Daddy,"

He met Melissa's gaze, but he couldn't tell what she was thinking. It was as if she'd closed the door to her soul along with the sliding door. But he didn't have time to deal with that right now. First things first.

"Gloria?" He held his arm out, inviting her to go before him. For a moment he thought she might refuse. That could be unpleasant for all of them. But then, shoulders squared even in defeat, she swept out, the unjustly accused queen to the very last.

"Gee, guys, you sure are quiet," Melissa told the dogs as she drove home a short time later. "Lots different from the trip there, eh?" She sighed and shifted gears. The dogs seemed to know something was not as it should have been. They were quiet and depressed. Hugo, his eyes mournful, watched her from the passenger seat. Little Stray huddled in a corner of the crate.

And Peter . . . his eyes as he'd told her good night, over Angie's golden head, they were not exactly mournful, but they were not the same eyes that had hovered over her own for a fraction of a minute until he kissed her. No, when she left, his eyes had been full of concern, and he'd looked as if he'd just fought a battle he'd not wanted to fight. And indeed, she guessed he just had. With Angie, still nervous, in his arms, they hadn't had time to talk, but he'd mouthed, "I'll call you," and she'd nodded.

"Hey, did you like going out through Peter's gate? Was it an adventure? You got to sniff all those bushes on the side of his house, didn't you? I know it was hard for you guys, not being able to say good night to Peter and Angie, but it was probably best this way. Angie was not feeling too secure just then. But you can give Peter kisses later, I'm sure." *And maybe I can give Peter kisses as well,* she thought. But she wouldn't say it out loud. There were things that were just too private to tell even the dogs.

* * *

Once home, she took off her shoes and padded over to the phone to check in with her answering service. No emergencies tonight. Good. Evidently, all her patients were healthy and well.

"Yo, Little Stray, do you like raisins?"

Hugo, hearing the magic word, heaved his body down from the couch and toddled towards Melissa. "Yes, Hugie my love, you may have some also."

But Little Stray, when presented with a raisin, sniffed at it once, twice, then sat down and looked expectantly up at Melissa.

"It's a raisin. You eat them. Hugo loves them. Watch." Hugo once again proved his prowess as a Grand Champion Raisin Catcher. "Too bad raisin-catching isn't an Olympic sport," she told him. "You'd bring home the gold every time."

Little Stray was not interested in raisins. She did, however, make it perfectly clear that something else would be quite nice.

As Melissa offered Little Stray a piece of dried cat food, which was accepted with the air of royalty, the phone rang.

"Peter," she whispered as she hurried to grab the phone.

But it was her cousin Madeleine.

"Hi M'liss, guess what. Her name is Lady and her owner's dead."

"Whoa! Madeleine, start from the beginning." Madeleine had a habit of starting conversations in the middle.

173

"Oh, okay. Sorry. I forgot. You need coherency, and ideas in consecutive order. You are a linear thinker. We're going to have to work on that. Gotta ask Sylvie to help you get over it—"

"Madeleine, you monster, stop teasing me."

"I'm not teasing you. I'm trying to tell you, but you are interrupting. Sheesh! Now. I told you I traced the Social Security number. It belonged to some lady. I called her but the phone was disconnected. Then I did some more checking and found that she'd died a few months ago. So then I tracked down the next of kin. A daughter."

"Good girl!" Melissa exclaimed in the exact tone she used when working with a dog.

Madeleine, who also trained dogs, knew exactly what that tone of voice meant. "Do I get cookies?"

"Yeah. But later. Now, tell me about this daughter."

"I like chocolate chip. Homemade."

"You'll get chocolate chip. Tell me about the daughter."

"And I don't want those cheap chocolate chips, you know, the generic ones. I want the realio-trulio chocolate chips."

"You creep!" Melissa exclaimed in exasperation. "You'll get realio-trulio chocolate chip cookies, and I'll even bake them myself. Now tell me about the blasted daughter!"

"Gee, M'liss. You sound sort of irritated. Maybe I'd better call back when you're in a better mood."

"I'm in a perfectly excellent mood," Melissa gritted out. "But you're making me very irritated. It's a good thing I like you."

"I like you too, coz. But you know, you shouldn't let yourself get irritated like this. You need to sort of hang loose, and stop trying to change the subject while I'm trying to tell you about this daughter."

"Good. So tell me."

"But remember, I expect a whole batch of chocolate chip cookies the next time I come to visit. And you better not skimp on the chips," she warned. "And you also better not burn them, or eat half the batter before you bake 'em."

"I haven't done that since I was a kid."

"Sure," her cousin jeered. "But I'm prepared to give you the benefit of the doubt. Now, where was I? Oh, yes. I tracked down the daughter. Fairly nice lady actually. About our age, decent job, family, two kids. Whole bit. She told me that when her mom died, her mom's neighbor was watching Lady until the weekend when the daughter was going to get her. But Lady ran off. Personally I think the neighbor was probably a flake or something. Anyway, the daughter was very relieved to find that Lady had been found and was in good hands."

"Did you tell her Lady had gotten hit by a car and had a broken leg?" The name sounded strange to Melissa, but looking at the dog, sitting very prettily with her head cocked, listening to Melissa's half of the conversation, the name fit.

"Yeah. She said she was glad the dog was being taken care of."

"So does she want her or not?"

"No." Madeleine's voice was definite. "She does not want the dog. She kept referring to Lady as 'the dog,' or 'it.' She's a cat person," she added, as if that explained it all, which it did. "So, dear cousin, it looks as if you have a dog. I told her you'd be happy to keep Lady until you could find a permanent home for her. Dontcha love how I volunteer you for such things?" Melissa could hear the familiar grin in Madeleine's voice.

"Yeah, Madeleine, you're a true pal."

"So what's this downer tone I hear in your voice? I thought you had a home for her."

Melissa looked over at Little Stray—no, Lady, she corrected herself—who had unearthed a rawhide bone and was stretched out on her stomach gnawing contentedly. "I *thought* I had a home for her," she said to her cousin.

"So what happened?"

"He has a little girl who is afraid of dogs."

"Bummer," Madeleine said cheerfully. "Looks like you've inherited a sister for Hugo. It'll do him good to have a sibling. Only, children can sometimes be sort of backwards about things, as you well know."

"I'm not backwards!"

"Yes, you are. Look how you'd rather be with dogs than with men. If that's not backwards, I don't know what is. Not that I don't love my dogs, but there are some things that men are just better at. You should get one sometime. Some of 'em make great pets."

"Madeleine, we've been over this before. I tried a relationship with a man and it didn't work. Didn't work big time."

"Hate to be the one to correct you, dear coz, but you're wrong. You thought you had a relationship with a man, but instead it was with Charming Michael."

Melissa groaned. "Don't you start too. I hear all the Michael-bashing I need to from Jessie and Sally."

"I know," came the chipper reply. "Where do you think I come up with some of my best bashing lines? Man-oh-man, that Jessie really does not like your ex-husband. I called her earlier tonight when I couldn't get you. She tells me this new man in your life is really quite a catch."

"You sound like he's a fish."

"Not at all, dear Melissa. Didn't mean to. How about my saying he sounds like quite a dish? Or a—"

"Stop it!" Melissa commanded, chuckling at her cousin's breezy attitude towards life. "There's no new man in my life. And even if there were, he has a daughter who is afraid of dogs. So any relationship with him is out of the question. Look, I gotta go now. I love talking to you but the dogs have to go o-u-t." It was a bold-face lie. Both dogs were quite content with their chewies. But she was just too tired to go through all this again.

"Okay. Take the darlings out and give them great big sloppy kisses from their Auntie Madeleine. Woody too. Love you, sweetie."

"I love you too, Mad," she answered. "Kisses to Bridget and Belle from their Auntie Melissa." Bridget and Belle were Madeleine's dogs. It was the ritual ending to their phone conversations. Someone who didn't know them would undoubtedly think they were completely eccentric.

After hanging up the phone, Melissa eyed Lady speculatively. "So you really don't have a home. Well, James," she said to her hero, "I wonder what you would do with a little girl who was afraid of dogs, and who had a grandmother who fed that fear."

But James was silent this evening. Probably because of the time difference between Hartley and the Yorkshire dales, she told herself.

"Lady," she said softly.

The sheltie jerked her head up in eager anticipation, then scrambled to her feet, clumsily because of her cast. The rawhide chewie was forgotten as she tapped over to sit in front of Melissa. The brown eyes were bright with inquiry.

"So you know your name. Good girl. It looks like you'll be staying with me for a while. Poor little love. No one wants you." She reached out to hug the warm furry body, smoothing over the places where she'd had to cut mats out. "Well,

I want you. You can live with Hugo and me. It might be tough, though. We don't have a nice backyard like Peter does." Then she couldn't say anything else, for tears were clogging her throat.

To say it had been an evening of ups and downs was putting it mildly, and the biggest down was Gloria barging in. First there had been the anticipation she'd felt at going to Peter's, the intimidation while driving through the neighborhood, the insecurities. Then seeing his house for the first time, and feeling as if she belonged there, that this was where she'd always wanted to be. And what a lovely house it was. Evidently Claire had had a terrific sense of style. From the brief glance Melissa had had of the living room, she could see that the colors were actually in a scheme, and nothing looked like a garage-sale special. Melissa gazed around the small room at her own shabby furniture. Peter had almost as many books as she did, and she'd recognized some authors. But his books were on shelves that were built into the walls, while hers were on planks and bricks. There was a special shelf, down low, for Angie's books, lots of them. She'd recognized some of those titles as well, from her own childhood. Then there was the yard, and the fence, she thought rapturously. The fence. A dream of a fence. The most perfect fenced-in backyard imaginable. And the man could cook. He even knew how to do dishes! Would wonders ever cease?

After the ice cream, which was a big hit, it

had been time for Angie to go to bed. Time for reading Angie a bedtime story, and singing a silly song. Angie had thrown her arms around her neck whispering something about a biggest bear hug of all. Then she'd had to kiss Angie good night before the little girl went upstairs. And some stuffed animals—Angie had insisted.

What would it feel like to tuck a little girl into bed each night? Hug a little girl tight each night? A little girl who knew the names of all the flowers in their garden, and who loved to be read to? She smiled to herself. She knew what it would feel like. She moved her gaze to the wall by her tiny kitchen, a wall that was plain, unembellished by measurements that marked a little girl's growing height. Her refrigerator held photos of her canine nieces, and Hugo, rather than pictures drawn in kindergarten. Pictures proudly presented by a six-year-old, who then had the honor of deciding whether to use the pumpkin magnet or the butterfly. It was an important decision. *Michael was wrong,* she thought. *I would have made a good mother.*

Just as Peter was an excellent father. *And,* she thought, *an excellent kisser.* She shivered at the memory of that kiss, that perfect kiss. Not that she had experienced a wide range of kisses. But even if she had, Peter's kiss would be at the top of the list.

Even if there was no future in it, even if she knew it wouldn't happen again—how could it, with a daughter who was afraid of dogs?—she let herself dream of possibilities just for now.

Tomorrow would be soon enough to face reality. But for now she'd let herself remember how soft his lips were, how giving and yet demanding as well. She'd felt something she'd not felt in a very long time. Something she'd not expected to ever feel again and so had closed off, put away in a box tied up with a ribbon. But now that box was opened. And she felt it. Desire. And though her experience with men was limited, she had experience enough to know that Peter had felt desire as well.

Chapter Eight

"What's that yucky smell?" Angie wandered into the kitchen trailing Senor Lemon, the yellow rabbit with the longest ears in rabbitdom.

"Good morning, my little lisianthus," Peter greeted his daughter. "That delightful aroma you detected is the burning of the pancakes."

Angie wrinkled her nose. "It smells terrible. And I don't feel like a lisianthus."

"Well, then, what are you this morning?"

"I'm a sunflower," she announced grandly, raising her face and arms as if to the sun, the stuffed rabbit dangling from her hand by one ear. With her golden hair and her green flannel nightgown, she did rather look like a sunflower.

"You know, it's almost time to pick out seeds

183

for spring planting. I was thinking about putting in some more trees. Maybe a peach tree." Peter shoved the offending pancakes down the disposal and turned the motor on. "There goes our breakfast."

"Make some more, Daddy," she commanded royally.

"Only if you help."

"Deal." She spat in the palm of her hand and held it out to him as he'd taught her long ago.

"You were a great help last night," he began as he carefully measured out the pancake mix.

She made a noncommittal noise, so he continued.

"You did a wonderful job of setting the table. Do you want to pour in the water?"

She poured in the water and he handed her the wooden spoon.

"Melissa sure knows lots of funny stories, doesn't she?" he went on.

"I like the stories about Woody the best."

"I like the one about Hugo eating her books when he was a puppy." He watched her carefully, and indeed, she drew her arms closer to her sides and waited. "You know, Hugo is really a funny dog. And he likes you a lot. I could tell. Remember right before dinner when you and Melissa were throwing the ball for him outside? Remember how much he liked that? Remember how he was smiling at you then?"

Peter flicked a couple of drops of water on the griddle and watched as they sizzled. "The griddle's hot," he announced. "Do you want to pour the first one?"

Angie managed to pour four pancakes without too much dribbling.

"Now we wait for them to bubble." Angie had pancake cooking down pat.

"I wonder if Melissa likes pancakes. Do you think she does?"

"Everybody likes pancakes. Even sunflowers like pancakes."

"I listened to the weather on the radio this morning. It's supposed to be another lovely warm day. How about a visit to the park?"

"Which park?"

He thought he detected a hint of hesitation in her voice.

"Oh, I thought the park by Melissa's clinic might be a fun place to go. There is that playground there, with the swings. You like swings."

"Will her dogs be there?"

His heart sank as he heard no joyous anticipation in her voice.

"Angie." He stooped down so he was on eye level with her. "Would you rather go to the park another day?"

She nodded, a look of sorrow in her eyes. She doesn't understand, he thought. She really does not understand what is happening. "Well, if we don't go to the park, what would you like to do?"

She pursed her lips while she was thinking. "Can I get my hair cut?"

Peter started. She'd never wanted her hair cut before. She'd always wanted it long, like Claire's had been. A suspicion crept into his mind. "Do you think you'd like short hair?" he asked casually.

"Oh"—she shrugged airily—"I think so. Maybe. Short curly hair." She moved her hand up to pat her hair, as if patting curls. Curls that wisped around her face like springy silk.

And he knew. "Like Melissa?"

"Yup."

His daughter wanted to be like Melissa March. Well, she couldn't pick a better woman to emulate. He felt a broad grin spread over his face. The morning was turning out to be glorious. "If you want to cut your hair just like Melissa's, we'll just ask her where she gets her hair cut and go there. How about that?"

His daughters eyes shone their answer. "Cool!" she said. "Did you hear that, Senor Lemon? I'm going to have short hair. I'm going to have short hair."

"But we might not be able to cut your hair today. It's Sunday, you know. Lots of places are closed on Sunday."

"Then can we go ice-skating?"

He gave her a quick hug. "Ice-skating it is, then," he agreed. "After breakfast I'll check the schedule for Sunday skating hours."

Angie put her pert little nose in the air and sniffed. "Oh, Daddy," she said. "I think we burned the pancakes again."

As Peter stared glumly at the second batch of pancakes going down the disposal, burned on one side, raw on the other, he heard the front door open. What in Sam Hill—

"Good morning, Peter, and how are you, my little precious angel?"

It was Gloria, a foil-covered plate in her hands. "What's that burning smell?"

Angie giggled as she hugged her grandmother. "We burned our pancakes, Grandma. Two times."

As she stood up from her hug, Gloria set the plate on the counter. "Then it's a good thing I brought a coffee cake for my darling little girl."

Why, Peter thought, did it feel like a gauntlet instead of a peace offering?

"Gloria, I wish you wouldn't—"

"Now, now, Peter, it's no trouble at all," she said as she took off her coat and draped it over the back of a chair. "Why, my little angel, you're not dressed yet. Why don't you run upstairs and put on that pretty dress I bought for you the other day. I'll make some scrambled eggs and it'll be all ready when you come down."

"Gloria"—Peter tried not to sound as angry as he felt—"Angie and I have already made plans for the day."

"But Peter, we've always spent Sundays together. Claire always insisted."

Peter thought it wise not to mention that Claire had spent her entire life trying not to disappoint her mother. "Angie and I have made other plans," he repeated firmly.

"We're going ice-skating," Angie piped up

cheerfully. "And I'm going to get my hair cut."

Gloria gasped. But this time, as her chin trembled, Peter watched her eyes. *She's trying to manipulate me,* he realized. *Just as she always used to manipulated Claire.*

"Angelina, darling, your hair is so lovely. It looks so much like your mother's. Wouldn't you rather keep it long, like hers was? Do you know, we could get you a new set of ribbons."

"I'm afraid that will not be possible this Sunday." Peter had to stop her before she made Angie feel guilty. "Angie, honey, I'm going to walk your grandmother to her car. I'll be right back." He scooped up Gloria's coat from the back of the chair and ushered her down the hall. He held the coat for her, then grabbed his jacket from the hall closet as he opened the front door.

In silence they made their way to her car. *The first one who speaks loses,* he thought.

"I only want what's best for Claire's daughter."

"She's my daughter as well," Peter answered evenly. "And as her only parent, I believe it is my responsibility to decide what is best for her."

"But you're a man. You can't raise a little girl by yourself. She needs the guidance of a woman. As Claire's mother, I feel it is my duty to help Angelina grow up to be a perfect young lady."

"Because Claire wasn't?"

She gasped. Her eyes wide with shock. "How can you say such a thing? Claire was a perfect lady, a perfect wife. And a perfect mother. I'm stunned that you could even think such a thing, let alone say it."

"But it's true, you know." Peter shrugged. In for a penny, in for a pound. "Claire was quite wonderful, and I loved her dearly. But she was not perfect. I ought to know. I lived with her for eight years."

Gloria pressed a hand to her heart, her face gone white. "Why—" she sputtered. "I lived with her too. I raised her. How dare you say you knew her better than I."

"You knew her as a daughter. I knew her as a wife. Not the same thing at all. She always wanted to please you, wanted to make you proud. Yet she always felt like a failure, as if whatever she did could not live up to your standards. I don't want the same thing to happen to Angie. I love her too much."

The older woman started to weep, tears cutting through the powder that covered the aged cheeks. "Don't you think I love her too?"

"I know you love Angie. And she loves you. That is not at issue here. What is at issue is that you and I want different things for her. As her father, I do have the responsibility to raise her to be the best she can be. Not perfect, that's not possible. None of us are perfect. I don't believe we are meant to be. But Angie will grow up knowing that she's a good person, a worthwhile person in spite of any imperfections. And if she wants to cut her hair, she certainly may."

Gloria sniffed, a royal sniff of disdain. "Then

I guess you don't need the assistance of an old woman. Peter, as long as you harbor these feelings towards me, I shall be unable to assist you with Angelina in the mornings and after school. When you come to your senses, you know where to find me. I am only sorry for her sake that she'll be without a woman's influence."

"Not necessarily. Melissa March and I are good friends, you know."

"That person who was here last night?" All traces of softness were gone from Gloria's voice now, replaced by a hard scorn. "What does she know about being a woman? She probably doesn't even own a dress! And think of all the germs she probably carries around with her. I imagine there are germs in your house right now from those animals that were here last night. Dogs!" She said the word as if it were an epithet. "And after a dog was responsible for my Claire's death."

All existence came to a sudden screeching halt. Suddenly things were clear. Suddenly it all made sense. This was why Angie thought her mother had been killed by a dog.

Flames of fury shot through him. "Claire died trying to *save* a dog's life," he ground out. "She was not killed by a dog."

"It's the same thing," Gloria replied with a sniff.

"There is nothing at all the same about it. If you truly believe that, then I have only pity for you." Peter's voice was cold as midnight in the dead of winter. When Gloria opened her mouth to reply, he cut her off. "It is time for you to leave. Good-bye, Gloria."

She stood for a full minute, glaring at him, as if he were some sort of bug she'd like to eradicate, an insect in her spotless life. Well, dammit, this was his life and she had no right to determine it. He refused to back down, even with her eyes stabbing him again and again, as if he were the villain and she the heroine.

At long last, back erect, head held high, she got into her car. "You'll be sorry!" The words were hurled at him. "I only hope Angelina doesn't suffer."

His daughter would not suffer, not as long as he breathed. But he would not enter into the childish squabbling.

He stood perfectly still as she backed her car out of the driveway and pointed it down the street. For the first time he realized how much he'd allowed his life to be determined by Gloria. Claire had always been a little afraid of her mother, and Peter had given in to many an argument to save Claire from having to deal with her mother's disapproval. Gloria had never raised her voice, yet her disapproval was very subtle, always clothed in soft words and smiles, leaving them to feel as if they had completely disappointed her.

How had he not seen it? Now it was so very obvious to him. Yes, he thought, in hindsight we all have 20/20 vision. He had been so caught up in his work, in his school, that he had left many decisions to Claire, and then to Gloria. A major chapter in his life, the part that had kept him closely connected to Claire, was over. No more Gloria in his life, at least not to the level that she had been before. He was taking charge of his life, and his daughter's. And perhaps this life included one very special veterinarian, two dogs, and a cat.

He was free. Not from Claire, for she would always be part of him. He would always treasure the time they'd had together, and he sensed that Melissa would understand that. No, he was free of the bonds that held him, tied him to the past. He was free of Gloria. He could live in the future now. A future of his own making. A future that might hold a lovely veterinarian whose hair carried the scent of peaches. Only then did he turn and head back to the house.

Maybe, before the ice rink opened, he and Angie could move the furniture around.

The front door opened and Angie stuck her head out. "Daddy, Melissa's on the phone." As he hurried up the walk his daughter continued chattering. "She says her friend cuts her hair. She says she'll ask her friend if she'll cut mine. She says she prob'ly will."

As he whirled his daughter up into his arms in a biggest bear hug of all, she whispered in his ear, "Can Melissa come skating with us?"

As soon as he said hello, she knew something was different.

"A-are you all right?" She didn't want to be pushy. "You sound a little unusual."

She heard a chuckle on the other end of the phone.

"I'll tell you about it later. Little pitchers, you know."

"Oh. The big-ears bit?"

"Right. But I'm so glad you called. Have you had breakfast yet? Angie and I have managed to burn two batches of pancakes and she's hopping up and down with severe hunger pains."

"I didn't know that hopping up and down was a symptom of severe hunger in humans. It isn't in cats and dogs," she teased.

"It is in six-year-old humans. So, have you had breakfast?" His enthusiasm was infectious. She caught it.

"No. Not yet. What did you have in mind?"

"Let's see. It's about ten now. How about if Angie and I pick you up in about half an hour. We can go out to one of those brunch places, eat until we are stuffed, and then, let's see." She heard a rustling of paper from his end. "Do you know how to ice-skate? There's public skating at the ice rink from noon until two this afternoon. Will you come with us?"

She paused. It sounded lovely, but still . . . "Is Angie okay with that?"

"It was her idea. She says it'd be stupendous if you came with us."

"Is she okay after last night?" As soon as it was out she wanted to bite the words back. "I'm sorry. I shouldn't have said that. It's okay. It's really none of my business." Still, he didn't say anything. Had she gone too far? Oh, why hadn't she learned all the right social skills when she was younger?

"Let's talk about that later," he said finally.

"I'm really sorry. I hope I didn't overstep my welcome."

"No. But you were right. We'll talk. See you in half an hour?"

Jean-Luc's mom had just picked him up, and all the clinic chores had been done. "I'll be ready and waiting."

"Melissa . . ." His voice was softer now, more intimate. She felt it soothing its way up her body. "Thanks."

"For what?"

"For . . ." There was a pause, as if she was searching for words. "For being a special person."

During a huge brunch, they talked about planting seeds, and books, and also the dogs. Melissa told Peter that Little Stray's real name was Lady and that she was adoptable. His face lit up like a young child's at a birthday party. Feelings of tenderness for him ran through her, as sweet as nectar.

"Give me a few days," he said, a surreptitious nod aimed at his daughter. "A few days to get things together."

Angie's interest in what was going on at the table next to them was too deliberate, too intense to be real, and Melissa's heart went out to the little girl.

Later, as she did up the laces on her skates,

Melissa realized she hadn't gone skating in years. The rink hadn't changed, though. The same "Do's and Dont's" sign graced the inner doorway to the ice, the air still smelled cold and rubbery, and the same old music blared over the loudspeaker. Angie found some of her friends and, with her father's admonitions not to do any hotdogging, immediately skated off with them.

Melissa was astounded at the number of people who greeted Peter with broad smiles and waves, and the number of people he introduced her to. Not all of them were adults. Peter seemed to know almost every child there by name. Though she knew a couple of the people from her practice, most were complete strangers. But they all knew Peter. It became very apparent that he was well liked and well respected in the community of Hartley.

And he skated like a dream.

"Where did you learn to skate?" she asked as they glided around the rink side by side. Though he'd reached for her hand, she wasn't quite ready to share their friendship in public.

"I grew up in the Cleveland area, remember? Lots of ice rinks there."

"Did you play hockey?"

"Sure did." He executed a hockey stop, shaved ice swishing, then took off a few steps in front of her and turned around so he was skating backwards. "And where did you learn to skate?"

"Right here. At this very rink. I grew up in the country, out of town a few miles. And you're not the only one who can show off." She likewise did a smart hockey stop, took a few steps forward, whirled around in a 360, then a half turn further, and skated backwards.

He wolf-whistled. "Hey, I'm impressed. We sure could've used you on our pee-wee team."

"I'm really out of practice, though. You're lucky I didn't fall on my face just now. The one you could've used was my cousin. She was the hockey player. I had to learn to skate as well as she could just to keep up with her. You know, the old keeping-up-with-one's-cousin bit."

"The cousin that found Lady's owners?"

"No, that is my cousin Madeleine. My hockey cousin is Madison Cartwright." She mentally braced herself for what would come next. People who knew hockey knew who Madison was. She was a legend in the making. Had been from the time she was Angie's age.

"Wait a minute." Peter stopped short on the ice, putting a hand on her arm to make her stop too. "Your voice got all tight just now. Is there something you don't want to talk about?"

She tapped the toe of her skate in the ice. It gave her something to look at while she didn't look at his face. "No. I guess not."

"You sound defensive."

"I'm not defensive." But she could feel herself bristling. She sneaked a peek at him. He was watching her closely, ignoring the people who were skating past them, around them. Ignoring the obnoxious music that was part of the ice rink.

"Madison Cartwright is your cousin?"

Melissa nodded. *Here it comes,* she thought. But it didn't.

"Don't you like her or something?"

"Madison? No. I love her. She's my cousin."

"She's considered one of the top goalies in her league."

Melissa nodded, still studying the ice, as if it were the most fascinating ice in existence.

"You seem to be defensive about it. You seem to be putting up a wall. Are you jealous of her?"

Could he really be different? She wondered. She took another quick peek. At least it was supposed to be quick. But her gaze met his, and his gaze locked with hers and wouldn't let go. Right now his eyes were staring deeply into hers, as if trying to read the very depths of her soul. A tiny flame of hope flickered into being. *Maybe,* her mind whispered, fanning the tiny scrap of light. *Just maybe.* "The three of us, Madison, Madeleine, and I, were all in college together." She wasn't sure she could go on. This was another one of those things she'd never told anyone, because it hurt so deeply.

Peter didn't urge her to continue, but even if she couldn't make herself meet his eyes, she knew he had his full attention on her, even with all the skaters whirling past. Well, nothing ventured, nothing gained. She took a deep breath and, making sure her voice didn't waver, continued. "Madison was the hockey hero. Madeleine was the most gorgeous girl on campus. And I was just . . . I was just plain me." She shrugged. "They used to call us Beauty, Brawn, and Brains. Guys used to come on to me a lot. At first I thought they were serious, but then I found out all they wanted was an introduction to either the Great Madison Cartwright, or That Gorgeous Babe who was my cousin."

She shifted on the ice, uncomfortable in the silence that followed, as if she awaited judgment.

"Then they were utter fools."

It was said with such complete sincerity that her heart, once she truly understood his words, sang out in bursting jubilation. She felt a huge grin break over her face. The tiny flame blazed up in her soul. *Yes!* her soul cried. *Yes, this man is different.* Suddenly she was filled with a happiness that was so strong it had to be expressed in energy. "Race you three times around the ice, Winthrop!" And she was off in a shot, with Peter, laughing, only skate lengths behind.

She won.

"You didn't even try."

He could detect the mischief in her voice. "I did," he protested, leaning heavily against the boards. "I did try. You're a faster skater than I am. Besides, I'm getting old and out of shape."

Her blue eyes twinkled at him. "Are you saying you're a geezer?"

He closed his eyes for a moment. "Almost. There are certainly days when I feel like a geezer." He led them off the ice to the stadium-style seats. They both sank down on the bottom row, leaning against each other to stay up.

Waves and washes of contentment sluiced through him. He felt a smile on his face. He was probably grinning like a fool. In a short few days she had brought him great happiness.

"Look." She pointed at the ice. "There's Angie. Wave."

His daughter waved back as she skated past with several of her friends.

"What is a collective word for girl?" she asked.

"Hmm. As in a gaggle of geese?"

She nodded. "A blunder of bulldogs, a swift of salukis, a dot of Dalmatians. A handful of hamsters."

He chuckled. Why, she loved words as much as he did.

"A puddle of puppies?" he offered.

"Absolutely. Girls? Let's see. I know. How about a giggle of girls. Oh, there they go again." She returned Angie's wave. "She skates very well. She obviously enjoys it."

"Don't tell your cousin the hockey player," he teased, "but Angie started figure-skating lessons last year."

"Don't tell the guys on Madison's team, but she has actually been known to watch figure-skating now and then."

The girls—the giggle of girls, he reminded himself—went around again. Angie was easy to pick out. She was the only one without a down jacket on. His thoughts screeched to a stop. His daughter did not own a down jacket. Gloria bought Angie's clothes. Gloria did not like down jackets. Gloria liked wool coats. Another change was coming.

"Are you in a rush to get home?" he asked.

She shook her head. "Nope. I'm free as a daisy unless there's an emergency when I check into my service. Why?"

"I would like to take Angie to buy a new down jacket. Only thing is, I don't know anything about girls' clothes. Gloria always did all of that." He took a deep breath and steadied himself. "Confession time here. I abdicated my role as parent to Gloria on more than one occasion."

She didn't answer. He risked a quick glance. She was watching the skaters.

"You used the past tense," she pointed out.

"Yes. Past tense." Short, surreptitious glances showed him her eyes were still on the skaters.

"How can I help?"

"Will you go with us to buy a down jacket?"

Her gaze met his. Her smile was in her eyes. "I'm not an expert on girls' dresses, but some of my best friends are down jackets." Her voice had dropped to a softness that stopped the world.

"I don't want girls' dresses," he said when time had started again. "Angie has enough of them. I want her to have common-sense, down-to-earth, no-frills jeans and sweatshirts. Clothes that she can spill paint in."

"But what does she want?"

He chuckled. He knew his daughter. "A down jacket."

Angie, after tearing around the ice for two hours, then exhausting herself in a shopping expedition at the mall, was sacked out on the living room couch, snoring lightly. Senor Lemon was in her arms, her brand-new bright blue down jacket on top of her.

Peter chose two mugs from the cupboard and reached for the pot of freshly brewed coffee.

Beckoning to Melissa with a mug in each hand, he led her into the family room. Close enough so he could hear Angie when she woke, but far enough away from her to give them some semblance of privacy.

"You moved the couch," she exclaimed.

"Angie and I moved it this morning. I always wanted it over here and decided now was as good a time as any. What do you think?"

"Makes for easy traffic flow," she said, then studied the couch. "I agree. I think it'll work out just fine."

Suddenly he was struck by an idea. "When Angie wakes up, maybe you'll look at the living room with me—to see how it can be rearranged as well."

She grinned at him. "You want my advice on arranging furniture? I'm warning you, I have absolutely no sense of style."

"I'm warning you, I'm willing to take that risk. If you'll help me."

She chuckled. "Buddy, you don't know what

you're asking. But if you're willing to risk my advice, I'm willing to give it."

Suddenly, he was filled with the urge to take her in his arms and hug her for all he was worth. But he held two coffee cups. Can't properly embrace a woman when your hands are full of coffee, so he did the only thing possible. He held out a mug.

Their fingers bumped, not altogether accidentally, when Melissa took the proffered mug. It was natural, comforting, no coyness about it, no teasing. He liked the way she closed her eyes and sniffed the coffee appreciatively, the way she kicked off a loafer and settled down onto the couch, her feet tucked under her. He liked the way she was able to make herself at home in his house. Her pixie face with its accompanying mop of curls shone up at him in invitation and she patted the cushion next to her. He sat.

"There must be a story behind this mug," she said, a smile in her voice. "Did Angie paint it?"

"Sally believes in allowing children to have a wide variety of artistic experiences. This past Christmas all the kids painted mugs for their parents, then Sally fired them."

Melissa turned the mug in her hands, studying it. "I see flowers, must be your garden. Birdhouses. But what's this over here?"

"It's a bee," he explained.

"Ah. Of course. I should have recognized it at once. It looks exactly like a bee."

"A blue bee," he pointed out.

"Probably some odd genetic mutation. Like

albino squirrels or something. I'll have to do a literature search for color mutations in bees. I'm sure some poor grad student somewhere did a thesis on it. I wonder if there are any other color mutations in bees."

He chuckled in delight. He'd never known anyone like her. "Drink your coffee before it gets cold."

But she gave it another luxurious sniff. "I love the smell of coffee." Her voice was rich and low, intimate. "It always reminds me of my childhood, of being safe and snug and taken care of."

There's a nice thought, he mused. *Taking care of Melissa.* "Somehow, you don't seem to be the kind of woman who wants to be taken care of."

"Oh," she said loftily. "There's taken care of and there's taken care of."

He felt a smile grow from somewhere deep inside him. "Which one don't you want?"

There was a subtle shift in her face, in her posture, in the way she held both hands curled around the mug. He knew that all kidding was over now, that he should listen very carefully.

"I don't ever want to feel smothered by being taken care of. I never want to not be able to make my own decisions, to have to rely on someone else for everything."

"Why don't you want to rely on someone else?"

"Because that gives people power over you. If you rely on them, and if they know it, they can use it to manipulate you to do what they want you to do. All in the name of taking care of you, of course." She took a sip of coffee, and he was fascinated by the way her lips pursed against the rim of the mug. "That's why it's so insidious. Because it's done in such a way that you're actually brainwashed into thinking it's for your own good. When you're in that situation, it's very difficult to see it. Which makes it even more dangerous."

He had a sudden hunch. "You're speaking from personal experience," he guessed.

She nodded, and took another sip of coffee.

"Want to tell me about it?"

Her eyes were shy as her gaze met his. "I don't want to bore you."

He set his mug on the table, then reached out for her mug. At last their hands were free. He twirled a strand of her hair around his finger, drawing her close enough for a very light kiss. At least, he meant it to be a light kiss. A kiss of friendship, of comfort. But it ended up being a little bit more. Then a lot more. As he lifted his head he eased his arm around her shoulders, snuggling her against him.

"Nothing about you could bore me," he murmured. "I think you're splendid." And she felt so very right, pressed against him like this. "I've told you about Claire. Why don't you tell me about whoever it is that makes you sometimes look as though you want to run away from me?"

She twisted in his arms to look up at him, her eyes large and round. "You're right," she confessed.

He nodded silently.

She settled back down against him and began to speak. "When I was in school, in the middle of vet school, I met a man who I thought was the answer to my dreams. His name was Michael. Jessie calls him *Charming* Michael because he's the kind of guy who always gets his own way by being particularly charming. Anyway, I fell for him. Hard. We got married. I don't really know why he married me. I'm not the kind of woman he usually prefers. It took me a whole year to realize that he was systematically charming me out of finishing vet school. Out of my dreams. He was trying to make me into what he wanted me to be. Something I wasn't. But it was very subtle. That's why it took me so long to catch on."

She stopped talking, so after a moment he prodded her. "What happened?"

"I left him, of course. Talked the vet school into readmitting me, finished my degree, bought the practice from old Doc Fields when he retired, and here I am, three years later. A realio-trulio veterinarian, struggling to pay off a clinic and a gazillion dollars in school loans. End of story."

He was not fooled. "But why do you sometimes want to run away from me?" Little wisps of her hair danced around as he spoke, his lips very close to her head. He gave in to the urge and kissed the top of that head, inhaling the soft fragrance of peaches. "Do I remind you of him?"

"No," she whispered.

"Then what?" He kept his voice as soft as

hers, once more pressing his lips to the crown of her head. He thought he felt her shiver in his arms, so he repeated the kiss.

"I don't want to jeopardize my clinic, my practice."

"By being involved with me?"

"Yes."

"Do you think that could happen?"

"It might."

"No. It won't. I know how much it means to you, and I want you to be happy."

"That's what Michael always said."

"But I'm not him."

"I know."

"But?" he prompted, streaming his fingers through the springy silk of her hair.

"I don't trust myself."

"Why? I find you incredibly trustworthy."

"Because . . ." She paused, as if willing herself the courage to continue. "Because I'm afraid I'm falling in love with you."

He smiled into her hair, closing his eyes to hold onto that scent. He loved peaches. He wanted to stay just like this forever, with her in his arms.

"My beautiful Dr. March," he murmured against her hair, then moved his lips down to her neck, around her cheek, to whisper words against her lips. "Let me assure you there is nothing to be afraid of. Because you see, my lovely Dr. March, I'm falling in love with you too."

"Daddy."

*   *   *

Melissa started at Angie's voice, and pulled slightly away from Peter. Then she caught the look in his eyes. She knew that look. But from the other side. *Love me, love my dog,* she'd always said. Well, for Peter it was *Love me, love my daughter.* She twisted slightly in his arms to see the little girl in the doorway. "Hi, Angie, we're talking. Come join us?"

The pressure of Peter's arm tightening around her shoulders told her she was right. She sought his gaze, and when she found it, was rewarded by the tenderness in his smile.

"It looked like you were kissing," Angie announced as she snuggled up onto their laps.

She heard Peter snort slightly as if he were trying not to laugh.

"Well, yes, we were," she admitted. "I hope you don't mind."

"I think it's gross."

"That's because"—Peter hugged both of them tightly—"you're six years old."

"I'll think kissing is gross when I'm two hundred," she announced grandly.

Peter's chuckle warmed Melissa's soul once more. Who'd have ever thought it, that she, Melissa March DVM, would be bantering about kissing with a man and his six-year-old daughter. Will wonders ever cease? *Hey, James,* she thought, *whaddya think of this? Maybe things can work out after all.*

"So," Angie said. "Whaddya want to talk about?"

"What would you like to talk about?"

Melissa, her ear pressed against Peter's chest, could feel his voice rumble.

"Oh," Angie said airily, "let's talk about our garden."

"What about our garden?" his voice rumbled.

Melissa let her eyes drift closed. She'd been awake most of the night worrying about Angie, worrying about Peter, just plain worrying. She'd just spent two hours skating, and knew she'd pay for it tomorrow in sore muscles. But right now she was secure, and all was well with the world. Angie was leaning against Peter, and her head was right under Melissa's chin. Her six-year-old hair smelled like baby shampoo.

"I was thinking, Daddy, that we hafta plant some more stuff."

"What kind of stuff? Please, my child, you must be more specific. If we went to the nursery and asked for more stuff, well, they'd look at us rather strangely, don't you think?"

Angie's giggle sounded like the ringing of a tiny bell.

"I was thinking, Ang, about putting in some more fruit trees."

"What kind?"

"Peach."

Melissa felt inspired to rouse herself to add her two cents worth. "I love peaches."

"I do too!" Angie crowed. "I do too!"

"And I wonder," Peter continued in a very casual voice.

Melissa was not fooled. Something big was

going to happen. She opened her eyes so she could listen better.

"I wonder if Hugo and Lady would like to help with the planting. I wonder if they like to dig holes."

There was silence.

This silence is not golden, she thought. *Not even tarnished brass.* No, it was like a tomb. As if all life had been euthanized.

Oh, her heart just ached for Peter. He wanted so much for his daughter to not be afraid of Lady. Life was sometimes so grossly unfair. She wanted to put her arms around him and hold him until the ache that she knew was also in his heart went away. And as for Angie . . . Angie sat on their laps perfectly still, as if she were holding her breath. Then she spoke.

"Was Hugo going to bite me?"

Relief coursed through Melissa. Even though they'd been over this several times before, Angie evidently still needed to hear it. Well, that was fine. Sometimes people needed lots of reassurance. And she promised herself that she'd give it every single time Angie needed it, for as long as it took. "Angie, I promise you, he was not going to hurt you," she said. "He was running to see you because he loves you. Because he was happy to see you. He was not going to hurt you."

Angie twisted around so she could see Melissa. Her forehead was creased in concentration. "Then why did Grandma say he was going to attack?"

Oh, no, Melissa thought. *What do you tell a six-year-old child?* There were many things she could say, based on only the few minutes she'd spent in Gloria's presence, along with the things Peter had told her.

"I think," Peter said slowly, "that your grandmother is afraid of dogs."

"Why?" Angie twisted around the other way, so she could see Peter this time.

"I don't know, honey. I wish I did." Melissa could hear the sincere regret in Peter's voice. She wondered exactly what he was thinking.

"Angie," Peter continued. "Did your grandmother ever talk to you about animals? About pets? Of any kind?"

"No. Only that they smell and don't belong in houses. And carry diseases. And"—her voice trembled and dropped to a near whisper—"that dogs sometimes attack people. And kill them."

Chapter Nine

"Good morning, Mr. Winthrop," Mrs. Calloway greeted him as he entered his office the next morning.

"Hello, Mrs. Calloway. I hope you had a nice weekend."

"Yes, I did. Oh, and I talked to Mrs. Elliott last night. She said she was going to be taking care of Angie for a while. Is everything all right? Your mother-in-law is not ill, is she?"

Trust Mrs. Calloway to try to ferret out what she could, Peter thought not without amusement. "No, she's quite well. Angie just wanted to spend some more time with her best friend." He in no way wanted his changed relationship with Gloria spread around the school.

"Well, that's good. Mrs. Elliott said Kaitlyn

was very excited about it. You know what an enthusiastic child she is. Kaitlyn is getting a kitten for her birthday and all she could talk about was the wonderful Dr. March who came to school on Friday." Mrs. Calloway beamed. "I told her that Dr. March is the vet I take my Clarence to. I wouldn't take him anywhere else."

"Yes, I believe you've told me that before." Peter tried to be tolerant. She had worked for him for several years, and he knew that under her slightly eccentric exterior she had the proverbial heart of gold. And she adored her geriatric dog. But she wasn't finished yet.

"You know she's single. Dr. March is, I mean," she added as if in explanation.

"Good morning, Mrs. Calloway," came Sally's cheerful voice.

"Good morning, Miss Foster. I was just telling Mr. Winthrop that Dr. March is a wonderful vet. Don't you agree?"

"Absolutely. Without a doubt. No question about it. None at all. Morning, Peter."

He gazed at the two women who were sharing the doorway of his office. "I thought the two of you never agreed about anything."

"Oh," Sally said loftily, "Mrs. Calloway doesn't realize that cats are the perfect race. Other than that we agree on lots of things."

"Now wait a minute, you young thing." Mrs. Calloway held up her hand. "You only think that because you've never experienced the pure devotion and loyalty of a good dog."

Sally shuddered theatrically. "Sorry. Slavish devotion is not my idea of perfect."

"Time out. Truce," Peter called. "It's too early on a Monday morning to start this."

Mrs. Calloway was quick to change direction. "She's pretty too, don't you think?"

"Who is?" Sally wanted to know.

"Why, Dr. March, of course," Mrs. Calloway answered.

"Yes. She's very pretty. Don't you agree, Peter?"

"Pretty" was not the word Peter would have used to describe Melissa. It was too weak a word, too common for a woman as vibrant and alive as Melissa was. But there was no way he would ever let these two women know that. "Isn't it time to get ready for the students to arrive?" he asked mildly.

He couldn't miss the look of speculation that passed between Sally and Mrs. Calloway. He decided to ignore it.

They decided to pursue it.

"You know, Peter," Sally continued, "Melissa is simply wonderful with children. She's a natural. She'll make a wonderful mother some day. She's very nurturing and caring. One of the reasons she's such a good vet."

Mrs. Calloway was quick to add her praises. "Oh, Mr. Winthrop, that's true. Watching her with hurt dogs, you can just tell that she'll be the perfect mother someday. And a good wife to some lucky fellow," she added sagely.

From behind his desk Peter eyed the two

women speculatively. "Are you by any chance hinting at something?"

"Who, us?" Sally asked with practiced innocence. "Hinting? Now what would we be hinting at? No. We're just sharing our thoughts with you." She waggled her fingers at him. "Time to get ready for the little darlings to arrive. See you later." And she disappeared down the hall.

"Was there something else you needed, Mrs. Calloway?" he asked pointedly.

She beamed at him. "Nothing at all. I'll leave you to read that report. Oh, and Mr. Ballentine called first thing this morning. He asked me to remind you that the school board would be meeting half an hour earlier than usual on Thursday night." She pressed her hand to her ample bosom. "Isn't it exciting? I just know you'll make a superb superintendent." With that parting remark she drifted out of his office.

Now where had she heard that? "It's not a done deal, Mrs. Calloway," he called after her. "And I really don't think you should assume anything."

"But everyone knows the truth, Mr. Winthrop," her voice called back to him.

Oh, no, they don't, he thought firmly. *No, they don't.*

"So how's your principal?"

"Just fine, Jess. How are you this morning?"

There was silence. Melissa looked up from the lab report that had just come in on the fax. "How are you?" she repeated.

Jessie's freckle face broke into a slow grin, delight shining in her eyes. "Well, color me thrilled," she said softly. "Good for you."

"Coffee ready?" Melissa asked, changing the subject before Jess said anything else. She really didn't want to discuss her relationship with Peter just yet. Even though Jessie was a very good friend, she was still unsure and hesitant to openly admit her feelings for him. Those feelings were too new, too magical. She wanted to hold onto that magic for a while longer before it became public property.

"Coming up." Jessie's shoes made squelching noises on the tile floor as she made her way down the hall.

Melissa turned her attention back to the lab report. The findings were not good. Melissa twisted around in her chair to look up at the photograph of James Herriot. A great lump formed in her throat. She had to swallow several times before she could speak. "Well, James, how do you tell an old woman that her cat is getting worse and is soon going to die?"

James, from his field of sheep, gazed on her with compassion, as he had many times before. And as before, Melissa closed her eyes and allowed calm and acceptance to flow through her.

She punched a number on her intercom. "Suzette, please call Mrs. Shoemaker for me. I have Sandy's lab report."

"Bad news?" Jess set a mug of steaming coffee before her.

"The worst possible." Melissa curled her

hands around the mug for comfort. "The new medicine isn't working. His blood count is out of control." She shook her head. "There's nothing else we can do. At least he's not in pain."

"Poor Mrs. Shoemaker," Jess murmured, leaning against the doorjamb. "That cat is all she has. And he's a nice cat too."

Melissa quickly took a sip of coffee and burned her tongue. Well, it would account for the sudden tears in her eyes. "Change of subject is needed here before we both turn into the proverbial watering pots." She took another sip.

"Okay. Change of subject," Jessie announced. There was a pause before she continued. "Remember last week when you told me you couldn't trust your judgment? I've been thinking about that for a while. Seems to me you trust your judgment every minute of every day. I trust your judgment also. So do all your clients. We all trust you to make decisions that are life-and-death ones." Her voice lowered, softened, and she leaned slightly towards Melissa. "You are very careful and methodical, and you have terrific intuition about hurt animals. You make good decisions based on the best information. That is why you're such a terrific vet, and why people trust you so much."

Melissa took another sip of coffee to cover her discomfort over the praise. She cleared her throat. "Good coffee this morning," she remarked casually.

"Think about it, will you, M'liss?" The intensity in her friend's voice was a palpable thing, filling the quiet between two good friends. Then Jess's voice became brisk and cheerful again. "So where is Lady this morning? I still think we ought to call her Rambette. Or Trampette."

Melissa cleared her throat before she answered. "Ah, you know her real name. But the lady's not a tramp. Just a stray. I understand you talked to Madeleine the other night."

"Yup. You have terrific taste in cousins, by the way. I heartily approve of them both. So where is our Lady Stray?"

"Upstairs with Hugo. But I want to bring her down to visit us in the back for a while today. She needs some socialization."

"I bet Hugo is in love."

"You got that right."

"And you?" she asked casually. Too casually, Melissa thought.

"I got that right too," Melissa answered, as if misunderstanding her. "Hugo loves everyone indiscriminately."

"I'll let that one pass, Melissa dear," Jess said with a smile.

"Oh, don't be so nosy."

"I have to be nosy," Jessie pointed out reasonably. "How else am I ever going to have any fun? We all know *my* love life's non-existent. Vicarious pleasure is the only pleasure I have."

"Well, you sure sound cheerful about it."

"Only way to be."

"Melissa," Suzette's voice said over the intercom. "Mrs. Shoemaker is on line two."

"Thanks, Suzette." Melissa gave Jessie a wry

grin as she reached for the phone. "This is the difficult part of being a vet. This is the part I hate." She was struck by the fierceness of her own voice and closed her eyes for a moment. She felt Jessie's arms around her for a brief hug before her friend went out, closing the door. Except for Sandy, Mrs. Shoemaker lived alone. There would be no one there to hug Mrs. Shoemaker.

Evidently the news about Sandy had spread throughout the clinic. The entire staff was more quiet than usual, more careful of one another. All of her staff—from Tom, the high school student who did the kennel chores, to Suzette, to Sara the groomer, to Jessie her loyal vet tech— loved Sandy. All of them had been pulling for his recovery. Sandy, along with Mrs. Shoemaker, was family. They were, Melissa thought, the best vet staff in the world.

Melissa spent the morning seeing patients. She gave shots, did puppy and kitten exams, and showed Mrs. Farjeon how to brush her dog's teeth—every day, she emphasized. She removed stitches from a spayed cat, confirmed the pregnancy of a lovely saluki bitch who was carrying at least four puppies. She prescribed medicine for ear mites in a crusty old cat who lived with an equally crusty old man. There was a rhythm and odd predictability to the day. It brought comfort to her heavy heart. Though she couldn't save Sandy, there were many other cats and dogs—animals she'd grown to know and love—that she could help.

Then, during a lull, she brought Lady downstairs.

"Hello, Lady," Suzette crooned, bending down and holding out her hand. "Do you remember me? I gave you a cookie on Friday. You liked it. Look, here's another one." All the clinic staff kept dried cat food in their pockets.

Lady looked at Melissa as if asking permission.

"It's okay," Melissa said. "Suzette is family."

Having received permission, Lady took a few steps forward, her cast tapping on the linoleum floor. She stretched her neck just close enough to quickly take the piece of dried cat food, then scuttled back to stand beside Melissa, where it was safe. She crunched delicately.

"Really pretty little dog," Suzette said. "So do you think Sally's principal is going to take her?"

"I think so. Probably."

"Well." Suzette sat down on the floor and pulled another piece of dried cat food out of her pocket to coax Lady closer. It worked. "If he doesn't take her, I bet my mother would let me." Suzette still lived at home.

"Thanks, Suzette. Tell your mom thanks also. But I think if Mr. Winthrop"—the formal name sounded strange to her ears—"doesn't take her, I'll keep her. She's been through so much in her short life that she deserves some constancy. Besides, Hugo is in love."

Suzette giggled. "Hugo would fall in love with a stuffed eggplant."

About a half hour before lunch, Peter called to ask if he and Angie could help her walk dogs that evening after work. She told him of course, that would be wonderful. It was a short call, however, for a cat was brought in with acute bladder stones.

Still, the sound of his voice wrapped itself around her heart, around her mind, like a cuddle blanket giving comfort and security and warmth throughout the rest of the morning.

At lunchtime she carried Lady upstairs to where Hugo waited. "Honey, I'm home," she called.

Hugo hove himself off the couch to stagger over to her, his tail wagging mightily.

"Raisins for you, and bagel and cream cheese for me."

She turned on the CD player and put in the Brahms violin concerto, humming along with it while she opened the refrigerator. "And guys, Ray brought the new issue of *Veterinary Medicine Review*. Terrific lunchtime reading. Oh, you guys want a taste of cream cheese? Okay. That's all. This is my lunch remember. I don't get to eat such lovely kibble for breakfast."

Curled up on her old couch munching on her bagel, Hugo at her feet staring hopefully, Melissa tried to concentrate on the journal article in front of her. *Genetic links to feline cystitis. What great stuff, terrific plot, wonderful charac-*

terizations, she told herself in encouragement. *It'll be almost as good as a Michaelson book*. But all her hype didn't work. Angie's small voice kept intruding. *"Dogs sometimes attack people. And kill them."*

It was a lovely evening for a walk in the park, Melissa thought several hours later. Angie, in her new jeans and jacket, was skipping ahead, but slowly, as if she was in deep thought. Hugo was waddling along, content to be in the company of people he loved. Lady's cast kept tap-tap-tapping. And Peter . . . Melissa smiled inside, hugging their new relationship to her heart.

Suddenly, still several steps in front of them, Angie stopped. Melissa and Peter stopped also, a couple of yards behind her, the dogs coming to a standstill.

Angie twirled slowly around and came to a stop facing them. Her face was a study in concentration. And indecision. "Hugo loves me?" Her voice was solemn.

"Yes," Melissa answered, equally solemnly. "Hugo loves you." Hearing his name, the bulldog pranced around in circles. "Hugo, sit," she commanded. "Stay." The dog obeyed, though his tail was still going mightily. Lady, unsure of what was happening, pressed her body against Melissa's leg.

"And he was not going to attack me?"

"No. He was not going to attack you."

There was silence for a moment while Angie

pondered this deeply, as if it were absolutely crucial to her. Melissa knew that it was.

"Does Lady love me?"

"Lady doesn't know you very well yet. But when she does get to know you better she will love you."

"Will Lady attack me?"

"No. She will not."

"Do you promise?"

"As best I can promise anything."

There was another pause, and Melissa waited through it, giving the child time.

"Is Lady afraid of me?"

Melissa eyed the little girl critically for a moment, knowing that Peter, next to her, was holding his breath.

"Angie, the best way to find out is to ask her."

"Ask Lady?"

"Yes. Ask her. And if you want to really know the answer, stoop down and put out your hand. Then she'll know that you're her friend. That's right. Palm down."

"Lady," she crooned in her little girl's voice. "Are you afraid of me? I won't hurt you."

It was Lady's turn to think things through. She leaned away from Melissa's leg, towards Angie, not sure, but willing to try. The little dog took a step forward, then another, until she was almost close enough to sniff Angie's hand. Angie held perfectly still, though conflicting emotions flitted across her face. "I won't hurt you," she repeated. "I won't throw sticks at you."

Lady took a quick look back at Melissa, for reassurance.

"Go ahead, Lady. It's all right."

Lady took a final step closer and delicately sniffed Angie's outstretched hand.

Melissa felt a slow smile form on her face, and from beside her, she could hear Peter begin to breathe again.

"It tickles," Angie exclaimed softly.

Peter hurried to his daughter's side, to kneel beside her, his arm going around her. *Don't rush her, Peter,* Melissa silently told him. *Don't rush either of them.*

Lady wagged her tail and stepped closer to Peter. He smoothed the golden fur on her head. "That's a good girl," he told her.

"Can I pet Lady?"

"Yes, my tulip. You most certainly may."

The next morning, Melissa woke up late. The blasted alarm didn't go off. She let Hugo and Lady out into the tiny yard, then raced back upstairs for a quick shower.

"Hey, you guys," Melissa called to the dogs as she was surveying the meager contents of her refrigerator. "Have you been stealing my bagels while I'm at work? This is the last one." The dogs came running, wagging their tails agreeably. "You know what this means? This means I have to go to the grocery store. I hate going to the grocery store."

The dogs looked at her in adoration.

"Yeah," she muttered to them. "I know. This

is just a ploy so I'll buy more raisins. Hugo, you've tried this one before."

She trotted back downstairs again, last bagel and cream cheese in hand, as her first patient pulled in the parking lot.

"Here's your cup of coffee," Jessie called to her.

"Morning, Melissa," Suzette chimed in from the reception area.

"I hate mornings," she grumbled, reaching for the appointment book.

"Take a good long slurp of coffee and you'll feel just fine. But it's very hot, so be careful not to spill it in your lap." Jessie stood in the doorway, arms folded across her chest, mischief in her face. "Late night, eh? Hope it was fun."

"Wipe that grin off your face, please," Melissa ordered with a mock scowl. "For your information, I was up late reading my book. Alone. And it was very good."

Jessie's face fell. "Gee. That's too bad. Here I thought you'd had a great late night with your principal."

"You're hopeless, you know that?" Melissa shook her head.

"Yeah. But I still like you."

"Okay, friend. I need a favor."

"Shoot."

"Thursday. Day after tomorrow." Melissa gathered up Woody from where he was sitting on the appointment book, his motor up to Mach nine. Rubbing the cat's ears, she studied the page. "We have a cat to spay, a dental on the

Yorkie, then the knee operation on that weimaraner, and then the lymph node removal on that old corgi. Probably only the cat, the weimaraner, and the corgi will stay here overnight." She looked up at her friend. "Peter asked me to take care of his daughter that night. He has some meeting that he can't get out of and his regular baby-sitter can't make it. Can you do the evening clinic check?"

Jessie put her hand on her heart in a typically melodramatic style. "To assist the path of true love, my dear Melissa, I would be only too happy to oblige." She grinned, delight shining in her eyes. "No prob." She trotted off down the hall whistling a sprightly tune. Off-key.

"Melissa." Suzette stuck her head in the doorway. Her usually sunny face was drawn with worry. "Mrs. Shoemaker is here with Sandy. She didn't have an appointment, but I told her I'd squeeze them in."

"Thanks, Suzette. That's fine. Why don't you put them in an exam room and I'll see Sandy in just a few minutes."

Well, James, Melissa said silently to her hero as she took another sip of coffee, *wish me luck with Mrs. Shoemaker*. This was always the most difficult thing in the world. Telling a client that their cat or dog was not getting better and, in all probability, would go downhill very quickly. This was going to be even harder than usual, because Mrs. Shoemaker and Sandy weren't just clients, they were family.

* * *

Annie Kimberlin

It was a long day, but finally clinic hours were over. There was just one more thing Melissa had to do, and there was no getting out of it. *Most people hate going to the dentist*, Melissa thought. *I hate grocery shopping.* She pulled her old van into a parking space and killed the engine. *Deep breath, Melissa. It'll soon be over and you won't remember a thing.*

The store was, as usual, brightly lit, posters and advertisements a visual scream. But she knew just where the bagels were. And the cream cheese, and raisins. The important things in life. Dried peaches also went into her cart, and then, on a whim, she craned her neck to see the directory signs hanging from the ceiling. Some chocolate chips, those mint ones, would be just the perfect reward for going grocery shopping. Hugo did tricks for raisins. Well, she went grocery shopping for mint chocolate chips.

Finding the aisle that held the baking ingredients, she took a direct path to the chocolate chips display. Maybe she should get two bags. She might need a reward for doing the laundry.

Suddenly, she felt a prickle at the back of her neck, as if someone were staring intently at her. She turned around to face an elderly woman, well dressed, fur collar on her coat, chiffon scarf draped around the neckline. The woman looked as if she'd just stepped out of one of those magazines for wealthy powerful women. Or at least out of a beauty parlor. The kind of woman who always made Melissa feel insignificant.

Then she realized it was Gloria staring coldly at her. Nothing even remotely friendly in those ice-blue eyes. She's trying to intimidate me, Melissa realized in surprise.

"Why, hello, Gloria. Lovely evening, isn't it?"

"Dr. March," the woman said stiffly. Barely civil. "I didn't expect you to shop here."

You expected me to eat dog kibble? Melissa thought. "It's the closest grocery store to the clinic, you know," she answered, trying to be pleasant.

The older woman glanced at the contents of Melissa's cart and sniffed derisively. "I expect you don't do much cooking."

Melissa merely smiled, suddenly at ease. "As a matter of fact, I don't like to cook."

The woman drew herself up. "My Claire was an excellent gourmet cook. She was the perfect hostess for Peter's many social engagements. In his new position he will be even more in the public light. The preparation for all those dinner parties are quite a challenge, you know. My Claire—" Her voice cracked, and for a second, the ramrod-straight shoulders sagged. The drill-sergeant demeanor was gone and in its place was an old woman. An old woman alone, and in pain.

Melissa was a healer. It was her vocation, her passion. Yes, her patients were mostly cats and dogs, but her heart went out to any creature in pain, no matter the species, no matter the temperament. Even a nasty dog needed comfort when it was hurt, and sometimes pain could make a normally nice animal bite. "I'm truly sorry for your loss," she said softly, instinctively reaching out to touch the woman's sleeve. "I know what it's like to lose someone you love."

But at her touch, the older woman sucked in a quick breath and the drill sergeant was back, looking down her nose at Melissa. "Indeed." Her voice was the epitome of haughtiness. "My son-in-law lost the perfect wife. And nothing will bring her back."

With that as a parting shot, the old woman maneuvered her cart down the aisle as if it were a tank.

Melissa stared after her. What an unhappy, nasty woman. Or perhaps she was just beginning to feel as if she were being replaced in Peter's life. Melissa glanced at her watch. Time to get home. Besides, she'd promised to take the dogs over to Peter's house this evening.

She reached for a third bag of mint chocolate chips. Reward for not giving into instinct when facing Major Gloria. She had better get used to Gloria, for someone that old was probably not going to change. You could teach an old dog new tricks, but sometimes people weren't as smart as dogs.

Well, she told herself briskly, *nothing you can do about Gloria. But you can make two dogs very happy by allowing them to run their little legs off in a terrific fenced-in backyard.*

Wednesday morning was bright and cheerful. A warm front had swept through bringing more mud and promises of spring. "Stand still," she told Lady. "I have to wipe your feet off before we go in." Lady was not impressed, but she tolerated it. Then Melissa carried her back upstairs for breakfast. "Sorry, Hugo, you don't have a cast, so you don't get carried. Besides, you're too heavy. Might as well cut out the poor-pitiful-me act." She blew him a kiss.

"My," Jessie remarked an hour later. "Aren't we in a cheerful mood today." She set the ritual mug of coffee in front of Melissa.

Melissa grinned at her. "Yeah. And I haven't even had my coffee yet."

"Gee, I hope it's not permanent, or you might not need my coffee in the mornings and I'd be out of a job."

"Don't start pounding the pavement just yet. I'm sure it's an aberration. And your job is totally secure until I learn to make coffee."

"Morning," Suzette's chipper voice rang out. "Did you guys see the crocuses in front?" She stopped in the doorway to Melissa's office as she shrugged out of her coat. "They're coming up. There are purple ones, and gold ones, and the daffodils look like they'll be out soon. Friday is the official end of winter, and spring is springing."

"And all the world is in love," Jessie sang out of tune, winking outrageously at Melissa.

"Go away," Melissa told her, laughing. "I have a report to write before clinic hours start."

* * *

Annie Kimberlin

Being in love with Melissa March, Peter thought, sitting behind his desk staring unseeing at the computer screen, was definitely a good thing. Good for all of them. Especially Angie. Last night she had given Lady several pats on the head. Had even asked if she could hold Lady's leash while they went for a short walk down the street. Later Melissa was in the backyard, under the porch light, throwing an old tennis ball for the dogs. Hugo was like a maniac about it, but Lady held back, a bit too shy to get in Hugo's way, and hampered by her cast. Melissa had beckoned Angie over. She'd lowered her voice as if the two of them were sharing a secret. "Hugo is quite irrational when it comes to playing ball. He doesn't want anyone or anything in his way Why don't you stand here, next to me, and toss this other ball over there, so Lady can get it without Hugo trampling on her."

Angie had agreed, so Melissa had hurled Hugo's tennis ball way into the back of the yard. "Throw yours now, Angie, while Hugo is going after his ball." And his daughter had thrown a tennis ball for Lady. Lady trotted after it, clumsily because of her cast. The sheltie picked up the ball delicately, as she did everything, and carried it back to Angie, slowing down to a walk when she came close to the little girl. By then Hugo was back, so Melissa hurled his ball again and he took off once more, snorting in glee.

"Now, Angie, tell Lady to give it."

"Give it, Lady," came Angie's piping voice.

And Lady dropped the ball.

230

"Tell her what a good girl she is," Melissa instructed, pulling a piece of dried cat food out of her pocket to hand it to Angie. "Now give her a cookie."

"You're a good girl, Lady. Here's a cookie. How does she know how to go get the ball? Melissa, can I do it again?"

So, between hurling the ball for Hugo, Melissa had taught Angie how to play ball with Lady.

Standing just inside the door, watching them, Peter had caught Melissa's eye. "Should I come out?" he'd mouthed. But Melissa had shaken her head no. So he'd watched miracle after miracle happening, his daughter and Melissa March, his heart filled to bursting with love for them both.

Angie had had her bath and had been read to. By Melissa. Had been tucked into bed along with all her stuffed animals, by Melissa, of course. And had even given Melissa a biggest bear hug of all. His daughter seemed as smitten with the vet as he was himself. *This is good*, Peter thought. *This is very good*. But what was even better was sitting close, on the couch, with Melissa. He closed his eyes and wondered what it would be like to have Melissa tuck him into bed. Wondered what it would be like to tuck Melissa into his bed. And crawl in with her. Those gorgeous eyes of hers, and her hair that was like silk, all springy and fine. Curls of silk.

After she'd left, late, he'd gone upstairs to his bedroom. There, on his bureau, was a pounded silver frame holding a photograph of Claire. It had been on his bureau, in that spot, since Claire's death. As if Claire were watching over him, protecting him. But now, on this evening, he took up the photograph, examining the woman carefully. Yes, he had loved Claire with all his heart and soul. His world had shattered when she died. He'd thought he never would be whole again. Then the possibility of someday loving someone else had seemed positively obscene. But time had passed. He had healed. He was a whole person again. He was ready to share his life and his love with another woman. Yes, he would always love Claire, but he would not have his house made into a shrine to her memory. He didn't want that. Claire wouldn't have wanted it either.

Photograph in his hands, he tiptoed into Angie's room and quietly made room for it on her night table—so she'd see it when she first woke up.

"Are you ready, Mr. Winthrop?"

He started. "Oh, Mrs. Calloway. I'm sorry. I didn't hear you."

"It's time to make the morning announcements."

He smiled to himself. He might be in love with Melissa March, but school was still in session. He moved into the outer office and picked up the microphone for the P.A. system. "Good morning, boys and girls." He began the day with an incredible sense of optimism.

*   *   *

Melissa was munching her bagel at lunch when she heard footsteps pounding up the stairs. Hugo and Lady started their canine chorus. "M'liss," It was Jessie's voice sounding out of breath as she tapped on the door.

"Knock it off, you guys!" Melissa told the dogs. The staff never bothered her if she was upstairs. It must be important, she thought as she opened the door.

Jessie was almost jumping up and down, a huge grin of delight on her freckled face. "Can I come in?" she asked, but she didn't wait for an answer. "Oh, I'm so excited—hi Hugo, hi, Lady—I can't stand it."

Melissa had to laugh at her friend. Jessie wasn't usually this hyper. "You're acting like a terrier. Now sit down and tell me what's happened."

"I can't stand it, I can't stand it," Jessie repeated. "I won! Isn't it wonderful!"

"Whoa! Start at the beginning. And sit down." She shoved a chair at Jessie. "Pet Hugo or something until you calm down. You'll burst a blood vessel and I don't know nuthin' bout burst blood vessels in humans."

"Okay." Jessie dropped onto the floor, ignoring the chair. Hugo waddled over to plop himself in front of her for scratching. "Hello, Hugo, you old lush."

"That's it. Take slow deep breaths. Now. You've calmed down. Tell me what's so exciting."

233

Jessie looked up at her, eyes shining. "I won the radio contest."

"What radio contest?"

"The one on public radio." She waved her hand in the air. "You really ought to pay attention to what goes on in the world, Melissa. I won tickets to the Chieftains' concert tomorrow night. The Chieftains. Imagine that. I actually get to go." She gazed off into the distance, into some imagined foggy, foggy dew, raising her arm as if reaching out for something only she could see. "And maybe there will be some tall young Scot, wearing a kilt. And he'll have Irish setter-colored hair. And he'll come up to me and say, in a very authentic and broad brogue, 'Excuse me, miss, but is this seat taken?' and I'll look up into his blue eyes, eyes the color of Loch Tay, and I'll say, in a wispy sort of voice, 'No,' and he'll be instantly smitten." She dramatically placed her hand on her chest. "Be still, my beating heart!"

"I'm sure it will happen just that way."

Hugo grunted. Then Jessie, dropping her persona, started scratching his head again. "Nah, all the good men are taken, and they don't wear kilts anymore." She sighed, a noisy sigh, full of discouragement and resignation. Her shoulders slumped. "I was just born in the wrong century."

Melissa tried to cheer up her friend. "You really wouldn't want to live without indoor plumbing, you know."

"And antibiotics. And tampons. Wouldn't

want to give those up." Jessie sighed another great big gusty sigh. "Still, you wouldn't miss what you'd never had."

Jessie looked truly morose. It was time to change the subject, Melissa thought. Friends don't let friends stay morose. "Well," she said brightly, "I think it's wonderful that you get to go to the concert. I know you'll have a terrific time. If they're selling CDs, make sure you get one for me, okay?"

Jessie's eyes grew more cheerful. "Okay. But if I go, I won't be able to do the clinic chores for you tomorrow night. Will you be able to manage?"

Melissa ran her hand down Lady's back. The spots where they'd clipped mats were becoming bristly. Lady wagged her tail and tossed her nose at Melissa in an affectionate motion. "It'll be fine. I'll bring Angie here with me, instead of going to her house. It'll work. You just enjoy yourself." She grinned at her friend. "And be optimistic, you may see some men in kilts after all."

"Yeah, maybe." Jessie didn't sound convinced. "But the men wearing them will probably be seventy-two, or have knobby knees."

Chapter Ten

Thursday was a long day. And emotionally one of the worst in history. But finally it was over, and at a couple minutes before five o'clock, Melissa pulled her battered van into the parking lot of Montrose Elementary School. She'd stopped by the library to pick up some books to read to Angie tonight. That would be nice. Kids' books were always about hope, about rightness in the world, something she needed right now. Speaking of right now, it was almost time to pick Angie up from the after-school program.

Melissa sat in the car for a moment, her shoulders sagging from exhaustion, and from something else, something deeper. Grief. After lunch, Mrs. Shoemaker had brought Sandy in to be put to sleep.

Damn! Melissa pounded the steering wheel. She'd become a vet to help save the lives of cats and dogs, and here was one of the most wonderful cats in the world, and she'd not been able to save him. She'd failed her patient, and his owner. It didn't matter that there was nothing she could possibly have done. Veterinary medicine simply could not cure some diseases. Melissa knew that if she called some of her buddies from vet school, they would have told her the same thing.

That wasn't the point. The point was, she *felt* as if she'd failed. Sometimes emotions and logic were at odds. This was one of those times.

Melissa swallowed hard, remembering Mrs. Shoemaker's quavery voice and shaking hand as she stroked Sandy while Jessie tied off the vein in the cat's front leg. "There, there Sandy, we all love you," the old woman had crooned. And it was true. The whole clinic staff loved Sandy. And also loved Mrs. Shoemaker, who always remembered them at holidays and brought platters of cookies. All baked with Sandy's help, she'd say.

In all honesty, at this point the decision to put Sandy to sleep was the best thing for him. To do anything else would be to let him suffer. It was just the best time for him to go. But still, it shouldn't have to be like this. There should have been something else she could do to save him.

When will we learn this lesson in human medicine? Melissa thought, staring out over the trees that lined the school playground. *That there are times when letting someone go is the most loving thing you can do.* Mrs. Shoemaker had held Sandy in her arms while Melissa slipped the needle in his vein. The elderly woman had petted him, her cheek resting on the old cat's head, tears streaming down the wrinkled old cheeks. Melissa had silently waited a few minutes, then held a stethoscope to Sandy's chest. He was gone.

"I had to be here, you know, Dr. March," she'd said, her voice weak and teary. "I've been with him all of his life, and I couldn't not be with him now, holding him, at the moment of his death." It was then that the woman had broken down in sorrow.

Melissa put her arms around the woman, who was still holding the lifeless body of her cat. Mrs. Shoemaker seemed so frail. "I know you couldn't," Melissa said. "You gave him the best life possible for a cat. And the best death. The very last thing he felt was your hand. He was a happy cat, up until the end. You are a wonderful pet owner. I'd trust you implicitly with any pet, Mrs. Shoemaker. Sandy was a very lucky cat to have lived with you."

After taking Sandy's body to the back room, Melissa had gone into her office and closed the door. She'd pulled an unprotesting Woody up onto her lap and swiveled her chair around so she could see the photograph of James Herriot. Woody, sensing she was upset, butted his head under her chin, his motor on high, the volume cranked up. "Well, James," she told her hero. "It's not always easy, is it?"

Standing among his sheep, James looked down at her with understanding.

Now there was a knock on the window of her van. Startled, Melissa looked up. Then she relaxed and, opening the door, climbed out. "Hello, Mrs. Calloway. How are you? And how is Clarence?"

"Hello, Dr. March. We're both fine, just fit as rain. And how are you these days? And how is Hugo?" The secretary had her immense pocketbook on her arm. Now she set it on the hood of her car and opened it to rummage through. "I know I have my car keys in here somewhere," she muttered. "There they are," she exclaimed, pulling them out of the depths of her handbag, a look of triumph on her face. The look turned to concern. "Are you all right, Dr. March? You look rather pale."

"Merely tired. Long day, you know. Surgeries on Thursday."

The woman relaxed. "Well, then, Angie will perk you right up. She is the most darling child. Mr. Winthrop told me you were taking care of her for him this evening. The school board meeting, you know. Time to interview for a new superintendent." She lowered her voice as if imparting a great confidentiality. "Mr. Winthrop would be an excellent superintendent. Everyone thinks so." A twinkle appeared in her eyes as she leaned closer to Melissa. "And you know, he's been so lonely since poor Claire died. Raising Angie alone and all. He'll make the perfect husband for some lucky lady."

Melissa grinned. "Mrs. Calloway, are you playing matchmaker?"

A look of theatrical shock crossed the woman's round face. She was as melodramatic as Jessie. "Matchmaker?" she gasped. "Not at all. I'm merely stating facts. Mr. Winthrop is definitely one of the best. And he's going places."

Melissa smiled and patted the woman on the arm. She could see through Mrs. Calloway a mile away, she thought affectionately. "Nice to see you, and give Clarence my regards. But I have to pick Angie up now."

"She's in the gym," Mrs. Calloway's voice said, floating after her. "Just follow the arrows on the wall."

"Thanks," Melissa called over her shoulder. "See you later." But Mrs. Calloway's words swirled around in her brain. Peter was going places? Superintendent? Then she remembered that in the grocery store Gloria had said something about Peter. What was it? She couldn't remember. She hadn't paid attention at the time, she'd been too busy trying to keep from being rattled by Gloria. Something about a new position. Peter certainly hadn't mentioned anything to her. But then, she reminded herself, he was not answerable to her. He didn't have to tell her everything. It wasn't as if they were married, she thought as she pulled open the doors.

Then she stopped short on the threshold of

Peter's school, Peter's world. Married to Peter Winthrop. What would it be like? Images of Peter floated into her mind. Peter laughing, his head thrown back, his shock of dark hair rippling in the breeze. Peter smiling down at her, his brown eyes seeming to enter her very soul. Peter holding a hurt dog in his arms, as carefully as he'd hold a child. And the look on Peter's face as he watched Angie doing some mundane chore. How he loved that child. What would it be like to be part of Peter's world? Part of Peter's life? Did she want that? Did she want to spend time with Peter, to share her days with him, as well as her nights? At the thought of sharing nights with Peter Winthrop she shivered deliciously.

Not only did she lust after his body, she lusted after his fenced-in backyard. *But you can't sell your soul for a fence*, she told herself. *Even for Hugo*. Being married to a vet was not easy. There would always be emergencies, and living with dogs and cats. How would Angie react to sometimes having dogs other than Hugo and Lady living with them, even temporarily? She hadn't gone into vet med for the bucks; she'd gone into it for the cats and dogs. Her life was devoted to them. Would Peter understand that? Yes, he'd understood when she'd had to call her service in the evenings to check for emergency calls. Yes, he'd understood why she had to drive her own van, so she'd be able to hurry back to the clinic at a moment's notice. But she'd never had to.

So she stood, deep in thought, holding open the door to Peter's world.

It all came down to trust. Everywhere trust. Her trust of Peter, his of her. Her trust in herself to have made the right decision to trust him. Angie's trust that the dogs wouldn't hurt her, and Lady's trust of Angie.

It isn't love that glues the world together, she thought suddenly. *It's trust. Trust in the human pack.*

Well, no use thinking about it now. She'd promised Peter she'd pick up Angie. And Angie was waiting. Angie was trusting that she'd be there.

Melissa walked through the door and let it thunk closed behind her.

"Will your friend really cut my hair? I like short hair. Kaitlyn has short hair, but it isn't curly. And Kaitlyn told me I can visit her kitten any time I want to. Isn't that great?" Angie had been cheerfully chattering nonstop all the way from the school, changing subjects and directions with the ease of the wind. Melissa had only had to make monosyllabic answers, assuring the child she was listening. But now, after having Sandy and Mrs. Shoemaker on her mind most of the day, the mention of Kaitlyn's kitten brought Melissa up short. She had an idea.

"Angie, where is Kaitlyn going to get her new kitten?"

"From the lady on the other side of Mrs. Calloway. Her cat had seven kittens. Is that a lot of

243

kittens? Kaitlyn says she's going to get a black and white one. But I think I'd rather have one that looked like Woody."

"Is there one that looks like Woody?" Sandy was—had been, she corrected herself—an orange cat as well. If there was an orange kitten in that litter that needed a home, well, she knew of a wonderful home that needed a kitten.

"I don't know. But Kaitlyn says there are lots of them," Angie was trying to be helpful.

Melissa decided to call Mrs. Calloway after dinner to find out the particulars about this litter of kittens. If there was a possibility of getting another kitten for Mrs. Shoemaker . . . Things were looking up all over the place.

Melissa turned into the clinic parking lot and drove around to the back.

"Is this really where you live? In your clinic?"

Melissa chuckled. "No, there's an apartment upstairs. That's where I live. But remember what your dad and I told you. We had to come here instead of going to your house because there are some sick dogs and cats that I'll have to check on from time to time."

"And can I really help? With the cats, I mean? And maybe with the dogs, but mostly I don't like dogs. Not in general. But I sort of like Hugo and Lady. But not dogs in general, so I am not sure I want to help your dogs. But I like cats in un-general, so I want to help with them. Where will Woody be?"

"Oh, Woody will be either downstairs in the

clinic, or upstairs with us. He likes to help cheer up the patients, you know."

"That's 'cos he's a candy-striper!" Angie crowed in glee. "A striped candy striper."

But Melissa only heard her with part of her mind. *Oh, no,* she thought. *Supper. With all the upset about Sandy, and then picking up Angie, I forgot to stop at the store and get something for supper.* Her shoulders sagged in defeat. And Claire had been a gourmet cook. She'd bet that Claire always had more in her refrigerator than bagels and cream cheese. Well, there was always that last bag of mint chocolate chips. Great supper. Bagels, cream cheese, and mint chocolate chips. And raisins. Always raisins.

She turned to Angie in the passenger's seat. "Say, Angie, I have a confession to make. I forgot to go to the store to pick up something for supper. So, I think we will just turn the old van around and go to the store." The grocery store was the last place on earth she wanted to go. But it couldn't be helped.

Angie's face wrinkled for a moment. Then it cleared. *She looks like Gloria,* Melissa thought in amusement, just for a second. At least, thank goodness, she hadn't inherited Gloria's temperament.

"I know what we can do," Angie announced. "We can send out for pizza. That's what my mom always did when she forgot to go to the store. An' that's what Dad and me do when we're hurrying. Pizza with everything on it. It's absolutely scrumptious."

245

Melissa looked at the child in amazement. "Pizza?" she asked. Claire the gourmet cook had sent out for pizza?

"All the time," Angie answered cheerfully. Then her face fell. "But please don't tell Grandma. It's a secret. Grandma doesn't like pizza."

"Angie, you have my word on it. I'll not tell your grandmother a thing. Girl, you just made my day. That is the best idea anyone has suggested in a long time. We'll send out for pizza."

She parked the van and hopped out. "Do you really like *everything* on your pizza?"

Peter wished he'd not had this dinner meeting before the school board meeting. He wished he could've stayed at school long enough to see Melissa—perhaps entice her into his office, behind a very closed door, where he could stream his fingers through her glorious hair and breathe in the scent of peaches. To hold her in his arms, to take that comfort and carry it with him through this evening's meetings. As it was, all he had was the memory of her voice, warm and soul-touching, over the phone at noon.

When had it happened? When had he come to the realization that he wanted to explore a forever with her? Was it the evening they'd moved furniture around? Or had the idea been there, unformed in his mind, from the very first instant he'd seen her, backlit by the headlights of her van as she took care of a dog he'd accidentally hit?

What would it take, he thought, to convince her that he wanted to explore a for always with her? The way to Melissa's heart was obviously through her dogs. *I'll just have to convince Hugo. That doesn't seem too difficult. Hugo loves my backyard. Of course, Hugo would probably love anyone's back yard if Melissa was there. That dog is utterly devoted to her*. He could understand that. He was becoming utterly devoted to her as well.

He would keep his devotion with him, tucked into the back of his mind as a knight took his lady's scarf into battle, for a battle tonight it might well be, he thought ruefully. He pulled into the restaurant where he was to meet the president of the school board. When, several years ago, he'd gotten his school superintendent certification, at Gloria's insistence, he'd really never expected this to happen. *Well, chin up, Peter, life is full of the unexpected*, he thought grimly as he firmly closed his car door and pocketed the keys.

Angie was enchanted with the apartment. She didn't seem to mind that the furniture was old and shabby, that the desk looked as if it had been in a dogfight and had lost. She didn't see the cracks in the plaster, or the faded curtains, the plank-and-cement-block bookshelves. She only saw, with the eyes of a child, the charming gabled windows, the apartment-sized refrigerator, and the clawed feet of the bathtub. This was, for Angie, magic. Then she saw the poster.

"Who's that?" she asked, staring up.

"That, my little friend, is James Herriot."

"Who's he?"

"Before he died a few years ago, he was a veterinarian in England who wrote books about being a country vet. And he's the reason I went into vet school." Melissa scratched Hugo's head. Hugo blissed out.

Angie's little mouth made an O. "Did he make you go?"

Melissa grinned at the literal six-year-old mind. "No, he didn't make me go, but he was the inspiration for me to go. You see, I grew up on a farm, way out in the country. And there were lots of animals on our farm. Dairy cows, and a horse, and ducks and pigs and dogs and cats." She patted her leg and Lady trotted over to join her, the cast silent on the braided rug. "James Herriot wrote books about being the kind of vet who traveled from farm to farm in England, taking care of the animals when they were hurt or sick. I read his books and decided that that's what I wanted to do when I grew up."

Angie frowned. "But you don't go from farm to farm," she pointed out. "Do you?"

"No. When I got into school, I decided to concentrate on small animals, dogs and cats mostly."

"And they come to you."

"Yes. Mostly they do." Melissa smoothed down the shaggy fur on Lady's sides. The golden fur was growing back. Soon, Lady would have a full coat of fur again. And there would never be mats in her coat again.

Angie came closer and sat down carefully on the couch. She timidly reached out to let Lady sniff her hand.

Melissa nodded at her approvingly. "That's it. Let her sniff. See, her tail is wagging, she remembers you. She knows you're her friend."

The little hand was the perfect size to stroke the golden head, Melissa thought. They were a good match, the gentle sheltie and the little girl. Both had reddish-golden hair and bright eyes; both had known loss at an early age. And both of them were learning to trust. Peter's instinct had been absolutely correct when he'd said that he somehow knew this was the dog to help Angie conquer her fear.

"But you went to Lady when she was hurt."

"That's because it was an emergency. And because . . ." Because she had heard something in the man's voice on the phone that had touched her, something she'd not wanted to look at, something that was electric and had felt destined. She did look at it now. She let that feeling of destiny invade her solitary being. She felt it, and acknowledged it. It was as real as real could be. Her life, and Hugo, Peter, Angie, and Lady, all entwined into one that was stronger and more beautiful than the parts alone.

"How long will Lady have to have her cast on her leg? When Joshua Martini broke his leg he had a cast forever. It was purple. Why isn't Lady's cast purple?"

* * *

Later, down in the clinic, while waiting for the pizza, Melissa showed Angie where they stored all the supplies. Angie was interested in everything, with question after question. In fact, the very act of asking questions seemed to be more important than the actual answers. Woody followed them closely, having learned that Angie had some pieces of dried cat food in her pocket and was doling them out periodically. Hugo, drooling, his gaze trained intently on Angie's pocket, and Lady were also in the entourage.

The bell to the clinic door rang.

"Pizza's here!" Angie crowed. "Pizza, pizza, pizza. I love pizza."

On the way down the hall to the door, Melissa felt like the Pied Piper. She was followed by a child, a drooling dog, a second dog tapping along on a cast, with a cat bringing up the end. She snapped on the light and opened the door.

"Hello, Melissa."

She felt as if the breath had been knocked out of her.

Lady backed up and began to bark, shrilly. Woody scampered over to hop up onto the counter, out of the way. Hugo danced around her feet.

"That's not the pizza man," Angie's surprised voice broke over her, smashing her thoughts, and allowing her to breathe again.

"Hello, Michael."

It had been a year since she'd seen him, and

he was just as godlike as he'd ever been, with his sunstruck hair and his skin bronzed to perfection, even at this time of year. Those perfect features were every photographer's dream. He smiled at her, and his smile was, as she remembered, blindingly bright, and sexy, and intimate.

"Can I come in?"

She backed away from the door, opening it wider to admit him. "Lady, knock it off!" But Lady evidently was an excellent judge of character, for Lady kept it up. "Sorry, Michael, come on in," she muttered. "Let me put her in the back. Angie, this is an old . . . um . . . friend of mine. Michael, this is a new friend of mine. Now c'mon, Lady, let's put you in the back. You too, Hugo. Let's go."

As she picked up the still-yipping sheltie and carried her down the hall, Melissa heard Angie's piping voice. "I'm Angie Winthrop. How do you do?"

And she heard Michael's answer. "I'm very well, thank you, Miss Winthrop. How are you?" Michael had lost none of his charm.

"I called you this afternoon, but your receptionist told me you were busy," Michael told her when she returned.

"Yes, I do elective surgeries on Thursday afternoons."

"And take care of children on Thursday evenings?" It was said with a charming smile. Evidently he wanted to make a point, yet not alienate her. He'd always said she didn't know

251

anything about children, which was why it wouldn't have been a good idea for them to have any.

"Melissa is baby-sitting for me because my daddy is at a school board meeting," Angie announced proudly.

Michael dropped to a knee in front of the little girl. "Oh. What does your daddy do?"

Angie's face shone as she told Michael, "He's a principal."

"That's a very good thing to be," Michael told her gravely. Then he got a thoughtful look as he stood up. "Winthrop, Winthrop." He caught Melissa's gaze. "He's expected to be the new school superintendent, isn't he?"

"What?" New superintendent? *Is this what Gloria and Mrs. Calloway had been hinting at?*

Michael grimaced in impatience. "Honestly, Melissa, if you'd pay attention to what was going on around you instead of hiding out with a bunch of dumb animals, you'd know what was happening in your own community. Don't you read the papers? They've been full of it. It's big political news. Very important position. Very influential." He turned his attention back to Angie. "So your father is the heir apparent, so to speak. I bet he will be having many more responsibilities soon."

"My daddy has lots of 'sponsibilities. He says he has three-hundred-sixty-eight kids."

"Well, then, pretty soon he'll be having even more. It's a good thing he found Melissa here to baby-sit you, so he can take care of all his new responsibilities." It was said slyly, with a hint of a smile on those perfect lips. "Don't you think, Melissa?"

No! Melissa's brain screamed. *No, it isn't true. That's not why Peter wants me. He wants me for myself. He told me he was falling in love with me.*

Of course, her mind answered. *What better way to get you to do what he wants than to tell you he loves you. Very clever man, that Peter Winthrop.*

I don't believe it.

Then you're a fool. And you know how awful you'd be at entertaining anyone without four legs and a tail.

Somehow Melissa kept her voice from shaking as she asked, "What did you want to see me about, Michael?" *And why did you have to come now, to ruin my life again? And why do I still let you?*

He reached into the inside pocket of his overcoat, pulled out a legal-sized envelope, and handed it to her. "You have to sign this."

So he'd finally found a buyer for their house, she thought numbly, as she scanned the document. She should be excited about it, knowing that her part of the money from the sale would pay off a good chunk of the clinic mortgage. But somehow things just weren't the same as they'd been five minutes ago. "I've had a tough day in surgery, Michael. I'll tell you what. Let me look this over tomorrow when I can decipher all the legal language, and then I'll call you."

"All right. You do sound tired all of a sudden.

Maybe this is too much for you." He waved his arm to include the clinic.

Anger blazed through her. "It's not *too much* for me. It's just been a long day. I'll call you in a day or so, when I've had time to read this carefully."

He held up his hands in mock submission. "Okay, okay, don't get excited. Give me a call. I suppose it can wait a day or so longer. I'll have to tell the realtor." He buttoned up his coat and headed for the door, then paused, his hand on the knob. He spun and positioned himself in front of Angie, and turned the glory of his smile on the child. "Miss Winthrop, it was a pleasure meeting you." He bowed slightly to her. Angie, with a giggle, bowed back.

"And Melissa, you'll do fine for a school super's . . . baby-sitter. Of course, you'll have to get yourself fixed up, new clothes and that sort of thing. And take a few cooking classes. But you're bright. You'll do just fine." He opened the door.

"Good-bye, Michael," she gritted out. The nerve of him. *Be fair*, she told herself clenching her fists so she wouldn't slam the door shut. *He's only telling the truth*.

Then Michael stuck his head back in, his smile flashing, his eyes twinkling, as if he weren't twisting the knife he'd just plunged in her heart. "Pizza man just drove up. Your favorite kind of cooking."

"Oh, goodie, oh, goodie, oh, goodie!" Angie chanted.

But Melissa wasn't hungry anymore.

*   *   *

Driving through the twilight on his way from the restaurant to the school board meeting, Peter concentrated on the road, illuminated by his headlights. Following a speck of light in the darkness, he mused philosophically about his life. It was a way of bringing closure to his life as Claire's widowed husband, and beginning a life as simply Peter Winthrop.

His life had changed on a night just like this. On an impulse he turned off onto Route 14, the road less traveled. He slowed down slightly and watched carefully to see the spot where he'd first found Lady, and Melissa, who had become his lady. There it was, just ahead. That spot right before that stand of trees. As he passed the spot, Peter briefly bowed his head, acknowledging that this was the place where his life had changed. Funny, it looked perfectly ordinary. Nothing unusual about it. A regular spot on the shoulder of the road, looking like every other shoulder spot in the county. And yet what had happened there had changed his life. The memory of his car striking the dog brought a suddenly sick feeling to his stomach—yet if it had not happened, he'd not have met Melissa. And that he found intolerable.

He felt a smile develop and grow on his face. He found himself grinning at the thought of seeing her again, of touching her again, of kissing her again. Yes, he'd kiss her again tonight, after the meeting. It would be his prize for surviving the battle. Kissing Melissa March would be his medal of honor.

After chattering through pizza, Angie accompanied Melissa downstairs to check on the patients. Melissa was actually glad for her company. She couldn't think too deeply about her life with Angie asking a new question every couple of seconds. She couldn't dwell on the feelings of desolation that invaded her being like a cancer growing out of control. If Peter were only using her, she'd simply not have anything to do with him. She'd have to remove him from her life, from her heart. Surgically, if necessary, like excising a malignant growth. She could do it. It wouldn't be easy, wouldn't be pretty, but it would be better done sooner than later.

Lastly, Melissa checked the newly spayed cat. "This is Entrechat. She's a Siamese kitty. She was just spayed." She gently rubbed the cat under her chin as she anticipated Angie's next questions. "That means she won't have any kittens. Look at this incision, Angie. See how the stitches are flat and clean. This is looking good, no puffiness or redness. That means there's no infection. Infection would not be a good thing."

"Did you sew the kitty with a needle and thread like a skirt?"

"Sort of like a skirt. Only I use very special needles and thread. Some needles are for clothes and some are for kitties."

"It's full of knots," Angie pointed out dubiously. "I can show you how to sew without knots. My grandma showed me how," she added helpfully.

Melissa's heart lurched. The little girl's eyes were so earnest, her face so serious. For a fleeting moment Angie looked exactly like Peter, and Melissa felt her heart lurch the other way. If Peter was to be no longer a part of her life, then Angie wouldn't either. That would be difficult, for she was truly a dear child. She'd followed Melissa's instructions very carefully, not touching the patients, and speaking quietly.

"Thank you very much for the offer, but this kind of sewing is different than clothes sewing. I need to have those knots there. But you're right. In clothes they wouldn't be a good thing at all. This is a special kind of thread, it will dissolve in about two weeks. We wouldn't want to use dissolving thread in clothes either." Melissa took a thoughtful look at the stitches in the kitty's incision. They were neat and precise—not at all like the knots she'd tied around herself and Peter, and Angie. Those knots had just seemed to appear effortlessly, yet now, those invisible knots seemed to be all messy and tangled. What did Shakespeare say about tangled webs? Something about deception. Who was the deceiver, and who was being deceived?

Was Peter just using her? How could she know for sure? She *had* to know. Because if that was the case, it wouldn't be fair for her to deepen her relationship with Angie since she'd be cutting off her relationship with Peter. Yet she simply couldn't distance herself from the child just because she no longer had a relationship with the father. She looked down at Angie's fair head, her hair in neat braids, and a rush of tenderness coursed through her. She did enjoy the little scamp. And there was one thing that Angie wanted that she could do.

"Hey, Angie, this is the last patient I need to check on right now. Let's go upstairs and I'll call Sylvie to see when she can cut your hair. Sylvie has a poodle named Jean-Luc. She cuts his hair too. After that we can share some of that leftover pizza with Hugo and Lady."

"Oh, goodie! I can have short hair!" Angie danced in a circle, but still quietly because they were in the treatment room. Then she suddenly stopped, arms upraised. She had a question. "Does Hugo like mushrooms?" She sounded dubious.

"Trust me. Hugo loves mushrooms."

Everyone had greeted him as if it were all settled, Peter thought ruefully as he sat down in the chair set facing the board members. Because it was an open meeting, there were many community members present as well. He knew most of them. Some of them had children in his school, some lived in his neighborhood. In the years he'd been principal at Montrose Elementary School he'd argued with some of them up one side and down the other. He'd always put the education of his students as his first priority, and he always tried to hire teachers who reflected that philosophy.

Harold Ballentine opened his notebook and flipped through some papers, tilting his head to see through his bifocals. As if from a distance, Peter watched Harold go through the motions of pulling out agendas and passing them around. The bang of Harold's gavel brought him back to reality.

"I'd like to welcome you all to this special board meeting to discuss the position of superintendent. As you all know, we'll be choosing a new school superintendent in the coming days. This is a major position in our community, one not to be taken lightly. We, the school board, are determined to make the best possible choice. We owe it to our children, the children of Hartley."

Peter let himself breathe deeply for a moment, conjuring up an image of a lovely wispy-haired vet, and the scent of peaches. The battle was about to begin. Hail, Caesar, we who are about to die, et cetera, et cetera.

Finally the last of the pizza was put away. Sylvie had been called—she'd be delighted to cut Angie's hair, how about tomorrow evening? Angie opened her visiting bag and pulled out a pair of fuzzy slippers shaped like lambs, Senor Lemon, and her own special pillow. As she undid the sticky fasteners on her shoes, Angie scowled.

"Why the face?"

"I want tie shoes. Dad says when I learn to tie I can have some. So I hafta learn to tie." Then she perked up. "Do you know how to tie shoes?" she asked hopefully.

"Sure do. Do you want me to teach you?"

"Yeah!"

So Melissa dug out a pair of her work boots. "These have laces that are pretty thick. They'll be easier to learn on. This might take a while, so you should put on your slippers to keep your feet warm."

At last the tying lesson was completed, and Angie was in possession of a very important piece of paper. It was a certificate, made up and run off on the clinic computer downstairs, that awarded Miss Angie Winthrop the degree of Shoe Knotter Excellent.

"Wait'll I show Dad. Now I can have tie shoes!"

They were all, human, canine, feline, curled up on Melissa's worn couch, bunched up like a litter of puppies. The library books were in a pile with them.

Melissa opened the first book, but before she could begin the story, Angie twisted around to look up at Melissa.

"Will you be my mommy?"

The words, coming out of nowhere, ripped through Melissa's heart. She would love nothing more than to be Angie's mommy, and Peter's wife. But not if he was just using her, needing someone to look after his daughter while he climbed the political ladder of success. And how would she ever know if it were so? Wouldn't there always be doubt in her mind? She mentally shrugged. She was really nothing to look at, she didn't wear makeup—didn't know how to wear makeup—and her hair was totally out of control. There was really nothing to hold a man's interest. And for one very long searingly painful moment, Melissa wished she were different, wished she were the kind of woman who could launch a thousand ships, or a hundred ships, or even a small fishing boat. But Angie was still looking at her with hope in her little blue eyes. It took her a minute to unclog her throat, and then she struggled to keep her voice from trembling.

"Oh, Angie, honey. I don't know what to say."

"Joshua Martini got a new mommy after his old mommy left. I want you to be my new mommy."

Melissa hugged the little girl tight, Woody between them. "I can't promise you that, but I can promise you this. I will *always* be your friend. And I am very honored that you would like me to be your mommy." *Even if Peter and I never see each other again,* she added silently. "But you know, Angie, your mommy loved you very much. And if she were here right now, I know she would be proud of you."

"She would?"

"Yes," Melissa said firmly. "She would be very proud of you." Melissa stroked the red-gold braids. "You have done an extremely difficult thing."

"I have?" she sounded pleased.

"Yes. You found the courage to face your fear. Remember how just a short time ago you were afraid of dogs? Well, look at you now. You've learned how to throw a ball for Lady, how to toss mushrooms to Hugo. You have become friends with two dogs. That is special because it took courage. Courage is a good thing to have. Your mother would be proud of you. And you know what? I'm proud of you as well."

Angie's forehead wrinkled up in thought. Then she asked, "Do you have courage?"

Now, that is the million dollar question, Melissa thought. *Out of the mouths of babes.* "Sometimes I have more courage than other times." *And when it comes to relationships with men I have no courage at all,* she added to herself.

"Well, I still don't like dogs in general," Angie said, as if reciting a mantra. "But I can like Hugo and Lady in particular. Just a teensy-weensy bit," she added. "Do you have courage sometimes, just a teensy-weensy bit? When there's something you're really, really 'fraid of? The biggest scariest thing of all?"

The biggest scariest thing of all. Well, we all know what that is, don't we, Melissa. Did she have the courage to trust in a relationship with Peter? Even a teensy-weensy bit? Melissa turned her gaze on the poster of her hero. *James,* she said silently, *did you ever need just a teensy-weensy bit of courage?* But this would take more than a teensy-weensy bit. This would take the biggest chunk of courage of all.

Melissa looked from the poster of her hero down into four pairs of eyes. They were all her friends. And now in their eyes, she read trust, affection, and love. All of them had known loss at an early age. Hugo had been rejected as a puppy, dumped at the shelter. Woody had been abandoned on her doorstep, a very sick cat. Lady had had who knows what kind of life as a stray, and Angie had lost her mother. Yet each one of them had found the courage to leave the past behind, to move forward.

She loved all four of them. Her heart wanted to burst with that love. She felt humbled that they had placed their trust in her. Could she do any less? As she gazed from one to the other of them, she was filled with the quiet certainty that if they all had the courage to trust, then she could do no less. She could—*would*—trust her own judgment. She could trust that Peter was not another Charming Michael.

"Yes, Angie." Her throat clogged, and she cleared it. "Sometimes I have just a teensy-weensy bit of courage." And she found herself smiling, yet wanting to cry at the same time. "Hey, Angie, I think I might just need some chocolate to keep up my energy while I'm read-ing all these books to you. Do you know there is a bag of mint chocolate chips in my kitchen just waiting for you and me to eat them up? Do you want some?"

Crossing the room, she chanced to catch a

glimpse of James Herriot. She could have sworn he winked at her. She winked back.

"Well, Peter," Sally said, coming up to him afterwards shaking her head. "I think it was an excellent decision." Sally usually attended school board meetings. She, being the conscientious teacher that she was, felt it was her obligation to know what was going on. He respected her for that. Lots of people worked for benefits, or to save up for retirement. He was lucky to have a building full of teachers who worked to teach.

"Thanks," he responded. "I think it was an excellent decision myself."

They walked out into the evening together companionably. "You're a terrific principal, Peter, one of the best—no. The very best I've ever worked for."

"Now, Sally, how many principals have you worked for?" he teased.

"Oh," she said loftily, "three. But," she hastened to add, "you're the best." She grinned at him. "Not very many principals take the time to visit the classroom and actually read to the kids. Gee. Imagine that. A principal who actually reads real books to the kids. What a novel idea."

He chuckled. "Pun intended?"

"Of course," she informed him with a saucy grin. "And now for something completely different," she said, making one of her quick switches from levity to gravity. "I think that if Lady comes to live with you it will be the best thing in the world for Angie. And you already know what I think of Melissa."

"Yes," he returned dryly. "You and Mrs. Calloway have both made it perfectly clear that you think she walks on water."

"But you, my dear principal, have not made it perfectly clear what *you* think about her." She turned to face him in the parking lot, and with the floodlights shining, he could see mischief in her eyes. "Don't think I'm being merely nosy. I have a vested interest in this, you know. I happen to consider Melissa one of my best friends. Even if she doesn't understand the obvious superiority of the feline race."

"Species," he corrected gently.

She tilted her head for a moment, considering. Then: "Nope. Sorry, Peter. Race." She grinned. "But don't try to change the subject." She took on a persona of mock fierceness, waving her arms for emphasis. "I want Melissa to be happy. And I freely admit that this is purely selfish on my part. She's the best vet in the world, and vets are as important to me as principals are, if not more so. I suppose more, actually, because I only work for principals. I entrust my cats to vets." She stopped and took on a persona of mock ferocity. "So, I don't want any possibility of her fading away in unhappiness. D'you understand?"

Did he understand? Would he be able to make Melissa March happy? Would he be able to keep her happy? Was he enough for her? He wasn't dashing, or heroic. He was perfectly content to spend his summers reading to his daughter, or puttering in the backyard with their garden. Would Melissa be content with such a prosaic person? Suddenly, irrationally, he wished for a horse and sword. But all he had was a middle-aged blue sedan. And, he brightened at the thought, a fenced-in backyard. Melissa loved his fenced-in backyard.

"Sally," he said. "D'you think Melissa can be tempted with a fence?"

He watched a slow grin spread over her freckled face. "Peter, my wonderful principal, Melissa would sell her soul for a fence."

He nodded. "Yup," he added, imitating her. "I thought so." He stuck his hands in his pockets. "See you in the morning, Sally."

He reached out to push the *play* button on the CD player. The strains of Brahms' Second Symphony filled his car bringing back the night when he had first held her in his arms. Arms that up until that very moment he hadn't realized were empty. Until he'd held Melissa March. The music of Brahms suffused his being, along with memories and images of Melissa: the scent of her hair, the taste of her mouth, the feel of her cheek against his. He glanced at the green glow that surrounded the indicators in the car and found that he was over the speed limit. He made a conscious effort to slow down. He couldn't wait to see her.

*   *   *

He should be here soon, Melissa thought, as she looked out the window down onto the street below. Angie was snoring softly curled up on the couch, Lady at her feet, Woody purring at her head. Hugo had been displaced temporarily by their guest, and had cheerfully unearthed an old sweater to curl up on. Now he, also, was snoring, albeit with more gusto than the child.

Soon, she thought. Soon Peter would be here. She couldn't wait to see him, to try out her new-found resolve, to show her infant courage—even if only to herself, to prove that she could do it, she could be brave, she could put the past behind her and go forward. She could, couldn't she?

Again he took the road less traveled, this time finding the spot easily. He ought to put up a marker, he decided. One of those tall obelisk things, and it should have a carving of a hurt dog on it. And the words *On this spot on a winter's night, while saving the life of a stray dog, Melissa March touched the soul of a lonely elementary school principal and he was lonely no more*. Such fanciful thoughts for an ordinary man. But they were his thoughts, he told himself. Somewhere in the day-to-day-ness of his life he had a speck of romanticism. Of course, Brahms with his lush sensuality helped.

Now that his future was settled, now that he could look to the future, he could ask her to join him in his life. What would he say to her first? What should he say to her first? What he really wanted to do was not say anything at all, but sweep her into his arms and fill his senses with her, fill his soul with her, as she had filled his heart.

Only a few more miles.

She closed the book in resignation. Even Michaelson's fantasy world couldn't grab her tonight. Not when she was waiting for Peter. The creaking of her old rocking chair accompanied the litany that set itself up in her head. He'll be here soon. He'll be here soon.

Suddenly, she had to do something. Anything.

She wandered into the small kitchen, poured the last of the mint chocolate chips into her hand, and scrunched up the bag. Hugo lifted his head at the sound. "No, buddy," she told him. "No chocolate for dogs. You know that."

Hugo, disappointed, snorted at her, then put his head back on his paws.

Melissa poured some apple cider into a pan and plopped in a cinnamon stick. Hot cider. Balm for the soul. Of course her soul, with its newfound courage, didn't need balm. But hot cider would be a nice way to welcome Peter. To welcome him into her life. Without hesitations. When would he get here? She glanced at the clock. Soon. Probably.

The normally bustling streets of Hartley were silent as Peter drove through the outskirts towards Melissa's clinic. He realized he'd never seen her apartment. Only the clinic. As if she had been keeping part of herself separate from him, private, untouched.

He saw the curtains at an upstairs window twitch as he drove into the parking lot. She was watching for him, he thought with a smile. He liked that idea, that she was waiting for him, watching for him. His senses began to whirl in the anticipation of fulfillment of his expectations.

He climbed out of his car. He shut the door quietly, not that there were any neighbors to disturb, but he knew that there were the patients in the clinic who might bark at the sound.

He was here at last, she thought with breathless anticipation as she trotted quietly downstairs, Lady in her arms because of the cast, with Hugo and Woody trailing along. She was afraid that if she left them upstairs, they might bark, might wake Angie. And besides, they were excited too. They could sense something big was going to happen. They didn't want to be left out.

She heard the sound of a car door close, and drawing her courage around her like a shawl, she opened the door to the clinic.

She stood in the doorway, the light from the clinic bathing her, surrounding her. Dog in her arms, dog and cat at her feet. My Lady of the Hurt Animals. His heart constricted suddenly, and for an instant he could not move, only stare at her hungrily, as if he were a pilgrim come to pay homage at her shrine.

Then somehow he was inside, with her and Lady in his arms, Hugo dancing around wildly barking, Woody daintily keeping out of the way of Hugo's flailing feet. "Where is Angie?" he whispered against her hair.

"Upstairs sleeping on my couch. Hugo, knock it off, you'll wake her up."

He breathed in the scent of her, then stopped with a start. Something was different. "Do I smell cinnamon?"

She put Lady down and wrapped her arms firmly around him. He reveled in her touch. He felt completed in her touch.

"It's the cinnamon in the hot apple cider waiting for you upstairs on the stove."

"I love hot apple cider," he murmured against her neck.

He felt her smile against his cheek. "I love hot apple cider too," she whispered, "but I love you more."

With his lips he traced a path up her throat, across her cheek, lingering on her eyelids. He felt her shiver deliciously in his arms, or was it he who shivered? When she raised her hands and with the lightest, most gentle of touches, streamed her fingers over his face, over his nose, lips, eyebrows, cheeks, memorizing the feel of him, he knew without a doubt that it was his own trembling. Suddenly the need for her was overwhelming, an explosion of sensation. His lips sought, found, and captured hers. He had won his medal of honor in her arms.

"Tell me, my dear Dr. March," he said at last, his voice husky with longing. "What would you think about spending the rest of your life in a house with a big fenced-in backyard?"

"I would love it."

"Even if that fence came complete with an elementary school principal and his daughter?"

She pulled away so she could look into his face. "Not the new superintendent of the Hartley school system?"

He shook his head slightly. "I turned them down. Gloria wanted it for me, for Claire, more than I ever wanted it for myself. I'm a good principal. I think that's where I can do the best job, where I can make the most difference in the lives of the students." Then he had a thought. "Would you prefer a school superintendent? If he had a fenced-in backyard, of course."

There was a pause. She stood statue still, her gaze locked with his, questioning him on a very deep, very elemental level. He did not know if the answers he had were the answers she sought. He could only give her honesty. He waited, not daring to hope, not daring to breathe, waiting while his future was decided.

When she answered him, it was with her lips, claiming his, her hands slipping under his coat to caress his back, drawing him closer and closer to her, into her, with her, until he had to gasp from the power of it. Then they stood, their arms, hearts, souls, entwined. Their breathing

Annie Kimberlin

slowed, stilled. She spoke the words he longed
to hear.

"The only backyard I want, will ever want, is
one that comes with you and Angie," She whispered the words, and he knew their life together
had begun.

Read on for a preview of Annie Kimberlin's next novel—coming Spring 1998 from Love Spell!

LONELY HEARTS

All of us have dragons. They come in a variety of colors and shapes and sizes. Some of them become our friends, others we merely learn to tolerate. Some of them stay deep in the caves of our hearts. As for others—well, sometimes we have no choice but to slay those dragons. And each of us must learn to be our own St. George.

Chapter One

Oh, no! Not again. Sylvie Taylor slumped against the front fender of her car and gazed morosely through the windshield to the driver's seat where she could see her keys, still in the ignition, dangle temptingly just beyond her reach. On the passenger seat she could see the two new bumper stickers she'd just brought home. One read *RUBBER STAMPS: Making the mail more beautiful one envelope at a time.* The other said *STAMP OUT NAKED MAIL.*

Jean-Luc, her white standard poodle, left off his prancing to pose in front of her, gazing adoringly at her over his shoulder, as if making sure she knew just how wonderful he was, and wagging his tail.

"I know, Jean-Luc. You love me even if I have

just locked my keys in the car for the gazillionth time." She reached out to touch the curls on his head. "Thing is, I can't get into the house either. So, we're just stuck here in the yard. Whaddya think about that?"

Jean-Luc's answer was to dance off after a butterfly for a few steps, then stop abruptly and begin sniffing the ground, following an unseen trail. He's probably looking for his ball, she thought. Well, a game of ball would just have to wait till she found a solution to her problem.

She turned her attention to her house. What would Princess Delphine do? Well, first of all, the Princess was not a scatterbrained dolt who locked her keys in her car, Sylvie thought sourly, purposely ignoring the obvious fact that the Princess didn't have a car. Or keys.

"Jean-Luc, come here and help me figure this out. I know the windows are all locked, because I'm sure I checked them before we left. But—" She snapped her fingers in triumph. "I didn't check the upstairs windows." She started off towards the detached garage. "Let's get a ladder and see." But Jean-Luc, hearing the magic word *ladder*, was already prancing ahead.

Several minutes later, after finally convincing her dog that he didn't want to climb up after her, Sylvie was on the roof. Her new sandals slipped on the shingles and she lurched, hand out, to avoid a fall. Well, no use complaining about it now; she'd known the sandals weren't practical when she'd gotten them. But she hadn't expected to climb the roof in them.

She carefully picked her way up and over to the first window. It was closed, wouldn't budge. She toured the roof, checking the other windows, only to come up with the same depressing result. She was thoroughly locked out. However, she did discover all sorts of grime ground into the wooden frames. Someday when she needed to work off some serious energy, she'd have to come up here with a scrub brush. Cupping her hand on the glass against the glare of the sun, she stared into her upstairs room. She could see her inks, pens, papers, stamps, but couldn't get to them. A fate worse than death, she decided melodramatically.

She wiped her now dirty hands on the seat of her shorts, then sank down on the hot roof and made a face. Rats! Now what could she do? Well, she told herself philosophically, it could always be worse.

She heard a crash, and a terrified yelp from Jean-Luc.

It was worse.

Heart pounding, Sylvie scrambled swiftly backwards down the slope of the roof scraping her knees on the rough shingles. "Jean-Luc," she called. "Are you all right?"

Then she saw him. Up on his hind legs, proudly pirouetting in his "I'm so very special" dance.

He was all right. She let out a sigh of relief. But it was short-lived. At Jean-Luc's feet was the ladder.

"What did you do?" she demanded.

It was a rhetorical question, for Jean-Luc loved climbing ladders. It didn't take a rocket scientist to figure out that he'd tried to climb the ladder and knocked it over. So now she was stranded on her roof, without a ladder, her keys in her car. And for probably the first time in her life, she'd actually locked all the doors and windows in her house before she'd left. What a time to be efficient. Evidently there was a new dragon in the land, come to pester her. "Dragon, thy name is car keys locked in the car," she muttered.

"Okay, Jean-Luc, I hope you're pleased with yourself. I'll probably die up here, and you'll have to resort to catching field mice and drinking rainwater to stay alive. Unless you learn how to jump over the fence. And that would take a major miracle."

Jean-Luc, looking quite pleased with himself, balanced on his hind feet again, and this time waved a front paw at her.

"Yes, you're extraordinarily cute and absolutely brilliant. But I should have taught you something useful, like how to break into my car. Or my house. Or how to track down one of Princess Delphine's knights in shining armor. I know she usually rescues them, but I'd sure like to borrow one to rescue me. Preferably," she told herself, "one who knows how to break into houses or cars."

But Jean-Luc wasn't listening anymore. He

was by the fence, on his hind legs, leaning over as far as he could, quivering and wagging his whole body Then he started to woof in excitement.

The woman, along with all of her friends, was completely, certifiably insane. As soon as he could arrange it he would request a different mail route. He wanted to leave the Crazy Lady and her crazy mail as far behind as possible. Just like a bad dream. The pity of it was, he liked this route. It was interesting, and was mostly tree-lined, which made it pleasant in the summer. He'd made several friends along the way, friends that he'd miss. Like little Joshua Martini, with whom he'd shared numerous knock-knock jokes since school had let out. But he wouldn't miss this lady. Oh no, he wouldn't This lady, along with every single one of the wacko people who sent her mail, was totally out of line.

First it was the plastic baseball bat. Without any wrapping. No box. Just the thing itself with the address label and postage stuck to it. Addressed to this Crazy Lady, from one of her equally mental friends. Then it was a beach sandal, but only one of them. He began mentally ticking off the things that had been sent to this woman, unwrapped, in the mail. A whoopie cushion, a pair of scissors, some rubber vomit, a Barbie doll, a toilet plunger, a dog bone. And that was just the beginning of the list. Today it was a can of Spam. Granted, the Spam wasn't as heavy as the cast-iron skillet had been, but that wasn't the point. Pieces of mail delivered by the United States Post Office should be properly packaged. And properly packaged meant the address was clearly written—*not* in rebus form—and easy to read.

Take that envelope he'd delivered last week. Some of the women postal workers had thought it was lovely. And he might have thought so too, if it hadn't been going through the United States mail. Of course, as soon as he'd seen it he should have known that one of her friends had struck again. The envelope was covered with a drawing of a living room, in full color, complete with snoozing dog in front of a fireplace. The address—when he'd *finally* found it—was written in tiny cursive script inside a drawing of a picture frame that hung on the wall over the fireplace.

And the postage. That was another thing. Postage belonged in the upper right-hand corner. Not scattered all over the envelope, not on the back of the envelope, or in the lower left corner, or in the middle of the address. Who did these people think they were to have such fun at the expense of the United States Postal Service? They were probably the same ones who always complained that the mail was so slow.

He heard the dog before he saw it. He knew she had a dog—the evidence was in the front yard, but the dog was always in the house. That was the only good thing he could say for her—that she kept her dog in the house. Now, he could see the dog—a white poodle—hanging over the fence, licking the air at him in greeting.

Wait a minute. It was Jean-Luc, the regular boarder at the vet clinic.

"Hey, Jean-Luc," he called. Then it hit him. Jean-Luc belonged to the Crazy Lady. How did someone as wacky as she was get such a nice dog? He'd always wondered what kind of a weirdo named a poodle after a bald guy. Well, now he knew.

Just over the fence where Jean-Luc was carrying on, she saw the mailman coming down the road. Hah! Knight in shining armor indeed! She started mentally playing with words, mailman, male man—now there was a redundancy for you.

He stopped by the fence to scratch Jean-Luc on the head, in just the right spot. How did he know where Jean-Luc liked to be scratched, she wondered. Then, still scratching Jean-Luc, who was showing all the signs of complete and abject adoration, the mailman raised his gaze to where it collided with hers. Collided, stuck, locked, and punched her in the stomach. Even from this distance she felt that pierce of con-nected-ness, that sense that she knew this man in some elemental way, that they were destined to play a part in each other's lives.

* * *

There had to be some mistake, he thought, staring up at her aghast. There on the roof was the unknown woman he'd seen two weeks ago at Melissa's wedding. Just as the music was starting, he'd caught some small movement out of the corner of his eye. He'd turned slightly, seen her, and his world had tilted. Her auburn hair, with tiny flowers and ribbons tucked into it here and there, had been like a frizzy veil, showering down upon her shoulders. Her face had had the barest sprinkling of freckles across the bridge of her delicate nose, and an expression of absolute delight in her eyes. She'd been wearing a filmy sort of dress, lacy and delicate, adding to the ethereal quality about her. She'd looked like a fairy, a sprite, a sylph. She'd been the princess of all the fairy tales in his childhood. Then he'd noticed that her hands were green.

He should have realized he was in for trouble. But never in his wildest moments had he imagined trouble this big. The will-o'-the-wisp whom he'd tried repeatedly to exorcise from his mind, who had haunted his dreams, flitted around the corners of his consciousness, teasing him, tantalizing him, was The Crazy Lady.

Her sandal slipped. She suddenly, painfully, and inelegantly found herself sitting on her rump. It was the proverbial bucket of cold water dashed on her soul. *Destiny indeed!* she mentally harrumphed. *Don't be absurd, Sylvie, this*

*is not one of Delphine's adventures. Much as you
may despair, this is reality.*

"Hello," he called up to her. "Are you all
right?" he added after a second, as if he really
didn't want to get involved but his mother had
drilled manners into him.

He had a slight accent. From somewhere on
the East Coast, New Jersey maybe.

"Actually, I'm sort of stranded," she called
back.

"Sort of? Or actually?"

She frowned. He was a comic, was he? "Actually. Jean-Luc knocked the ladder down and
the windows are locked, so I'm stuck."

"Did you do such a thing?" he asked Jean-Luc
with obvious familiarity.

"You seem to know my dog," she said, then
instantly cringed, hearing the challenge in her
voice and not liking it.

Once again he raised his face to her, and she
had a fleeting image of the rays of the sun re-
flecting from his eyes.

"I deliver mail to the Hartley Vet Clinic. Jessie
and Dr. March introduced me to Jean-Luc last
winter when he was boarding there. What a
nice dog," he added, more to Jean-Luc than to
her.

"Yeah, well, this 'nice dog' has a warped sense
of humor. He knocked over my ladder."

"It was probably just an accident." He left off
scratching Jean-Luc and straightened, one
hand on his hip, the other shading his eyes

against the shine of the sun, his feet planted firmly on her sidewalk.

She felt a twinge of annoyance. He could at least offer to put the ladder up for her instead of standing there staring at her as if she were green. Or as if he thought she might turn into one of the Princess's sorceresses and fly away. Maybe his mother hadn't taught him manners. It wasn't a matter of male chauvinism, nothing to do with the fact that he was a man and she was a woman. Oh, no. It was simply common courtesy. If she'd been walking down the street and found someone stranded on a roof with their keys locked in their car, she'd offer to put their ladder back up for them.

"Would you like me to put the ladder back up for you?" he offered.

She bit back any number of scathing comments. Destiny or not—and the whole idea of destiny was absurd, she reminded herself, that was something that happened in Delphine's world, not hers—she needed that ladder. Besides, she wanted to see him up close. "That would be nice," she finally said. "I'd appreciate it."

He undid the gate latch and slipped into her yard, careful not to let Jean-Luc escape, she noticed. He easily slung his mailbag off his shoulder onto the ground and strode purposefully over to the ladder.

Now that he was closer, she could see his face better. It was an interesting face, full of planes and corners. Two dark slashes for eyebrows, short dark hair in the kind of waves that probably felt springy. When he looked up she saw his eyes were a startling blue, a bright blue, a clear blue, almost, but not quite, turquoise. Blue that had the clarity of watercolors rather than the thickness of markers. She itched to draw this face, to capture it, to make something of it. A sorcerer perhaps, or a prince . . .

"You need a longer ladder." His voice came to her, breaking into her musings. "This one is barely long enough to reach the roof. That's why Jean-Luc was able to knock it over so easily." He set the ladder against the house, pushing against it firmly a couple of times, to make sure it would stay put.

She stared at him dumbly. What was he talking about? And had she really heard a hint of disapproval in his voice?

"The angle from the ground to the roof is too short to give you any stability." He looked up. "I'll hold onto it while you climb down."

How silly of her to think that he disapproved of her. He didn't even know her. And she didn't know him, so there.

Carefully, because of her slippery sandals, she swung one leg over the gutter and with her foot reached out for the ladder. The gutters were full of leaves, she noticed in annoyance. Have to clean them out again. Just one more thing she didn't have time to do. She swung the other leg over, conscious of her bare legs, wishing that she had long pants on, feeling somehow vulnerable in shorts. Then, irritated at herself for feeling that vulnerability, she took charge of herself. She was acting like a ninny, she told herself. He was just the mailman. She caught sight of him holding the ladder steady, and a rush of awareness swept through her. He was the male man, yes, he was a very male man indeed. *Get a grip, girl*, she told herself sternly. Male man indeed. As if it were some kind of accomplishment.

Now he noticed that her hands weren't green anymore, and her legs, oh, those legs were long and slender. They were coming down right in front of his nose, lovely legs, lucious legs, looking smooth and silky . . . He felt his eyes glaze.

Jean-Luc let out a sudden bark, startling her. Her sandal slipped on the rung of the ladder. She felt herself pitching wildly, straining helplessly to grasp at anything that was stable. She was falling. Knocking into something hard. Landing. On top of the mailman. The male man.

Then he was sprawled on the ground and she was on top of him. And he hurt. Badly. He sucked in a sudden breath. It was difficult, there was something heavy on his chest. The pain was so bad he saw red. It took him a moment to realize the hurt was coming from his ankle.

"Are you all right?" Her face was hovering over him. "I'm so very sorry! I'm such a klutz!" Her face disappeared for a second as she scrambled off his chest, but there she was again, concern in her gray-green eyes. "Can I get you something?" She frowned. "No, I guess I can't. I'm still locked out of my house. Damn!"

He wasn't seeing red anymore, and the pain was receding to the proverbial dull roar. It was still excruciating, but somehow he was able to detach himself from enough of the pain to be able to think, to speak coherently. Maybe.

"My ankle," he muttered.

Instantly her face disappeared again, but he felt her hands on his leg. They were surprisingly gentle. "It looks twisted," she reported. "I think you need to get your shoe off. In case it swells, you know."

He squinted against the brightness of the sky to see her framed against the light. She was sitting on her heels, a considering look on her face. "It might be easier if you let me do it," she said.

Do what? he wondered fuzzily as he felt a furry muzzle sniff his cheek. Jean-Luc, he realized.

"Is that okay?" she asked. "Jean-Luc, go away. Do you want me to take off your shoe? I'll try not to hurt your ankle."

"Sure," he muttered, closing his eyes.

New and sudden burst of pain. His eyes flew open wide. The Crazy Lady was killing him. He had to get out of here before she succeeded.

"Almost through," she said cheerfully.

Almost through killing him. He knew he should have traded routes. First it was Spam, now it was death. All because of the Crazy Lady.

Chapter Two

It wasn't easy, getting that shoe off. Of course, he was a mailman, Sylvie reminded herself. He walked all day and probably didn't know about rosemary footbaths. She tossed the shoe aside and threw a quick glance at his face. His eyes were squeezed closed. Oh, no, she'd hurt him after all. "I'm sorry, I didn't mean to hurt you," she said apologetically. "But your ankle is really swelling."

"It's okay." His voice was gritty and tight. "No problem."

"Well, I'm afraid it is a problem. You see, I can't drive you to the hospital because my keys are locked in my car, and I can't get in my house to call the ambulance because my house is also locked. But if you wait here, I'll trot next door to the Mathesons' and see if I can use their phone."

She heard a sudden barking. But it sounded as if it were from inside her house. Sylvie frowned, looking around. "Jean-Luc?" she called.

Jean-Luc's furry head appeared in the living room window. His mouth was open in a doggy grin and he appeared to be very pleased with himself.

"Jean-Luc, how did you get inside?" Sylvie demanded.

Jean-Luc woofed.

How could he possibly have gotten in? She sifted the possibilities through her mind. Aha! She came up triumphantly with a gem. The dog door. But wait a minute. She'd locked it. She *knew* she had. She specifically remembered locking it. Didn't she?

"Wait here," she told the mailman, "I'll be right back."

Trotting around to the back of the house, she saw Jean-Luc halfway out of the dog door, grinning at her.

"You brilliant creature!" she crowed. "What a good boy you are. The good guy dog saves the day. Whaddya think, can I get through that door?"

Jean-Luc was enthusiastic at the prospect of his mom wriggling through his very own door. "I know, I know," she told him. "You've never seen me do this. Well, there's a first time for everything." She scraped her leg on the metal of the dog door. "Ouch!" Quick inspection proved no permanent damage. Then she was in.

Running through the house to the front door, she unlocked it, swung it wide open, and pushed out, letting the screen door bang closed. The mailman was right where she'd left him.

"Okay, got to get you into my house so I can—"

"No."

"What?" She couldn't possibly have heard him correctly.

"I said no. Just please, leave me here," he said in a voice that was tight as a spring. "Call the Post Office, ask for Harvey Schmedlapp. Tell him what happened. He'll send someone right over."

She put her hands on her hips and gaped at him in amazement. "I can't do that."

"Why not?"

"Well—" she sputtered. "It wouldn't be neighborly. It wouldn't be helpful. It would be despicable, that's why. My house isn't the Bates Motel, you know," she pointed out.

She caught his scowl. Maybe he thought her house really *might* be the Bates Motel. Well, sheesh! She was just trying to help.

"I'll be just fine," he practically growled at her. "And I won't be offended."

A low rumble of thunder muttered overhead. Sylvie glanced up at the sky to see dark gray towering clouds racing towards them. "You'll be very wet."

She watched the emotions shift on his face as he too saw the thunderheads. He obviously was not happy about this. Well, too bad. All she wanted to do was help him. Why was he getting all bent out of shape? *Because he's a man*, she told herself. *Men don't like to be in situations where they're not in control*. He was not in control, therefore he didn't like it.

"Okay," he said at last. "But you'll have to get my mailbag and bring it in as well."

"Got it," Sylvie sang out as she trotted dutifully across the lawn. She intended to sweep the mailbag up gracefully and whoosh it to safety. She grabbed the shoulder strap and swung. The bag didn't budge. What was in here? Man-oh-man, what kind of muscles did it take to haul one of these things around all day? Surreptitiously she snuck a peek at him. He was watching her, his eyebrows a slash over those clear blue eyes.

How could she do this under such intense scrutiny? "You're looking at me like my brothers used to."

"How is that?"

"As if you're waiting for me to fail so you can bully me about it." She faced him squarely, legs apart, hands on hips, her stance just daring him to laugh at her.

He did. Well, actually it was more of a painful chuckle. Surprisingly, it sounded nice, deep, soft, and she wondered what his laugh would sound like if he weren't hurting. For an instant she felt a fleeting sense of intimacy with him.

Big whoops! Hold it, Sylvie! First destiny, now intimacy. Change of subject real fast now.

"How do you haul this thing around? What's in here?"

"Cans of Spam."

"What? Spam? Really?" *Other* people sent Spam in the mail? Ignoring the pound of sarcasm in his voice, she surreptitiously peeked inside the bag, edging the flap wider so she could see better.

"You can't snoop in there. It's illegal," he pointed out.

Instantly her hand jerked back out. "I'm not snooping," she lied. "I just wanted to make sure the mail wouldn't get wet." She felt the first light drops of rain on her cheek. "Oh, no. Here it comes. This is not going to be pretty," she warned him, "so don't even bother to watch." She felt her face turn red with exertion as she put all her meager strength into dragging the bag across the lawn. Forget trying to carry it. Forget any semblance of grace. He must be incredibly strong. Of course, Princess Delphine would've been able to carry it, no problemo. She would have cast an itty-bitty spell to make it as light as a feather. *Well, Sylvie girl,* she told herself, *reality rears its ugly head once more.*

Finally, with one last burst of determination, she hauled the bag up the step to the shelter of her front porch and slumped over for a second to catch her breath. Then she scampered down again and over to the mailman.

"Can you lean on me?"

Since he probably outweighed her by a hundred pounds, the suggestion was patently absurd. But, she noticed gratefully, as a drop of rain ran down her cheek, he didn't laugh.

Somehow the two of them, working together, got him struggling to his feet, then in a sort of hobble, over and onto her porch, where he sank down on her porch swing, out of the rain.

She was staring at him with wide eyes that were full of concern. It made him uncomfortable, and he shifted on the swing. His ankle was propped up on one of those rattan stool things, with a giant-sized bag of frozen peas wrapped around it. Frozen peas, of all things! She'd insisted on it. Still, he had to admit, she was only trying to help. Yeah, after she'd tried to kill him. He closed his eyes, as much to escape the expression on her face as to make himself relax.

"Who do I need to call?" she asked.

He kept his eyes closed. "The Post Office. Ask for Harvey Schmedlapp. Tell him what happened."

By the banging of the screen door he knew she'd gone into the house and he was alone. For a moment he listened to the whooshing sound of the rain on the roof, and from the distance came a mutter of thunder. A slight breeze wafted the delicate scent of lilacs across the porch. Then the rain came running off the side of the roof in a sheet, making a splashing sound on the ground below. Her gutters were obviously clogged. He concentrated on the sounds of the rain, willing his mind away from his throbbing ankle. There was another, softer door bang, and then he felt a wet nose thrust into his hand. He opened his eyes.

"Hi, Jean-Luc," he muttered. "Yup, I really did myself in. No, you don't need to take care of me. I can take care of myself, thank you." Still, he smoothed down the curls on the dog's head. He'd been taking care of himself for years, he thought somberly, and he always would. There was no one else to do it, hadn't been for a very long time. Foster families, even the good ones—and he'd had a good one—didn't exactly make for a nurtured life. Helen and Philip were good to him, they treated him like their own children. But they just weren't his own parents. No matter how much they tried, no matter how much he'd wanted to believe otherwise, he was alone in the world.

Still, if he allowed himself to peer into the seldom-visited corners of the deepest part of his mind, he would find memories of his mother reading and singing to him at bedtime. Smelling of lavender and roses, she hugged him close, and whispered that she loved him more than anything in the world. He knew, without a doubt, that he was cherished. But those memories were kept well guarded, away from the light of day, like precious jewels.

Another bang of the screen door, this one

loud, demanding his attention. The Crazy Lady was standing in front of him, an innocent smile on her face, a tall glass in each hand.

"I thought you might like some lemonade while you wait. I talked to Mr. Schmedlapp. He said someone would be here in about fifteen minutes to get you. They'd have to get the mail back to the Post Office before they took you to the hospital. So I told him your ankle was really swelling up, and he said I could take you. To the hospital."

Oh, no! "He asked you to take me to the hospital?" How could Harvey do this to him?

"No." There was impatience in her voice, and she waved her hand as if in explanation. "I told him about the swelling and I offered to take you to the hospital so you don't have to wait while they take care of the mail." She looked pleased with herself. "He said it was very kind and thank you," she added pointedly when he didn't respond.

He cleared his throat. "Yes, it is kind of you. But I don't want to put you to this trouble." He wasn't going to tell her that he was sure she'd probably find another way to kill him. Furthermore, he was not going to the hospital, but that was none of her business.

"No trouble," she said breezily.

Oh, it'd be trouble for him. He groaned to himself. He had to find some way out of this. He'd blame it on the bureaucrats. "I need to go with Harvey. I think there's some kind of policy about it. Something to do with liability." He hoped she'd believe him. He never had been good at lying.

A frown wrinkled her forehead. "Oh. All right. I guess you have a point. I wonder why Mr. Schmedlapp didn't say anything about it. Well, this glass is sweating and my hand is getting wet, so please take the lemonade."

All at once he saw, not The Crazy Lady, but the wispy sprite who had been haunting his dreams. The fine features, clear, almost translucent skin, perfect eyebrows perched over perfect moss-green eyes. And her hair, wild and free, and all the existing colors of red, scattered about her shoulders. Hair that screamed out trouble. And it was wet. Perfectly formed raindrops scattered all over the filmy stuff.

He took the lemonade, anything to make her stop hovering over him.

Jean-Luc, sitting prettily at her feet, barked.

"Oh, all right, Jean-Luc, here's one for you." The Crazy Lady stuck two fingers in her glass and pulled out an ice cube. She tossed it to Jean-Luc. He caught it on the fly, then settled down to stare off into the distance while he crunched it delicately.

"Your dog eats ice cubes?"

"Yup. He thinks they're a treat. He also loves frozen peas. That's why I always buy giant bags of them." She settled into the wicker chair next to the swing. Next to him.

To put some distance between them, he

shifted his gaze down to the glass in his hand. There was a quartered lemon at the bottom, and something purple floating on the top. "What's that?" he asked, not wanting to sound ungrateful, but afraid he did.

"Violets. I think they're pretty with lemonade, don't you? Here, Jean-Luc, have another ice cube. Now lie down. Good boy."

"They're perfectly edible," she continued over the sound of Jean-Luc's crunching. "I usually freeze them inside ice cubes, but I haven't had the chance to do that yet this year, so I just picked some fresh ones."

Jean-Luc grunted from his spot on the porch. The Crazy Lady nudged him with her foot. It was bare, he noticed. And her toenails were painted bright pink. Then he realized what she'd said. She'd just gone outside in the rain to pick violets to put in lemonade? That explained her wet hair. He looked from the violets in his glass to her. She had raised her glass to her lips, but now she paused.

"What?" she asked.

"I've just never heard of putting flowers in lemonade."

"Oh." She sounded surprised. "I've always done it. But only with violets, because they're the prettiest. The dark purple ones, that is. I have white violets too, but they don't go well with the yellow. I could always use rose petals, I suppose, or nasturtiums, but I like violets the best."

Lonely Hearts

He was right the first time, he thought as he watched her take a sip. She was crazy. A poodle named after a bald guy, cans of Spam in the mail, and flowers in lemonade. He didn't even want to think what other wacky things she might do.

"I have some elder ointment that would be good to put on your ankle, if you'll let me."

"What?!" He sounded terrified, even to himself. This was ridiculous, he thought. "No, thank you," he answered stiffly. "I'll wait for Harvey, and he'll take me back to the Post Office." Then I'll go home, he thought to himself. I'll surely be able to drive in a short while.

"But," she protested, "elder ointment has been used for sprains since, oh, for hundreds of years."

"Not by me."

"Well, of course not, but by your ancestors."

"Not my ancestors." He was sure of it.

"Did your ancestors come from anywhere near England?"

He nodded.

"Then chances are they did use elder ointment. It's probably as old as England."

He decided to stall her, take another tack, until Harvey could get there and he'd be safely out of her way. "Which is why it's called *elder* ointment? Okay, tell me. What is the stuff? Any relation to *younger* ointment?"

She chuckled. "Very good. You're quick, even when you're in pain. It's an ointment made from leaves of the elder bush, and red poppy flowers, and some other stuff. Very soothing."

"Probably because of the poppies," he muttered.

"Very likely," she agreed cheerily. "I have some all made up, I'll just get it." She looked ready to scramble out of her chair. "Really, it helps."

She obviously was not getting the picture. "No, thank you." He said the words very clearly and distinctly, so she couldn't possibly misunderstand. "I'll just wait here for Harvey." He realized he had to find some way to get rid of the bag of peas before Harvey arrived. Even if they *did* make his ankle feel better, he wasn't going to let anyone see him attached to a bag of frozen vegetables.

She made a big production of lifting up the bag of peas and scrutinizing his ankle. He braced himself in readiness, but she didn't touch it. "It looks pretty awful," she offered.

He closed his eyes again and leaned his head against the back of the porch swing. "It feels fine, just a little sore," he lied through his teeth. No way was he going to admit how much he hurt. Anyway, it *would* feel better tomorrow, he promised himself. Tomorrow was Saturday. He'd have the weekend to rest. Then he'd be fine. He had always been a good healer.

She didn't answer. In fact, she was silent. Well, that's a first, he thought sourly. But whoa. Wait a minute. She really seemed to be trying to make him feel better and he was behaving like a heel. The wicker from her chair creaked in annoyance. He opened his eyes just enough for a sidelong glance. She'd huddled up in the chair, feet drawn up on the cushion, ankles crossed, arms wrapped around her knees. All the cheeriness was gone from her expression. The sparkle had left her eyes. Now he *felt* like a heel.

As a peace offering, he took a tentative sip of his lemonade. "Hey, this is really good." He took another, fuller swallow.

"You sound surprised," she said somberly.

"I am. What brand is it?"

"Brand?"

"Yeah. You know. What brand of lemonade?"

She mumbled something.

"I didn't catch that." What was wrong with her now? he wondered.

"It's not a brand. It's fresh. Homemade."

He felt his mouth drop open and closed it. "You just made this?"

She nodded.

So that's why there was a quartered lemon in the bottom of the glass. No one had ever made him fresh lemonade before. And then gone out into the rain to pick violets to put in it, even if he did think it was a dumb thing to do. And he'd been treating her as if she were a blight on the earth. Well, she was a blight on the earth, but he didn't have to treat her like one. No one had gone to such trouble, any trouble, for him in a very, very long time. He swallowed the great lump that suddenly sprung up in his throat.

"Thank you," he said gruffly. "It is truly excellent lemonade. The best lemonade I've ever had." No response from her. He tried again. "Life gave me lemons, and you made me lemonade."

There, he thought triumphantly, he saw a grin. A small grin, but it was a start.

"I feel responsible for hurting you," she said in a small voice, shrugging her shoulders up as if in supplication. "If I hadn't fallen off the ladder you wouldn't be hurt. The least I could do is make you lemonade. And I only offered to give you some elder ointment because I know it really does work."

"Tell you what, why don't you let me have some to take home. And I'll try it. I promise. Okay?"

A hint of that sparkle returned to her eyes. "Okay."

Chapter Three

The next morning Sylvie carried her mug of tea upstairs to her rubber room. This was the heart of her house, where she created the designs that had made her company, Some Enchanted Rubber, a household name among rubber-stampers.

She absently took a sip of tea as she picked up one of the sketches she'd sweated over until the early hours. It was the mailman. Well, it really wasn't the mailman, it was a sorcerer, but his face was unmistakably the face of the mailman. His stance was proud, robe billowing in an unseen wind, arms upraised as if challenging the powers of the universe to deny him anything. Yes, she thought with great satisfaction.

This was a good one. It would make a terrific rubber stamp.

She picked up another drawing, also of the mailman. This time he was a prince, reclining against a cushion, his eyes closed. He appeared to be asleep, but in the lines around his mouth, in the slash of eyebrows, there was a look of unacknowledged pain. The clothes were travel worn and stained. His fingers curled protectively around the strap of a leather pouch, on the ground, at his side. This one would go wonderfully with the stamp of the succoring maiden, the one where she was kneeling, holding out a bowl of something or other. Yes. She could see it now. The Prince in Pain and the Succoring Maiden. It was as if the two images were meant to be used together. Perhaps with one of the dogs looking on in concern. Maybe a window in the background; she had several castle windows to choose from. Or maybe the crowd of onlookers.

This was the magic, the power, of rubber stamps. People were free to choose their art, free to combine stamps, in an endless number of possibilities, to create entire worlds of their own. And no two pieces of stamped artwork were ever exactly the same.

So. It was a done deal. These two new designs would go in her next supplement. "The question is, Jean-Luc," she said to her poodle, at her feet as always. "How can I incorporate them into the Adventures of Princess Delphine? Let's see, Delphine, along with her faithful canine companion, Halcyon, can come across a prince hurt in the woods, so of course they'd have to care for him. After all, the Princess has a savior complex. But then, Jean-Luc, my very own faithful companion, how does the wizard come into it? Is he a good wizard or a bad wizard? What's the relationship of the prince and the wizard? They look alike, so they're obviously related. Brothers? And my other new design, the one of that dragon. Where does the dragon come into all this? Perhaps the prince was hurt while trying to slay the dragon."

One of the things that made Sylvie's stamp company unique was the ongoing adventures of the Princess Delphine and her faithful companion, Halcyon, that introduced every new stamp. Sylvie put out a catalog every year, and then every three months she put out a supplement of new stamp designs—and the newest installment of the story. Stampers loved her story. Some of them even wrote to her suggesting possible stamps and story twists. Well, she had her new stamps—the dragon, the wizard, prince, and a couple of others. But she had to come up with names for these new characters. Names.

Oh, my goodness! She had no idea what the mailman's name was.

She'd never even introduced herself. There hadn't been time. Mr. Schmedlapp had driven up as soon as she'd handed the mailman the pot of elder ointment. He'd thrown a hasty thanks over his shoulder as he'd hobbled out into the rain, to the truck, leaning heavily on the postal official's arm. That was the last she'd seen of the mailman. The male man.

Suddenly, she had to find out who he was, to find out how he was doing, what the doctor had said. After all, it was really her fault he'd been hurt. She would call the Post Office. But wait— Jessie! He said he delivered mail to the clinic, and knew Jessie and Melissa.

Letting her drawings flutter to the table, she raced downstairs to the phone. She knew the number by heart.

"Hartley Veterinary Clinic."

"Hi, Suzette, this is Sylvie. Is Jessie free?" She put her hand down on the counter. On the sticky counter. Sticky from the sugar she'd spilled last night while making lemonade. Only it wasn't in granular form anymore, it was solid. She poked at it with a finger. It had mixed with dripped lemon juice and was now a dried smear of sticky yuck. She grabbed a dishrag, got it wet, wrung it out, and slopped it on top of the dried sugar. That would soften it. She'd wipe it up later.

Jessie's voice came on the phone. "Hi, Sylvie. Going away again? Do we get that great guy dog for the weekend while you jet off to some faraway place and hawk your rubber stamps?"

"No, nothing like that. Not until next month. Say, Jess, you know that person who delivers your mail?"

"Ray?"

"Is that his name?" She tried to sound casual.

"Tall, sort of rangy, dark curly hair, drop-dead-gorgeous blue eyes, wonderful sense of humor but sort of shy?"

Shy? He hadn't seemed shy yesterday. He'd been rather grouchy, but then he'd been hurt, and besides, the rest fit. "Yeah. His name is Ray? Do you know his last name?"

There was silence for a second or two, before Jessie spoke again. "Say, Sylvie, are we . . . ahem . . . interested in Ray?"

"No!" Sylvie protested. "Of course not. And get that sly tone out of your voice right now. Nothing like that at all. He just got hurt in my front yard yesterday, and I want to find out how he is doing."

"Hurt?" Sylvie could almost hear Jessie's ears perk up. "How hurt?"

"He sprained his ankle. At least I hope he only sprained his ankle."

"How'd he do that? I know you don't have any gopher holes in your yard. And I don't think Jean-Luc would trip him. Jean-Luc likes him."

"No, nothing like that. I, um, I sort of fell on top of him."

Another silent pause, then a low whistle. "You fell on top of Ray? Man-oh-man, I'd sure like to fall on top of him. Studly, yes, but I like him too," she camped in a very faux Irish femme-fatale accent.

Sylvie felt her face turn red. Good thing Jessie

wasn't here or she'd really never hear the end of it. "It wasn't like that, silly. I was climbing down my ladder, I slipped, and I fell on top of him."

"Okay, spit it out. The whole story this time, not just the Good Parts version. Believe me, though, falling on top of Ray must've been a Great Big Good Part."

"Stop it!" Sylvie pleaded, chuckling in spite of herself. She told Jess the whole story. What there was of it, which wasn't much, she reflected. "Anyway," she ended, "I want to find out how he's doing."

"Yeah. I *really* believe you. Okay. Have it your way. Say, you wanna know where he lives?"

"Sure." She tried to sound as if it didn't really matter one way or another. She didn't think she succeeded.

"You know that corner apartment on the other side from mine? The one with all the roses? The one that faces the park? That's Ray's. And before you ask," she teased, the grin sounding clearly in her voice, "the answer is yes. He lives alone. Now, Sylvie, go forth and—um . . . make sure you have a very good time. Just don't forget to tell your Auntie Jess all about it. Oh, wait'll I tell M'liss that you have the hots for Ray. She'll die! We've wanted him to find someone for just ever."

"Jessie," Sylvie wailed, "I don't have the hots for him! I just feel responsible for what happened. I just want to make sure he's okay. Nothing else, not at all. No hots. You know how I feel about romantic relationships. They don't work."

"Sure, Sylvie. Anything you say."

Hanging up the phone, Sylvie realized she probably shouldn't have called Jessie at all. Jessie was a dear friend, but had a bizarre sense of the romantic. Oh, well, no use fretting, what was done was done. And speaking of things getting done, she had to do some chores, put some more elder ointment in a jar to take over to Ray.

She turned his name over and over in her mind. Ray. What a neat name. A slice of sun piercing the darkness, carrying light, like a promise, through the clouds. A ray—the vehicle through which life-giving light came to earth. Shadows and colors and light. She was an artist. Light was very important to artists.

Suddenly she realized she was staring at the phone. Where was her mind today? Let's see. She would take him the ointment, and a loaf of that onion herb dill bread—she had some in the freezer—and she'd make a card. Yes! That was it. She'd make him a one-of-a-kind-rubber-stamped-hope-your-ankle-is-better card. She turned abruptly and trotted back upstairs to her rubber room.

She quickly surveyed the shallow shelves, filled with the three-thousand-plus rubber stamps, that lined the walls. She picked out her ladder stamp, and that one of the falling woman. A house that could pass for her house. Hmmmm, which Poodle should she use? She didn't have a mailman stamp, but one of the ordinary men would probably work if she colored his clothes blue, and over here were several bitty stamps of postcards and letters. On to the section of shelves that held weather stamps. She needed some towering clouds in the sky, threatening rain. What color inks would be best? She pulled open the drawer where she kept her ink pads arranged by type of ink, and then by color. She chose grays, blues, and greens for the grass and trees. Oops! She almost forgot her lilac bush. Grab that stamp and some purple inks.

Purple and blue reminded her of a bruised ankle. Ankle! She waltzed over to her shelves labeled "Body Parts" and picked out a big foot and ankle stamp for the inside of the card.

When she had assembled her stamps, inks, and pencils, and decided on just the right paper, she gave herself mood music. *Sgt. Pepper* on the CD player. Singing along loudly and off-key about the Lonely Hearts Club Band, Sylvie started on the card. Intent, excited, full of anticipation. It would be perfect! He would love it.

He took the card that she held out to him. He recognized the scene right away, of course. The ladder, the poodle, the falling woman, the man looking up, even the lilac bush. When he glanced down at her—she barely reached his shoulder—he also couldn't miss the look of expectation in her uptilted face. She evidently expected him to say something.

"Where did this come from?" he asked.

"I made it," she announced.

She made it? "How?"

"Stamps. I'm a rubber-stamp artist. Surely you've noticed the envelopes I get, and the ones I send. And it's my business, you know."

"What is?"

"Rubber stamps. I own a rubber stamp company. You know. Some Enchanted Rubber. It's my company."

He shifted his weight on the crutch, hopping a bit, trying not to jar his hurt ankle. She clutched a large paper bag in her arms. She'd shifted it a couple of times since they'd been standing here. It looked like it might be heavy. He should offer to take it from her. After all, he had been drilled with manners when he was growing up. He should invite her inside. As if he were a normal friendly man and she were a normal friendly woman.

He sighed. He didn't want her in his house. He didn't want anything to do with her. This time he really was going to get her—the sprite he'd seen at Dr. March's wedding—out of his mind. He had to. She was—his thoughts came to a screeching halt. He'd been about to tell himself she was driving him crazy.

Stalling for time, he opened the card. Inside, under the image of a purplish bluish foot, in lovely handwriting—handwriting that if possessed by the general population and used on all their mail would make his life much easier— were the following words: *"Short ladders cometh before a fall. Thank you for rescuing me. Sylvie Taylor. P.S. Jean-Luc also says thanks. You saved him from a dismal future diet of nothing but field mice."*

He really didn't want to do this, but he had no choice. After all, he owed it to Helen, his foster mother, to do her proud in social situations. "Do you want to come in for a minute?"

"Sure," was her chipper reply. "I brought you some goodies."

"More frozen peas?"

"Is that sarcasm I hear dripping from your tongue?"

She was sure a saucy little thing.

"Jean-Luc and I are friends," he pointed out reasonably. "I just don't want him thinking he has to guard his treats from me."

When she chuckled, he inexplicably warmed to the sound. He discovered an answering smile coming from somewhere deep inside, a smile that would explode if he didn't let it out.

"Wow!" she said in mock amazement. "You can actually smile. Cool!"

He shrugged. "Not much to smile about in the last twenty-four hours."

Instantly, all amusement vanished from her face. He found himself fascinated by the way her eyes got large and wide. The way her hand flew to her mouth. "Oh, I'm sorry. I forgot to ask. What did the doctor say? How's your ankle?"

To evade the question, he turned clumsily, trying not to trip himself with the crutch, and held his front door open for her. "Come in."

DON'T MISS OTHER *IT'S A DOG'S LIFE* LOVE SPELL ROMANCES!

Rosamunda's Revenge by Emma Craig. At first, Tacita Grantham thinks that Jedediah Hardcastle is a big brute of a man with no manners whatsoever. But when she sees he'll do anything to protect her—even rescue her beloved Rosamunda—she knows his bark is worse than his bite. And when she first feels his kiss—she knows he is the only man who'll ever touch her heart.

___52213-6 $5.50 US/$6.50 CAN

Molly in the Middle by Stobie Piel. Molly is a sheepdog, and unless she finds some other means of livelihood for her lovely mistress, Miren, she'll be doomed to chase stupid sheep forever. That's why she is tickled pink when Nathan MacCallum shows up. Molly knows from Miren's pink cheeks and distracted gaze that his hot kisses are something special. Now she'll simply have to herd the two together, and show the silly humans that true love—and a faithful house pet—are all they'll ever need.

——52193-8 $5.99 US/$6.99 CAN

Dorchester Publishing Co., Inc.
P.O. Box 6640
Wayne, PA 19087-8640

Please add $1.75 for shipping and handling for the first book and $.50 for each book thereafter. NY, NYC, and PA residents, please add appropriate sales tax. No cash, stamps, or C.O.D.s. All orders shipped within 6 weeks via postal service book rate. Canadian orders require $2.00 extra postage and must be paid in U.S. dollars through a U.S. banking facility.

Name_____
Address_____
City_____ State_____ Zip_____
I have enclosed $_____ in payment for the checked book(s).
Payment <u>must</u> accompany all orders. ❑ Please send a free catalog.

Heart's Magic

Flora Speer

Bestselling author of ROSE RED

In the year 1122, Mirielle senses change is coming to Wroxley Castle. Then, from out of the fog, two strangers ride into Lincolnshire. Mirielle believes the first man to be honest. But the second, Giles, is hiding something–even as he stirs her heart and awakens her deepest desires. And as Mirielle seeks the truth about her mysterious guest, she uncovers the castle's secrets and learns she must stop a treachery which threatens all she holds dear. Only then can she be in the arms of her only love, the man who has awakened her own heart's magic.

___52204-7 $5.99 US/$6.99 CAN

A Faerie Tale Romance

The Mirror & The Magic

CORAL SMITH SAXE

Bestselling Author Of *A Stolen Rose*

Sensible Julia Addison doesn't believe in fairy tales. Nor does she think she'll ever stumble from the modern world into an enchanted wood. Yet now she is in a Highland forest, held captive by seven lairds and their quick-tempered chief. Hardened by years of war with rival clans, Darach MacStruan acts more like Grumpy than Prince Charming. Still, Julia is convinced that behind the dark-eyed Scotsman's gruff demeanor beats the heart of a kind and gentle lover. But in a land full of cunning clansmen, furious feuds, and poisonous potions, she can only wonder if her kiss has magic enough to waken Darach to sweet ecstasy.

_52086-9 $5.99 US/$7.99 CAN

A Faerie Tale Romance

Someone's Been Sleeping In My Bed

LindaJones

**WHO'S BEEN EATING FROM MY BOWL?
IS SHE A BEAUTY IN BOTH HEART AND
  SOUL?
WHO'S BEEN SITTING IN MY CHAIR?
IS SHE PRETTY OF FACE AND FAIR OF
  HAIR?
WHO'S BEEN SLEEPING IN MY BED?
IS SHE THE DAMSEL I WILL WED?**

The golden-haired woman barely escapes from a stagecoach robbery before she gets lost in the Wyoming mountains. Hungry, harried, and out of hope, she stumbles on a rude cabin, the home of three brothers; great bears of men who nearly frighten her out of her wits. But Maddalyn Kelly is no Goldilocks; she is a feisty beauty who can fend for herself. Still, how can she ever guess that the Barrett boys will bare their souls to her—or that one of them will share with her an ecstasy so exquisite it is almost unbearable?

_52094-X $5.99 US/$6.99 CAN

BESTSELLING AUTHOR OF
LONGER THAN FOREVER!
FOUR WEDDINGS AND
A FAIRY GODMOTHER

Only a storybook affair like the marriage of Cindy Ella Jones and Princeton Chalmers could lead to three such tangled romances—and happily ever after endings:

BELINDA

Kidnapped from the wedding party, the lonely beauty will learn how a little love can tame a wild beast—even one as intimidating as Cain Dezlin, the handsome recluse.

LILITH

Thrown together with Frank Henson, a seemingly soft-spoken security guard, self-absorbed Lilith will have to learn that with love and respect, there's a prince waiting behind every toad.

ROBERTA

The shy redhead's heart has been broken by a wicked wolf once before—and now that Maximilian Wolfe has shown up at the wedding she is determined to get to her grandmother's before the big bad Frenchman can hurt her again.

_52114-8 $5.50 US/$6.50 CAN

Dorchester Publishing Co., Inc.
P.O. Box 6640
Wayne, PA 19087-8640

Please add $1.75 for shipping and handling for the first book and $.50 for each book thereafter. NY, NYC, and PA residents, please add appropriate sales tax. No cash, stamps, or C.O.D.s. All orders shipped within 6 weeks via postal service book rate. Canadian orders require $2.00 extra postage and must be paid in U.S. dollars through a U.S. banking facility.

Name_____
Address_____
City_____State_____Zip_____
I have enclosed $_____ in payment for the checked book(s).
Payment <u>must</u> accompany all orders. ❏ Please send a free catalog.